Coalbridge

A novel

Cover photograph: Copyright Connor Wilkins.

ISBN 978-0-473-57635-6 (POD Amazon)

ISBN 978-0-473-57636-3 (Kindle)

ISBN 978-0-473-57637-0 (iBook)

ISBN 978-0-473-59835-8 (EPUB)

ISBN 978-0-473-59834-1 (Paperback)

Facebook.com/christinapersicoauthor

christinapersicowriter@gmail.com

This book is many things.

It is a culmination of hours of work. It is, as cliche as it sounds, a labour of love.

It is, hopefully, mildly entertaining. I hope it touches someone's heart in a positive way.

But most of all, you reading my book is a long-held dream come true.

Thank you.

CP x

Chapter One

The darkness always seemed darker in the wilds of the English countryside. There were no streetlights and the moonlight was hidden.

Darkness, however, was an ally tonight. It was an aid in being inconspicuous.

'Is this the right place?' A voice said. It was hardly audible over the wind.

''Course it is. I know it like the back of my hand.'

'I'll thank you to address me properly. Where was the *Sir*?'

'My apologies, sir. I wasn't thinking.'

'Yes, well, enough talk. Let's find this place.'

Their footsteps were silent in the soft dirt. They walked slowly towards their goal. Dim moonlight, dappled by cloud cover, made their target stand out as a mass against the sky.

'That's the one, sir.'

'Must you keep up your needless talk? I can see, you know.'

The underling decided against replying. He had thought this assignment would be a lot more pleasant - 'You're vital to this operation – one trip and you'll be home free,' he'd been told. He wasn't enjoying the attitude, but the money would be the result.

They approached the large stone stable. It was an impressive building, large enough to house 30 horses. As far as they knew there were about a dozen in there now.

'How much noise will these things make when the light is turned on?' The superior voice asked.

'Not much, sir.' He wanted to leave off the last word but felt he should pick his battles. 'They're used to people. Trusting. Most of them, anyway.'

They reached the heavy door. The underling reached into his pocket and produced a key. It opened with hardly a squeak. Rustles and soft whinnies indicated the animals' surprise as the light was flicked on. The two people went inside and quickly shut the door. This had an element of daring, they knew, but they had systems in place for a quick exit.

The underling led the way past the blinking horses to the fourth stall on the left side of the aisle. A big black stallion looked at the intruders mildly.

'Hey, big boy.' The underling held his hand out to the horse, palm up with a small handful of grain.

The thoroughbred's ears went up in recognition. He whickered at the sight of the grain. He lipped it off the man's palm and munched quietly.

'That's it?' The superior asked impatiently.

'Should be. We might want to wait and see if--'

'Is it completely necessary? We're tempting fate, the longer we stay here.'

'Well, it's safer, but not completely necessary, no.'

They retreated towards the door and turned off the lights. The underling paused a second to make sure the horses were settling, then slipped out and locked the door behind him. Then they made off through the trees towards their transport.

A small blue hatchback sat on the side of the country road. The superior got into the passenger seat and opened the glove box. He removed an envelope and handed it over.

'I think you'll find it all there,' he said. Condescension hung from every word; it was his style. 'But remember the pact or that money will be history. And so will you.'

The second man nodded. 'Yes, sir. Thank you.'

The car started and drove off, and the second man stood there, leafing through the cash. Yes, he was better off, but at what cost to that place behind the trees?

Chapter Two

Few things were as aesthetic as autumn in the south of England.

The leaves were turning all the colours between green and red on the spectrum, and there were so many of them. Rural Somerset was a picturesque place year-round, but October seemed to bring a special effect.

The farming town of Long Ashton, North Somerset, was particularly beautiful at this time of year. It reminded James Blackman of home, and that was why he liked it. That and the handsome homestead, Manorbrook, that he now owned.

His success as a three-day event rider had enabled him to purchase this lovely piece of land. It had an excellent stable block, a nice ranch house, and was conveniently located within driving distance of several good events, and close enough to Bristol for flying. And the leafy ruralness reminded him of Masterton, where he grew up and his parents still farmed on 12 acres in the ruggedly beautiful North Island of New Zealand.

This morning was planned as a training session for the younger mounts. He had three, and he was sure that two of them would be good eventers. He wasn't so sure about the third, but his teammate Jadin Steele, a friend from Masterton pony days turned fellow international rider, was certain there was something in the horse.

Jadin periodically installed himself in James' spare bedroom by way of cost-saving when he was in the area. Since he had taken a fancy to the young thoroughbred, James had him riding her.

Currently, James had seven horses in total, three of which were under his name. The other four were owned by others – like an owner and jockey arrangement. The arrangement worked well for both sides; most owners were hands-off but they still got the rewards and recognition of the horse's success.

James headed down to his 'office', as he fondly called it. The house was on a small rise, and a grassy incline led down to the stable, exercise arena, and miniature cross-country course. Most of the obstacles in the cross-country training area were natural – logs, a ditch, hillocks. The arena held a set of showjumping poles, and dressage training occurred around those. It was not on the scale of an actual event, but it served the purpose.

He expected to see Jadin out on Clarabelle, the young grey mare, but instead, his friend came running back towards the house. 'Jimmy, call the vet. Coalie looks terrible.'

James' pace quickened. Coalbridge was his pride and joy, a gorgeous black thoroughbred stallion who had brought him most of his major wins. He was a once-in-a-lifetime horse in the mold of Mark Todd's double Olympic champion Charisma. 'What's wrong with him?' He jerked open the stable door.

'I don't know. He looks really sick and he's not eating or drinking."

James approached the stallion and bit his lip. Coalbridge looked smaller than his 17 hands, almost shrunken. His eyes were dull, and he let out a plaintive cough.

'Hey, old man.' James took the stallion's halter and rubbed his nose. What was wrong with him? He'd been fine yesterday, hadn't he?

'Vicky,' he called, looking around for his head groom. He looked at Jadin. 'Is she here?'

'Yeah, outside somewhere.' He stuck his head out the door. 'Hey, Vick, come here, can you?'

The girl came through the door, her red hair tied back in a long straight ponytail. She had worked for James for four years, taking care of his mounts and doubling as an exercise rider. She lived with her husband, a course designer, ten minutes away.

'Hi, boss,' she said. 'I checked all the beasts last night, about 8pm, before Brett picked me up. Coalie was fine then, sprightly and looking for more food.'

James shook his head sadly. 'And Caitlyn wasn't here any later, I assume?' Caitlyn was his other groom, younger and newer to the job, but with excellent horse sense for her 19 years. She also happened to be James' niece.

Vicky shook her head. 'Don't think so.'

James sighed and rubbed the horse's ear. 'We'd better call the vet in.'

Dr Mark Clinton had been looking after Somerset's equine population for twenty years. He came within half an hour and looked Coalbridge over. A frown creased his forehead as he stood back and looked at the horse.

'Well,' he turned to James. 'It looks like it could be colic, but I'd like to take a manure sample and see if anything shows up.'

'Okay.'

'I'll get this to the lab, and I'll be in touch in a couple of days.' The vet patted the horse's neck. 'In the meantime, don't let him eat for a while and keep a close eye on him. Get as much fluid into him as you can - I'll give him fluids before I go.'

'Okay. Thanks, Doc.'

James looked at Jadin as the doctor retreated. 'Well, this wasn't the start to the morning I expected.'

'No.' Jadin shook his head. 'You ready to get the kids out now?'

'I guess. You want to ride Clarabelle?'

'Uh-huh. My boy needs a run later, but I can do that first.'

'His boy' was his top ride, a hardy warmblood cross named Delaware. The steady grey had won at Pau, the second-last five-star event of the year before the season moved down under to Adelaide, and seemed to be entering his prime. Warmbloods had come into their own as sport horses in the last thirty years, and while there was still the odd full thoroughbred, the majority of top eventers were now crossbreds.

They saddled up and took the horses down to the ditch. Clarabelle sniffed around the reeds and responded to Jadin's hands on the reins perfectly. James' feisty Patriot, on the other hand, lifted his front hooves and switched his tail.

'Hey, stop it.' James brought his chin almost to his chest. 'If you learn to listen, mister, we'll get through this a lot quicker.'

After an hour of work, they cooled their mounts down and took them back to the stables. James checked on Coalbridge. He looked no better, and Vicky's best efforts to get him to drink had failed.

'Can you try, Jimmy?' She was genuinely upset. 'He listens to you.'

'This isn't your fault, Vick. Stuff happens.' James took the bucket. 'He was fine when you checked him.'

She shrugged. 'I know. But I don't like seeing him like this.'

'Neither.' James patted her shoulder and swung open the lower stall door. Coalbridge raised his head and looked at him with disinterest. 'C'mon, big fella. Try some water.'

Coalbridge wasn't interested. James took his halter and gently lowered his head. When his nose touched the water, the stallion jerked his head up, something he never did. James had handled him since he was a yearling; he was as amiable and obedient as a dog.

'Come on, Coalie. Have a try.' He rubbed the horse's forehead for a few moments before again lowering the stallion's head. Coalie shook his head, splashing water over his owner's hand. James tried a couple more times, but the big black would have none of it. With a sigh, he left the water in the stall and shut the door. 'If he won't take anything soon we'd better call Mark back.'

By the time they'd finished with their second round of horses, Coalbridge still wasn't drinking. James and Jadin went up to the house for lunch, and James dialled the vet.

'Tell you what, James,' the vet said, 'I'm going to push that test through and get you the results in the morning. Keep trying to get him drinking - those fluids will keep him going for a while. The big thing is if he goes downhill.'

Caitlyn came after lunch to help with the afternoon run and joined the crusade to get Coalbridge drinking. Now 19 and out of school, her natural love for horses led her to become James' official groom. She was not sure where she wanted to take her life, so a gap year working for her uncle was the current plan. Coalie liked her but he wasn't interested in ingesting anything. James put his forehead on Coalie's. 'Come on, old man. You need to be okay.'

Coalie nodded off again. James went out to see Caitlyn on Marksman, his back-up horse, in the dressage arena. She and the chestnut gelding had a lovely connected rhythm, and she was very good at the subtleties of the discipline.

'You changed your mind about that riding career of yours, Catie?' James asked as his niece brought Marksman to a stop outside the arena.

She shook her head, long blond ponytail swishing behind her helmet. 'It's a great lifestyle, but I just don't have the dedication.'

'Graduating Year 12 and 13 with Honours?' James raised his eyebrow.

She grinned down at him. This was not their first discussion on the topic. 'No, Uncle Jim. I haven't changed my mind. Working with horses, riding here and there, is great. Riding and training all day as you do, no.'

Mark Clinton's assistant came by in the late afternoon to check on Coalie. James had managed to wheedle a bit of water into him, but not enough. Coalie stood quietly through a couple of injections and James was told he'd get a call in the morning with any results.

The extra fluid seemed to brighten Coalie up a little, and he was a little more interested in his surroundings. James made sure he had extra water for the night before locking up. When he went back down to check him again at 10:30, the big horse was dozing, his water a third down. James gently patted his neck. 'Good boy.'

The phone rang just after eight the next morning. The gravity in the good doctor's voice was a surprise. 'James, I'm afraid this isn't as simple as we thought.'

Chapter Three

Amy Williams hoisted her saddle onto the back of her thoroughbred gelding and tightened the cinch. The sun had broken through the typical English cloud, and she was ready for some warmth.

She patted her horse's neck and opened the stall door. Chester tossed his light grey, almost white head and followed her out. She lifted her eyes to the dancing clouds. The English countryside was unlike anywhere else. It wasn't unlike her native Waikato, but she wasn't homesick. Not for more than the landscape, anyway.

Chester tugged at the reins, wanting to pick up the pace. She let him into a trot and started posting as they entered the arena. His dressage needed work, but she hoped his jumping was close to where it needed to be for them to compete on the English circuit. He'd won Puhinui, the biggest three-day event in New Zealand, but Britain held the best competitions in the world.

She put Chester through his paces, trying to keep him light on his feet. He was a full-blooded, old fashioned thoroughbred, which meant he didn't have the refinement of the warmbloods. Ex-instructors had warned her he'd never make it in England for that reason, but she had to give it a shot. Elegance wasn't everything.

She just hoped she'd at least do enough to justify the relocation. Few people had supported her decision to move halfway around the world to try eventing full-time. Her parents, still fighting after a bitter divorce, just used it as ammunition.

'Are you out of your mind, Amy Margaret?'

Amy shook her head and cooled Chester down. Putting him back in his box, she ran her hands down his leg. Nothing there to worry about, thank goodness. She was always on alert for a flare-up of his old racing injury. He went straight to investigate his feed.

She shut the half-door and leaned on it, watching him. When she was busy, it was easy to be confident about what she was doing. But when she had nothing to do except go home to her flat, the worry came back. She patted Chester and turned to go. At home, she tossed her work clothes on the floor and pulled on her sweatpants. Sometimes she missed home, her friends and fellow ex-Pony gang; yet other times she was relieved to have the distance.

She got out ingredients for stir fry and turned on the radio, but didn't hear much over her thoughts. She wasn't sure how long she'd be in England. But she knew she had to try, or she'd have always wondered.

Their first competition would be a small one-day event in Dorset. Chester was a good horse, but it would be an uphill battle to make her way up.

She wouldn't have it any other way.

James Blackman stared at the phone in his hand as if it might bite him. 'What do you mean? It's not colic?'

The vet cleared his throat. 'Not necessarily. But there appears to be traces of arsenic in Coalie's system.'

James blinked. 'Arsenic?'

'It seems too concentrated for a mistake.'

'So what then?'

'I can't say that for sure, but it looks like this might have been deliberate.'

James froze. 'What?

He heard the vet's sigh over the line. 'Well, I'll analyse this a bit more to make sure. But in all likelihood, if it was a natural accident and he's found some on your property, another horse would also have had a nibble and be feeling off. I think we need to get the police involved. But first I'm going to come and flush out his stomach.'

James hung up and ran a hand over his face. He looked up to see Jadin walk in. 'Any update?'

James blew out a deep breath. 'Doc says it could be deliberate.'

Jadin's jaw dropped open. 'Like poisoning? Crikey, that is awful.'

'And frightening,' James muttered. 'It means someone has broken in and done it deliberately.' His eyes went to Jadin and skittered away.

Jadin opened his mouth as if to say something but then shut it again.

'What?'

'Nothing.'

James grabbed his arm. 'You know something?'

'No!' Jadin jerked free. 'You think I wouldn't tell you if I did?' His voice was barely above a hiss.

James sighed. 'But someone seems to have betrayed me. The lock wasn't damaged like it had been ripped off. Someone got in with a key.'

'And if this was an inside job, we're all under suspicion,' Jadin said.

'Yes.' His jaw was tight, and his eyes hard.

Jadin leaned against the wall. 'So what now?'

'That's what I asked Mark. He said he'd run a few tests to be sure, but we'll probably have to get the police involved.'

'Darn.'

'Tell me about it.' James grabbed his jacket and shrugged into it. 'Well, the show must go on. Are you coming?'

'Yeah, guess so.'

They checked on Coalbridge, who still looked lethargic but Vicky had got him to drink a little. James stroked over the soft ears. 'We'll find the scumbag who did this, old man,' he murmured. 'Without a doubt.'

They took the youngsters out for some dressage work. James cantered his trainee, Faststarter, easily across the arena, signalling a flying change halfway down. The horse switched gaits effortlessly. He glanced up to see Jadin's grin from where he was working another novice. 'That's some dancer you've got there. When are you going to find a new name for him? Can you imagine the poor commentators?'

James laughed. 'Any ideas?'

'Well, just an idea, but he's black, like Coalie - what about something else - bridge? Like Darkbridge?'

'Nice idea. But between you and me, I'm saving the bridge suffix for when Coalie's retired to stud.'

Jadin looked at him in surprise. 'And how come I've never heard about this breeding career of yours?'

James grinned. 'It's not going to be a big thing. At least I don't know if it will. But I'd like to breed a couple of my own from him.'

'Wow, the things you never know about a guy…'

'Oh come on,' James laughed. 'What did you think I'd do, just put him out to pasture?'

'Well, not exactly.' Jadin grinned. 'Can I get dibs on a foal?'

James laughed. 'It'll be another ten years, but sure.'

Vicky met them as they dismounted by the hot walker. 'Your mobile's buzzed a couple of times, Jim.'

'Okay, thanks.' He hurried to pick it up. Mark Clinton: Two missed calls.

He pressed redial. 'Hi, Mark. Sorry I was down in the arena.'

'No worries. We've run a few more tests, and I think it's reasonable to say there may have been deliberate sabotage. It's much too concentrated.'

'There's no arsenic around here anyway.'

'Well you never know, sometimes things can go unnoticed. But I don't think that's what we're dealing with.' The vet cleared his throat. 'Jim, if this is what it looks like, we need to get the authorities involved.'

James rubbed the back of his neck. 'I don't want to be stuck in the middle of a storm.'

'I know, and we'll do what we can, but this is inevitable. Calling Steve probably isn't a bad idea, either.'

Steve Merkell was the chef d'equipe for the New Zealand eventing team and oversaw a lot of the ins and outs of the sport and the media. 'Yeah, okay.'

'Seeing as I'm the one with the evidence, I'll call the cops and let them know what's going on and get back to you.'

'All right. Thanks, Mark.'

Steve Merkell sounded understandably taken aback.

'Someone's got into your barn and poisoned your horse?' He repeated.

'Looks that way.'

'Wow, okay.' There was a pause. 'Well, for starters, we'll keep this as quiet as we can. We probably won't even tell the other riders at this stage.'

'Jadin already knows.'

'Right, well, that can't be helped. Who else?'

'Only my groom and the vet, Mark.'

'Okay. Have you involved the authorities?'

'Mark's calling the police.'

'Good. Why don't you call me back once you've talked to them.'

He'd barely hung up when his phone buzzed again. It was Mark.

'A couple of investigators are coming to talk to us at your place. They want to talk to everyone involved, so that includes Jadin and Vicky.'

James sighed and leaned against the door frame. 'Okay, when?'

'Later this afternoon. How's Coalbridge?'

'Vicky's got a bit of liquid in him but she doesn't think it's enough.'

'Okay. I might bring something to keep him hydrated.'

James wandered out and summoned his groom and teammate to tell them the news. He didn't suspect Jadin or Vicky for a second, but he wasn't looking forward to the drama of a police investigation.

One thing was sure, no one was getting to Coalbridge again. He'd been putting off installing security cameras, figuring the stable was locked up and alarmed, but clearly, that wasn't enough.

There was something surreal about seeing a police cruiser pulling up his driveway. He watched as two officers, a man and a woman, emerged from the vehicle. The man approached and held out his hand.

'Hello, I'm Inspector Gavin Willbrook. This is my partner, Constable Tessa Martin.' The woman came forward and shook his hand with a sympathetic smile. 'You have a poisoned horse?'

'James Blackman. Yeah, we found my horse Coalbridge poisoned yesterday morning.' They walked towards the barn, where he introduced Mark, Jadin and Vicky. 'Mark says it's too much to have been accidental.'

Constable Martin flipped over her notebook. 'Can you elaborate on that, Dr Clinton?'

'Mark, please,' he corrected pleasantly.

'Mark. Go ahead.'

Mark detailed the results of the bloodwork and the level of concentration. James made himself pay attention.

'Any signs of a break-in?'

They looked at James, but he looked at Vicky. 'You were the first one down this morning, right?'

She nodded. 'It was all locked up, just like normal. The only thing different was how sick Coalie was. He was fine when I checked him the last time last night.'

'And what time was that?'

'Just after eight,' Vicky said.

'And where did you go after that?'

James bristled but said nothing.

'Brett...my husband picked me up and we went home. About ten minutes away.'

Tessa Martin flipped her notebook shut. 'Can we see the horse's environment?'

Vicky led them in. 'Sure, this way.'

The two detectives looked closely around Coalie's stall before Inspector Willbrook took out a camera and snapped pictures. James' jaw tightened. His barn was now a crime scene.

They talked some more to the vet as they looked the horse over, then asked about Jadin's whereabouts. Tessa turned to James. 'Is there anyone you can think of who would want to harm your horse? Or sabotage you?'

James shook his head. 'Not that I can think of. There's usually a lot of camaraderie in eventing circles. Of course, everyone wants to win, but I wouldn't have a clue who would take it this far.'

'What about disgruntled employees? Personal enemies?'

James thought about it. 'No, I don't think so.'

'Anyone you've recently let go? Even something like that can elicit revenge.'

'Well, I recently lost a couple of grooms, but they both resigned. I've only been here a few years and haven't fired anyone.'

'Their names?'

'Clive Ressler and Lucy Murchison.'

'And where are they now?'

'I don't know any addresses, but Clive's working for Cole Kendrick, the British rider. Somewhere in Essex, I think. And Lucy went back to London.'

Tessa Martin scribbled in her notebook.

'Anything else any of you can think of?' Gavin looked from face to face. Nobody offered.

'Well, call me if you think of anything,' he added, handing a card to both James and Mark. 'We'll be in touch.'

'Thank you both,' James said.

'Not a problem.' Tessa smiled warmly at him. 'Take care, all of you.'

He watched wearily as the car disappeared down towards the road. He heaved a sigh. 'And so it begins.'

Jadin squeezed his shoulder. 'We'll handle it, Jimmy.'

'Oh, I know. But the whole thing is a pain in the neck.'

'Ain't that the truth.'

'You riding any more tonight, Jim?' Vicky asked, holding Coalie's head as the vet took out his syringes.

'No, I think we got it all done.' He glanced questioningly at Jadin, who nodded.

James watched as Mark injected his horse. There was a minuscule flinch, which was a good sign.

'Well, you're a trooper, old man.' The vet patted the soft black neck as he repacked his bag. 'Looks like he's on the mend, James.'

James smiled. 'That's a relief. Anything you need a hand with, Vick?'

She shook her head. 'Don't think so. Just feeding and topping up the water. Won't take me long.'

'Okay then. Thanks for everything, guys.'

He and Jadin headed up to the house. 'You know,' Jadin started as they kicked off their boots on the porch.

James groaned. 'Why do I not like the sound of your tone?'

'I cannot fathom why,' Jadin deadpanned in his best imitation of an English lord. 'However, as I was saying, that nice constable wasn't wearing a ring.'

'What do I care whether or not he's married?' He opened the fridge and popped open a can of Coke.

'Not the Inspector. The constable. The female officer.'

James rolled his eyes. 'Don't start.'

'Just saying, she seems very nice.'

James flicked him with his Cola. 'What do you want for dinner?'

'Let's order takeaways. I'm exhausted.' Jadin sank onto the sofa.

'Yeah, pretty long day.' James swirled his drink. 'I'm thinking I'll call the security people tomorrow. I need some cameras installed.'

'Good idea.' Jadin rubbed his neck. 'I can't believe someone you know has done this.'

'Me neither, but how else could they have gotten in clean?'

'No windows they can slip in?'

James shook his head.

'But still...how did they open the padlock?'

'Got to the keys somehow.'

'Who else has a key? You and Vicky?'

'Yeah, and a couple of teammates.'

'Any missing?'

'No.'

'So someone's nicked a key and had it copied.'

James looked wearily at his friend. 'You may be right. But how do we prove that?'

'Ask the key companies?'

James raised an eyebrow. 'Every place in the county?'

'Well, we start in Ashton. This place can't have more than one locksmith.'

'If it has one at all. Probably got it done in Bristol.' He ran his hand over his face. 'Boy, this is exhausting.'

'What d'you want for dinner?'

'Doesn't bother me. As long as it's edible. Do you want to order? I'm taking a shower.'

'Sure.'

They theorized some more over their noodles, but they just went around in circles. If someone had duplicated a key, it would be very difficult to find.

'Of course,' Jadin stabbed his fork towards his friend. 'Someone could've been paid to get the key copied and get it to the perps, but they're not directly involved.'

James snorted. 'That's pretty involved.'

'You know what I mean.'

'Yeah, but that still means someone I know has betrayed me.'

'True. But it's possibly a more feasible explanation than if they are conspiring against you themselves.' He shrugged. 'Money can be a huge incentive.'

'Oh and that makes it less disloyal.'

'That's not what I meant.'

'Sure it wasn't.'

Jadin stood up then, a storm in his usually placid blue eyes. 'You don't trust me, do you? You haven't ruled out the possibility that I did this.'

'Of course I have. Jade, we've known each other for how long…'

'Which counts for nothing, apparently.' Jadin threw his napkin back onto the table. 'We've been like brothers since we were ten. That's nearly two decades, in case you hadn't realised that. I don't know what you think of me, but for the record, I would give my life before I betrayed you.'

'Jadin-'

'Forget it.' He stalked out of the room.

James put his head in his hands. He was stressed and he'd taken it out on Jadin. But he didn't think for a second he was guilty.

But someone was. He wasn't going to like it, whatever happened.

Chapter Four

James sat mindlessly in front of late-night TV. Jadin had never returned and he was too tired to deal with it. He knew he hadn't been free of fault but his friend was assuming a lot too. The digits on his mobile had clicked to 00:00 by the time he switched off the TV. He was dead tired but had too much on his mind for sleep to come easily. He was also half concerned the perps would come back.

Vicky had volunteered to bunk down in the tack room, but there was no way he'd let her. He thought of doing it himself but he figured they wouldn't be back two nights later.

Can't sleep anyway. Might as well.

He dug out his sleeping bag and collected a couple of throw pillows. He locked the door behind him and trekked quietly down the rise to the barn. The sky was clear and beautiful, but the events of the past few days made the darkness seem eerie. He unlocked the barn and slid the bolt shut behind him. A few of the horses stirred, and he checked quickly on Coalie, who was dozing. He meandered to the tack room and settled in.

He listened to the stillness, broken only by the occasional snuffle or rustling of hooves in the hay. He thought over his argument with Jadin. They'd had a lot of fights over their twenty years of friendship, going back to whose pony looked better before the in-hand class. But there'd never been a question about loyalty. They'd always had each other's backs. But if it was him, what better way to throw you off his trail? No way. James put his head back and went to sleep.

He was woken by the stable door unlocking and heeled boots tapping towards the feed room. He sat up and checked his watch. It was just after six.

Vicky walked past, stopping suddenly when she saw him. 'Oh, it's you,' she said. 'I thought for a second we had another intruder.'

James grinned. 'Sorry. Morning.'

She leaned on the doorjamb, studying him. 'Get any sleep?'

'A bit. But hopefully, I won't have to repeat it. I'll give the security people a call today.'

'Good idea.' She walked away, then stuck her head back in. 'Would you like some hay and energy feed, too?'

'Very funny. I think this morning calls for a proper English breakfast.'

He walked into the house to the smell of eggs and sausages. He walked into the kitchen just as Jadin tossed some bacon into the pan. 'You read my mind.'

He could see Jadin pause.

James took a breath. 'Jadin, I'm sorry. I'm stressed by what's going on, and the fact that it has to be someone I know. But I honestly don't suspect you.'

He heard Jadin exhale. 'Well, I probably made some assumptions too.' He turned to face him. 'Sorry.'

James took a step further into the room. 'So...can I have some breakfast?'

'Sure.' He smiled, but it was replaced by a frown. 'Where did you sleep last night? In the barn?'

'Yeah, in the tack room. Wasn't completely sure they wouldn't come back.'

'Oh. You look like you did.'

'Gee, thanks.' He wandered over to the message machine. The light wasn't showing. 'No messages, I guess.'

'Well, it's only six twenty. I'm pretty sure most detectives work nine to five unless they're in homicide or something.' He flipped the bacon. 'Besides, this is a tough case. There's no evidence.'

'A sick horse.'

'Yeah, but that doesn't point to who did it.' He glanced at James over his shoulder. 'Have you thought about the fact of Clive and Lucy leaving?'

James looked up from checking his emails. 'They didn't do it.'

'You're sure? How well do you know them?'

'Well enough.' James straightened up and glanced at the clock. 'I'll ride Patriot, then come back up here and call the security company.'

'Rightio.' Jadin slid the breakfast onto a plate.

Coalbridge seemed more like his old self and was starting to nibble at his feed. Vicky reported he'd drunk most of his water overnight.

James stopped long enough to talk to the horse and rub his ears. 'We'll have you back out running before you know it.' Coalbridge nudged his hand, looking for carrots, his favourite treat. 'Sorry, Coalie. Maybe tomorrow.'

Patriot was lively, tugging on the bit and dancing in place. James kept him standing still outside the arena for 30 seconds before walking in.

'He looks great,' Jadin said from outside the ring. He leaned against the rail, holding Delaware by the reins. The big grey gelding looked on with the air of a benevolent professor supervising a student.

'He was good. Very good, weren't you, old lad?' Patriot tossed his head as they passed the other horse. 'I think there's hope for him yet.'

James cooled down Patriot slowly around the outside of the ring so he could watch Jadin on Delaware. The 12-year-old was one of the few horses in the world he'd have bought for himself without question if he could. 'Over my dead body' was Jadin's reply to any enquiries from rich owners. He wasn't a flashy horse, but he was about as grounded in all three disciplines as one animal could be. Probably even more so than Coalbridge, as much as James hated to admit it. He didn't have Coalie's flair, but with that sometimes came a few mistakes. James turned Patriot back towards the barn, making a fuss of him for his effort. He was fairly certain Patriot only did things for food but it couldn't hurt.

He left the horse in Vicky's capable hands and jogged up to the house to call someone to install security cameras. He'd always been sure locking and alarming the stable was enough; eventing didn't have the dirty underbelly that racing had. But he was taking no more chances.

After getting the promise of a quote later that day, he headed back down to the barns. He and Jadin spent the afternoon leisurely working with the youngsters, taking it slow and letting them adjust to new things at their own pace.

James clipped his horse to the hot walker. 'When are you heading back to York?'

'Not soon enough for you, apparently.' Jadin grinned at him as he removed a saddle.

'That's not what I meant. Just wondered.'

Jadin followed him to the tack room. 'Probably Saturday, straight from Portbury. Are you still taking Marksman?'

'Sure, why wouldn't I?'

'Well, it's been a bit disruptive around here is all.'

'Yeah, well, I'm not letting them stop me.' He glanced at his watch. 'Speak of the devil... he's due for a decent run today.'

Jadin slung another saddle over his arm and headed for his horse's box. 'Can't believe we're into another season already.'

'Neither can I. And only another year to the Olympics.' James opened Marksman's stall door. The tall chestnut nickered at the sight of him.

'You going over to Kentucky this year?' Only two of the six five star-level events worldwide were outside of Europe -

Kentucky and Adelaide. The calendar started with Pau in October, followed by Adelaide in November. Kentucky took place the following April, followed by Badminton in May, Luhmuhlen in June, and Burghley in late August or early September. It was a somewhat lopsided season but was meant to allow riders in different time zones and seasons to compete. Jadin and Delaware had won Pau three months ago, but James had won the overall Classics standings for the last two years.

'I'm not sure. I was going to take Coalie, but I'll have to see how he is. Seeing as I'm leading the points anyway, it's no big deal,' he added with mock pompousness.

'Sure, sure, boast away. Del and I will get you yet. You're not taking Marksman?'

The horse pricked his ears at the mention of his name. 'Smart boy.' Jadin stopped outside the stall to pat his nose.

They clipped the horses to the hot walker and James went back to the rickety little desk in the tack room to go over his plans for the Portbury four-star in two days. He would run Marksman in the top event, as well as one of his younger horses, Lacklustre, a bay eight-year-old, in the three-star. Jadin would be taking only Delaware so there would be plenty of room in the four-horse trailer. Vicky walked in and added another bridle to the stack in the corner. 'There, I think that's all you should need.'

'Thanks, Vick. You're sure you don't want to come?'

'Nah, that's okay. I'll keep the fires burning here.' She brushed a strand of hair back from her face. 'But I'll use my seniority to get dibs on Kentucky and Badminton.'

James chuckled. 'You get first pick anyway. But I'm not sure about Kentucky this year.'

'Really?' She opened the portable tack locker and started packing.

'Yeah, just not sure about taking that long a trip. I was going to take Coalie, but we'll have to see how he goes.'

'What about Badminton?'

'I'm planning to take both him and Marksman. So again, not sure I want Coalie to do a big trip only three or four weeks out. I wouldn't have even attempted it with Marksman.' The horse didn't mind riding in a trailer but he hated flying. The two times he had, he'd had to be sedated so he didn't go mad when the engines started up.

It was only a fifteen-minute drive to Portbury, so it should be an easy trip. Then they'd drive into Bristol where Jadin would fly back to York. Delaware was an easy traveller, so Jadin made a lot of journeys by air, to James' unending envy.

The security company came that afternoon and installed cameras and alarms right around the property. The technician showed James how to work the cameras, which ran on a 24-hour reel and fed to his desktop.

The next morning Coalie was doing well, looking around for his feed when James opened the stable just after seven. He was fidgety, so he put him on the hot walker and studied him. He wasn't quite his usual pristine self, but he was moving well and tossing his head around, playing with the ring. Definitely on the mend. It was good to see before he hit the road.

James and Jadin were the only two members of the New Zealand eventing team who had made the trip to Portbury. It wasn't one of the larger events, but they both felt it was a good starting point for the English eventing season. James noticed that Markus Klinnsman, the Swede who was second to him in the overall FEI Classics series, had brought two of his horses including his top mount Vertigo.

Dressage day dawned with rain drizzling over the greater part of the county. Marksman wouldn't mind in the least, but Lacklustre hated a sloppy arena.

Thankfully James and Lacklustre were second in for the three-star. Lacklustre kept snorting and tossing his head as they warmed up, trying to get the rain out of his face. As James tried to hold him in a piaffe, trotting almost in place, Lacklustre decided to just stand still. James held in a groan and nudged him forward again, wondering if he should just scratch him, but decided against it. At this stage of the gelding's career, the experience was the most important thing. And running the English eventing circuit, he'd better learn to tolerate rain now and then.

Their dressage test was horrendous.

Lacklustre kept moving when he was meant to stop, stopped when he was meant to keep moving, and flat out refused to do a flying change. Their score was 51.00, over twenty points behind the leading rider on 25.00, and the majority of the field was still to come.

Lacklustre's ears were pinned back to his head as they returned to the stables, snuffing like an angry freight train. James dismounted and tried to calm him down but to no avail. Catie came up to take the reins. 'Sorry, Uncle James. I'll lead him out.'

'Careful he doesn't bite your head off,' James muttered as he returned to the trailer to sort himself out for the four-star. He checked his watch. He still had a couple of hours before he had to be back on Marksman, so he decided to run back to the accommodation and grab a shower.

Marksman was in a much better frame of mind. The rain didn't bother him at all. They produced a nice flowing test, putting them second with two-thirds of the class gone.

James gave Catie the reins so he could hang around and watch Jadin. Delaware looked a little clunky, but they completed a decent test, placing tenth.

Jadin shook his head as he walked his horse out of the ring. 'Well, that would've stunned the audience.'

James grabbed the reins as Jadin dismounted. 'It wasn't that bad. At least you made your flying changes.'

Jadin chuckled dryly. 'Yeah, I guess so.' He took the reins. 'Just as well you can jump, Del.'

The rain was heavier overnight and the cross-country track would be muddy. Lacklustre would be grumpy the whole way around, but their score was beyond salvaging anyway. A muddy track might assist the sure-footed Marksman.

The three-star class went first, which only chopped up the track further. They were early in the next run, but Lacklustre was definitely in a foul mood. James held the horse firm in the starting area while Lustre fidgeted. The starter gave the signal and James released the reins. Lacklustre bolted forward as if he'd heard a shotgun.

His canter was choppy as they made their way to the first obstacle, but at least he jumped it. James pulled him down to a trot to even out his stride, then let him back out to a canter. Lacklustre was still grumpy but he was running and jumping. James rode above his withers, keeping a tight hold on the reins on the slippery ground.

James' main worry was the three-part water jump; an obstacle into the lake, one in the middle and one out of the water. It was a tight line with only three strides between jumps, and Lustre wasn't always the quickest on his feet.

As they approached the water James pulled back on the reins, slowing Lacklustre down fractionally. The horse jumped in and James' breath caught in his throat as he felt a rear hoof catch on the jump. Lustre stumbled as he landed but launched himself over the island jump. James sat back, not interfering as the horse got his feet under him. They made it over the third element and James exhaled, taking the time to pat the horse's neck as they cantered away.

Lacklustre continued to motor around the course, and they made it to the finish with no faults and no time penalties. James thumped the horse's neck as they eased back to a trot.

He may have his issues in the dressage arena but he was certainly proving he could jump.

The rain had stopped by the time he went out on Marksman for the four-star, but by this time the course had gone beyond muddy to sloppy. A few competitors had decided to scratch, but James knew Marksman could handle a wet track. Jadin warmed up Delaware nearby; he would start his run next after the three-minute interval. Delaware was also a good runner in the mud. 'Good luck, Jimmy,' he called.

James saluted him. 'Same to you.'

Marksman danced about in the start box, eager to get going. James watched the starter and nudged his horse forward. Marksman tackled the course like the pro he was. James clenched his teeth as they approached the water, but the horse cleared it easily. 'Good boy.'

Marksman popped over the last jump and they cantered towards the finish, again clear and within the time. James slowed the canter then brought Marksman to a walk, glancing at the board for his score and also to see how Jadin was going. The camera cut back to Jadin's round as Delaware approached the water.

James held Marksman still for a moment to watch. Delaware's bold strides carried right up to the base of the entry jump and he popped over like it was cavaletti. He cantered towards the island and seemed to take off too early, but he went over. James frowned as Delaware approached the exit jump, looking off stride. He jumped, but his left back leg caught the top of the wood.

It was like watching a car crash. Delaware's front feet hit the ground scrambling, trying to regain his balance, but his back leg was still caught and he fell. Jadin had tried to hold him upright but lost his grip and slipped out of the saddle, falling heavily to the ground.

James' gasp was inaudible over the gasps of the crowd. Delaware scrambled to his feet and limped a few feet away, but Jadin's form remained motionless on the ground.

Start moving. Get up!

He watched the activity on the screen, stewards running up to catch the horse and medics approaching Jadin. The ground announcer's voice broke into his thoughts, explaining that the cross-country was on hold while they took care of the accident. 'Good round, Uncle Jim.' His niece's blond head came into view. 'Want me to take him?' She followed his gaze, and her face fell. 'Oh, no.'

Jadin was still lying motionless as the medics gathered around him and the ambulance pulled up. There was a sombre hush over the audience as the possible severity of the accident started to register. James was suddenly aware of how tightly he was holding the reins and relaxed his hands.

He realised Catie was still standing there, one hand on Marksman's bridle. He shook his head as if to clear his brain and swung his leg over the saddle. 'Sorry, Cate. Sure, you can take him.' Something flashed on her left hand and James stared, his brain unable to process what he saw.

Caitlyn must have noticed his expression because she quickly removed her hand. 'I'm...sorry, Uncle Jim. I was excited to tell you but…'

James took a breath; it was all too much to take in right now. 'I'm sorry, sweetie. We'll talk later, okay?'

Caitlyn was looking weirdly at him, probably because he seldom used any terms of endearment. 'Okay. Tell me about Jadin, when you know, please?'

'I will. I'm going to find out where they'll take him.'

He glanced again at the screen, but it had gone blank. He swallowed. *Don't let it be that bad.*

Chapter Five

Amy double-checked her bag and her appearance one more time before marching towards the door. Today she and Chester would tackle their first event on English soil. It was exciting, but it also scared the wits out of her. The next few months would be the Litmus test. And if she wasn't good enough, this whole expedition had been wasted.

Chester loaded into the trailer without any hesitation, and they got onto the road, wipers slashing across the windshield. Thankfully Chester didn't mind the wet.

She turned on the radio for company. It had certainly been a lonely few months in England.

She missed Mickey. They had been close since intermediate school, and they went through the Pony Club grades together. She was the closest thing to a sister she'd ever had, and in her family, she had needed one. The fighting started when she was at intermediate school, and she'd sometimes felt like a pawn in a messy divorce.

Amy felt Chester shift in the trailer as they went around a corner. Horses became her lifeline when she reached her teenage years. She spent most of her free time at the Pony Club, helping care for the horses and equipment. Some days, she would go and stay at Mickey's nice, normal home.

She envied her immensely. Mickey had two parents who loved her, her brothers and each other. She loved sleeping over at their house, playing castles in the treehouse and telling ghost stories with the boys at bedtime.

She'd once asked Mickey if her parents could adopt her.

Mickey said she didn't think so, but she'd be her sister forever.

Sixteen years later, she was still upholding her end of the bargain.

Amy saw the showgrounds in the distance and pulled off the highway. She didn't feel sorry for herself anymore, at least not often. But she was still angry and that was hard to let go of. She pulled to a stop at the gate and gave her name to the attendant, who showed her where to park her trailer. She stopped in the designated area and got out of the truck, taking a moment to study her surroundings. In many ways, it reminded her of a country show back in the North Island, only busier.

She let down the ramp and led Chester down. He stopped at the bottom, surveying his new surroundings. When he appeared satisfied, she led him around to stretch his legs. They still had ninety minutes before the dressage started.

She glanced around surreptitiously herself as they walked. It seemed like a relaxed atmosphere, almost like a family day like the A & P Show back home, but more competitive. Some of the horses seemed quite top-notch.

The rain had stopped by the time the dressage got underway, but the arena would still be muddy. She warmed Chester up carefully, keeping an eye on his troublesome left foreleg. The vet had warned her he could go arthritic in that leg, so she took extra care.

She watched a couple of entrants before her, impressed with the standard. This tiny event could easily match the three-star at Puhinui. She knew it was probably a bit below Chester's level but she wanted to ease him in slowly. There was plenty of time.

He walked into the ring with just a trace of arrogance. She kept him still a fraction longer than necessary just to remind him who was boss, then eased him into a trot.

The test went well, she thought, considering he hadn't competed in a few months. His flying changes were still a bit rusty but they were improving. They placed second.

'That's a good horse,' the woman in the next trailer commented as they returned for a break.

'Thank you. He's not bad but he's still learning,' Amy said, stroking the grey ears.

'Has he done much eventing?'

'Quite a bit back where we come from, but it's another level up over here.' She removed his bridle so he could have the bit out of his mouth between stages.

'Well, good luck.'

'Thanks, same to you.'

Amy grabbed a bite of lunch before warming up for the cross-country. This was Chester's strongest phase. He was a good jumper but sometimes didn't pick up his feet enough over the more delicate show jumping poles.

The ground was muddy but in decent condition. Chester flew around almost as if the standard was beneath him. They never came close to any time penalties.

The rain came again by the time they got to show jumping, and it was unpleasant all around. Several riders decided not to bother, but Amy pressed on. An outdoor spring sport in England was bound to have some rain now and then, and one couldn't just turn tail before the Badminton show-jumping because of rain.

She could hear Mickey's voice in her head. When, not if.

She was drenched by the time they went into the arena, and Chester was starting to get temperamental. He hit the first jump, and the round spiralled downward from there. He knocked down six out of twelve.

She brushed him dry in the trailer, analysing the performance in her head. The rain and his bad mood had certainly contributed, but there was still work to be done. Despite the elements, she was disheartened. She'd thought he - they - were better than that.

James flashed his New Zealand Olympic ID at yet another official, his indignation growing. His best friend was still lying on the cross-country course and he was being stonewalled. Someone finally allowed him to take care of Delaware. He approached the horse slowly, his eyes darting to the ambulance where Jadin was being loaded. He still hadn't moved. James was a praying man but seldom had he prayed this hard.

He took Delaware's reins, soothing the horse with his voice. The attendant told him that the horse had injured his back leg. Dropping the reins to the ground to keep him still - a Western riding trick Jadin had taught the horse years ago - he moved to the rear left leg and gently ran his hands over it, noting Delaware's flinch as he touched the fetlock.

'Easy, old man.' He returned to the horse's head and stroked his neck. 'Let's get you back to the stable and ice that.' He talked to the horse, as much to give himself something to think about as to calm Delaware. The ambulance pulled away, lights flashing.

He saw a medic that had stayed behind and approached him as fast as he could with Delaware's limp. 'Sir, excuse me…' He produced the same eye-catching ID. 'I'm Jadin Steele's friend; I'm here with him this weekend. Can you tell me how he is?'

The medic looked at him. The weariness in his expression was frightening. 'They're taking him to St Michael's in Bristol. You'll have to take it up with the doctors there.'

James pleaded with him. 'I have to take care of his horse first. He'd want me to do that before I came to some waiting room. Please.'

The medic looked at him again, then sighed. 'All right. Strictly off the record...'

'Yes.'

'It looks like he may have been partially crushed in the fall. He's unconscious, probably has a few broken ribs. There's also, erm, a good chance he may have a severe spinal injury.' James swallowed. 'How bad is it? Is his--' His voice caught. 'His life in danger?'

'That depends on the head trauma. At this stage, I'd say he was critical.' His expression softened slightly. 'I'm sorry, son.' James nodded, sucking in a deep breath. 'Thank you.' He turned back to Delaware and stroked his face. 'Come on, Del.' The walk back to the stable was slow with Delaware favouring his leg. It gave Jadin too much time to think. The fall repeated itself in his head in slow motion. The camera hadn't caught Jadin hitting the ground; they'd had the opposite angle. Maybe that was just as well.

Delaware walked slowly, his head hanging. He didn't seem to be in too much pain; he had only a slight limp. James wondered how much the horse was aware of. They certainly understood more than what most people gave them credit for. James loved his horses and he was sure they loved their riders back, as much as a dog would.

'He'll be okay, old boy.' He rubbed Delaware's sweaty grey neck as they walked. The horse was still breathing heavily from the run but it was slowing down. They made it back to where Delaware was stabled next to Marksman and Lacklustre. Caitlyn came running out and took the other side of Delaware's bridle. 'Is he okay?'

James sighed. 'I squeezed a bit of info out of one of the medics.' He gently backed Delaware into his stall and slipped off the bridle, looking at his niece across the neck. 'It's not good, Catie.'

'Oh.' He saw a few tears well in her eyes. Jadin had been Catie's friend ever since he let her ride his horse when she was seven.

'I'll go up to the hospital, but Jadin would want me to look after Delaware first. There's nothing I can do for Jadin right now.' He moved back to strip off the saddle and blanket.

'Is Del okay?' Caitlyn asked, stroking the horse.

'Seems to be except for that off hind. He was limping on it.' Jadin brushed the now-dry saddle area. 'Can you get me an ice boot?'

'Sure.' She let herself out of the stall. Something glinted on her hand, and James remembered the ring.

She came back and they bandaged the limb. Delaware just stood there. 'He looks glum,' Caitlyn observed.

'I know. I think he knows Jadin's hurt.' James rubbed his ears and the horse nosed his hand. James gave him a piece of carrot.

'I'll feed them all soon. Anything special before tomorrow?' Caitlyn asked.

Tomorrow. James wondered how he'd come back and show jump. 'No, just the usual.'

She nodded and let herself out of the stall. James finished brushing and did the same. 'So, you want to tell me about that ring?'

She looked abashed. 'I'm sorry. Today's such a bad time.'

'Not your fault. It will give me something else to think about. And I do want to know.'

'Okay.' She looked down at the diamond. 'You know that guy Wilson I was seeing?'

James raised an eyebrow. 'The jockey?'

'Uh-huh. We, well, got kind of serious.'

'I dare say.'

'He proposed yesterday after we had dinner.'

'Ah.' James cocked his head for her to follow as he returned the gear to their tack box. 'And you said yes.'

She blushed a little. 'Yeah.'

'So…' He locked the tack box and turned to face her. 'Is he good for you?'

She nodded.

'What do your mum and dad say?'

'Mum loved him from the start. Dad took a while but he is a lawyer.'

'Doesn't mean he's not right.'

'No, but I could be engaged to the King of England and he'd find some fault. It's his job.'

'What didn't your dad like?'

'Why, so you can back him up?'

James had to grin. 'I can neither confirm nor deny.'

Caitlyn sighed dramatically. 'Worried about his income. Worried about his 'temperament'.' She added the air quotation marks.

'And you don't think it's too soon? In your life or the relationship?'

'Uncle Jim, I'm nearly twenty.'

'You have no idea how young that is.'

"Whatever. Yeah, I'm sure. It'll be a long engagement, anyway.' She raised her eyebrows at him. 'What is this, the Spanish Inquisition? I already have two parents you know.'

James grinned. 'Hey, I was only seventeen when Melanie had you. I always thought I was the hip, cool uncle.'

Caitlyn laughed. 'You are. But you went old-fashioned on me as soon as you saw the ring.'

'Well, you went and got engaged on me.' He punched her shoulder lightly. 'Look, Caitlyn, in all seriousness, if you're happy and you love him, then I'm all for it.' He grinned at her. 'But I'm not going in to bat for you against your dad.'

'Oh, I think he's come around.' She twisted the ring.

'Well, I guess congratulations are in order, young lady.'

She grinned coyly. 'Thanks.'

James checked his watch, feeling his mood deteriorate as they switched topics. 'I'm going to head up to the hospital. You need help with anything else?'

'Nah, I'll be fine. I'll feed and pack up.' She twisted her hands together. 'Can you text or call when you know anything?'

'Of course.' He gave her a sad smile and squeezed her shoulder. He headed for the parking lot, then paused and turned back to her. 'Jadin loves you too, you know. You've always been his honorary niece.'

She smiled through watery eyes. 'I know.'

The boots thumped to the floor and the gear bag followed. Only extreme self-control kept her from slamming the door. Amy collapsed on the couch and shut her eyes. On top of their dreadful jumping round, Chester now had heat in both his front legs, which could be tendon or ligament injuries. If they didn't come right in the next couple of days it could be more than a slight sprain.

She was still damp and dirty, so she headed for the shower. Her favourite vanilla shampoo wouldn't hurt her frame of mind either. She decided she needed something to enjoy today, so she ordered from her favourite Thai place.

Feeling more relaxed, she sat down in front of the TV with her Phad Thai. The news was just reaching the sports segment, and she watched all the football highlights with disinterest before they moved on to the more interesting stuff.

The presenter's demeanour darkened. 'International eventing rider Jadin Steele is in critical condition after a fall at a small three-day event in Portbury, Somerset. Steele and his mount Delaware fell at the third element of a water treble on a wet course.'

Amy's hand flew up to her face as they replayed the accident. 'Steele was attended to by medics at the scene before being taken by ambulance to St Michael's Hospital in Bristol. No further medical information has been released.'

Amy sat back hard. As a teenager, she had idolised Jadin Steele and James Blackman. They were riders in their twenties, from her tiny country, making waves in the big leagues of eventing. That was everything she wanted to do; everything she had packed up her life in Waikato for.

And critical condition? There was a possibility he could die? That was scary.

She knew that eventing was a dangerous sport. She'd certainly broken her share of bones over the years. But she'd never really thought of it as life-threatening, the way she did racing. In light of what she'd just seen, her day suddenly looked a whole lot better. She felt for his family and his teammates, the people she wanted to join one day.

She finished her food and thought about calling Mickey, but decided sleep was a good idea. She stared at the ceiling, the lights from the TV making eerie patterns. Or maybe everything just felt eerie today; someone was fighting for his life for doing the same thing she did.

Chapter Six

James was going to go mad if someone didn't tell him
something soon.

They had played the next-of-kin card. He'd explained that
Jadin's family all lived thousands of miles away and he was
the closest thing Jadin had right now, but they'd still insisted
on calling his parents first, waking them from a dead sleep in
the middle of the night to tell them their son was fighting for
his life.

James had at least been able to talk to Tom and Judie. He'd
explained the fall the best he could and assured them he'd take
care of Jadin. They wanted to fly out immediately but he
thought they should at least wait to know more.

One more reason you'd better not dare die on me, Jadin.

As far as he knew from the first doctor an hour ago, Jadin had
been in surgery for his brain injury. It seemed he would then
be moved to traction as they tried to gauge how badly he'd
damaged his spinal cord.

The possible scenarios ran through James' mind and he shook
his head as if to clear it. He couldn't imagine Jadin paralysed,
or worse. Once, years ago, they'd joked about what they'd say
at each other's funerals, depending on who died first. They had
been in their early twenties, their dreams were within their
grasp, and death seemed a long way away, if not an
impossibility.

He got up and paced the room again. Another doctor appeared
and looked wearily at him, setting off alarm bells in James'
head. 'Are you here with Jadin Steele?'

'Yes.'

'Are you next of kin?'

James clenched his teeth, half annoyed and half dreading how serious that meant it was. 'No, but his parents are in New Zealand and waiting for news. I have medical power of attorney until they get here.' He produced his ID.

The doctor nodded crisply. 'All right, let's have a seat.'

James sat, rubbing his hands together.

'Jadin was partially crushed when his horse fell on him. He has three broken ribs on his right side, and some brain trauma also on that side.' He cleared his throat. 'We had to go in and drain some bleeding from his brain, but we won't know how severe the damage is until he wakes up.'

James nodded. 'What are the possibilities?'

The doctor sighed. 'If there's no more swelling, there's a chance there will be no permanent damage. But there is a chance he will need therapy. He may have memory loss, or there might be some more permanent problems, like learning how to talk again.'

James clenched his teeth. 'What about his spine?'

'He has damaged several vertebrae, I'm afraid. There's a chance...' The doctor paused, but James guessed what was coming. 'He may not walk again.'

James sat back against the chair, jaw set. The idea of Jadin wheelchair-bound and unable to speak properly was repulsive. And yet, he suddenly realised there was a silver lining in the doctor's speech. 'But his life's not in danger?'

'The brain trauma doesn't appear to be as bad as we feared. Assuming he wakes up in the next 48 to 60 hours, he should be out of the woods.'

James let out a breath. That was one relief. 'Is there anything else?'

'Cuts and bruises that will all heal.' The doctor looked down at his clipboard. 'We're keeping him in the ICU as a precaution for now, until we know for sure about his brain injury. You can see him if you're not too long.'

James had seen his closest friend lying immobile on the cross country track, but somehow the sight of him in a hospital bed, hooked up to tubes with a wire monitoring his brain, was ten times worse. It made it all more real. He approached cautiously as if the figure was a stranger. It was so far removed from the Jadin he knew.

He sank into the chair beside the bed. 'Hey, Jadin.' It seemed weird to be saying such familiar words in such a surreal situation. 'I took care of Del. He's fine, just a bump on his back leg.' He reached over and took his hand. 'I talked to your Mum and Dad too. They're okay. I'll call them back in a minute and update them on how you're doing. They'll probably fly out tomorrow.'

He'd heard those in a coma could sometimes hear what was said to them, so he pressed on. 'Caitlyn's upset for you too. You've always been her friend. She's engaged, you know. Oh heck, you probably already know; she probably told you before me. I gather he's a nice enough guy; I just worry that they're rushing things. Well, if he doesn't treat her right, he'll have you on his tail, along with me and her dad.'

A nurse appeared in the doorway and signalled for him to leave. He squeezed Jadin's hand and stood slowly. 'Hang in there, buddy. You're gonna be okay.'

He walked past the nurse and back out of the ICU so he could use his cell. He knew it would cost an arm and a leg to call back to New Zealand but this was one of the times that was unimportant.

He talked to Judie, repeating what the doctor had said as gently as he could. Jadin wasn't in immediate danger, so they would fly out later that afternoon New Zealand time, arriving at Bristol tomorrow night.

'I'll come in and get you,' James said, ignoring their protests. 'Or Caitlyn might like a drive.'

'Oh, Caitlyn Holland is still working for you? How is that darling girl?' Judie seemed glad for another topic to latch on to.
'She's good. She's just got engaged.'
'Oh really! And who is the lucky young man?'
'He's a jockey.'
'Oh, how nice.' Her tone sobered. 'Oh dear, I am terrible, getting all excited at a time like this.'
James smiled. 'No, Judie. It's what Jadin would want.'
He heard her sigh. 'You're right. Okay, we'll see you or Caitlyn at the airport tomorrow night, your time. Thank you for everything, Jimmy.'
Something in the familiar way she said his name made him wonder how long it had been since they'd talked to each other. Too long, certainly. 'No problem. Have a safe flight.'
He checked on Jadin again before heading home. They'd been close enough to Portbury that they hadn't needed a hotel. He called Caitlyn from the car, wincing as he realised how late it was. 'Sorry, Catie. I didn't look at the time.'
'No, I would've wanted to know. How is he?'
'Stable, for now.' He gave her a brief rundown, hearing her gasp at the spinal damage. 'But we don't know a lot for sure yet.'
'Oh heck, Uncle Jim.' Her voice sounded small. 'I just can't imagine Jadin…'
'I know.' He started the motor. 'Get some sleep, okay? You could come up and see him before the jumping in the morning.'
'Okay. Goodnight.'
'Night, honey.' The endearment slipped out. He rarely called her anything but her name, but they'd all had a reminder of just how short life was.

Amy got up earlier than usual so she could check on Chester's legs before work. They were still warm to the touch but not as bad as the night before. Hopefully, it wouldn't be anything serious; this adventure was just beginning.

She parked in the secured lot and walked into her work. She enjoyed her job as a receptionist in a newspaper office; it was interesting work, even though she had no career aspirations in the field. She'd done similar work back in Waikato.

'Morning, Amy.' Her fellow clerk, Tori, was the closest thing to a friend she had in England. 'How was your weekend?'

'Well, okay. I took my horse out to a one-day event, but he had a brain explosion while show jumping.' She booted up her computer. 'Hurt himself, too.'

'Ouch. Sorry to hear.' Tori glanced at her. 'Are you okay?'

'Yeah, fine. It's his legs; a tendon sprain or something similar.' She opened her inbox and scanned the unread mail, trying to pick out the most important ones. 'How was your weekend?'

'Oh, all right. Gardening, the boys' football. The usual.' She typed away with her long, manicured nails. 'My ex wants to change custody, though.'

'Oh. You have a problem with it?'

'Not really. If the boys don't mind. They do need their father.'

'You know, I admire that you two aren't playing the boys against each other. Too many couples do that.' *Like my mum and dad.*

'Yeah, that was one thing we both agreed on. Our problems aren't their fault.' Tori paused reflectively. 'Sometimes I even wonder if we were too hasty breaking up.'

Amy looked at her. 'If you feel that way, maybe you should reconsider.'

Tori smiled ruefully. 'It's probably too late.'

'Oh, he's remarried?'

'No. It's just been too long, and too many issues.'

'You never know. If you still love him, it's worth a chance.'

Tori smiled at her. 'You sound like you speak from experience.'

A face flashed in Amy's mind. 'In a way, yeah.'

Tori studied her. 'You still love him. Whoever he is.'

Amy sighed. 'Look, it's been so long now that I'm not even sure if it's love. Or even if it was then.' She groaned to herself at the stack of mail and started sorting. 'But I still think about him, yeah.'

'So are you going to take your own advice?'

Amy grinned guiltily. 'Well…'

Tori laughed. 'Yeah, I figured.' She spun her chair to look for something in her drawer. 'So why not?'

'He's halfway around the world.'

'Ever heard of the internet?'

Amy rolled her eyes. 'No, way out in the wilds of Waikato we use Morse code.'

'Funny.' Tori shrugged. 'Look, I happen to believe you're right. If you still care, it's worth a shot.'

Amy shrugged back. She still thought of Damien a lot. They'd been best friends once and headed perhaps for something more, but life had got in the way. In his case, his dream to go into the Navy; in hers, the decision to upend and chase rainbows on the other side of the world.

'If I should try, just maybe you should too,' Tori said.

The ringing phone saved her from having to reply. 'Enfield Gazette, Amy speaking.'

The day dragged on. The heavens opened just after lunch, which didn't improve anybody's mood. There didn't seem to be much work to do, so Amy went through her emails for anything she'd missed.

She fed Chester and cleaned his stall. His legs were still warm, so she reapplied the ice packs. She frowned when she realised he hadn't finished his food from the morning.

'Are you sick, old boy?' She brushed his fetlock out of his eyes. He didn't look ill or droopy, but she headed to find a thermometer just in case.

His temp was 100 exactly, so he didn't have a fever. She checked him over but couldn't see anything amiss, so she refilled his feed and water and watched him eat. This time he finished it.

She gave him a last pat and headed for home. She hoped his legs would come right in the next day or two or she'd better get the vet to have a look.

She hoped it wasn't anything serious. She loved her horse, but there was no point being here if she didn't have a mount.

And now, in a strange way, she didn't want to go home.

Chapter Seven

James arrived at the event ground far earlier than needed to give himself something to think about. He checked on Delaware and bit his lip when he saw him keeping the weight off his back foot. He stepped into the stall and Del nosed his shoulder. 'Hey, old man. It's sore, huh?' He ran his hand down the leg and removed the ice pack. The leg was swollen from knee to fetlock and hot to the touch.

'Oh, man.' He went to get another ice pack and carefully strapped it on. Delaware flinched at the contact.

'Better call Mark, hmm?' He stroked the horse's neck. 'Let's take you on a bit of a walk so I can clean up, okay?'

He clipped a lead rope to his halter and led him slowly out of the box. Delaware wouldn't put weight on the leg. James led him slowly towards the paddock, and Delaware was happy enough to nibble on the grass but he wouldn't walk around. James called Mark Clinton as he went back to clean the stalls. Lacklustre was in a much better mood this morning, so hopefully, they could jump a decent round. He wasn't worried about Marksman; he was good in the third phase.

He had all three horses fed, groomed and the stalls cleaned by the time Caitlyn showed up at eight. 'You've taken my job,' she said when she saw Delaware eating.

James shrugged. 'I needed something to do, so I figured you could have the morning off.'

'Could've left me in bed then.'

'Sorry, you still need to get them ready.' James stroked Delaware's nose. 'Did you go up and see Jadin?'

She nodded. Uh-huh. The nurse says there's no change.' She patted Delaware's nose. 'How's this boy?'

'Leg's pretty bad, hot and swollen. I've called Mark.' He ran a hand through his hair. 'Suppose I'd better find something to eat before I have to jump.'

Caitlyn frowned. 'You haven't had breakfast?'

'Nah, I wasn't hungry.'

Caitlyn shook her finger at him. 'You seriously need to find me an aunt.'

James gave her a look. 'What does that have to do with my breakfast?'

'A woman in the house will make sure you eat your meals.' She spoke with the air of an old-fashioned governess.

'Yes, ma'am.' He rolled his eyes. 'How about you quit lecturing me and start saddling Marksman?'

'Oh, all right.'

Mark came straight out, saying he'd had a quiet morning. He carefully ran his hands over Delaware's leg. 'And you said he won't put weight on it?'

'No.'

He palpated the leg gently. 'I don't think it's broken. But I think the tendons are badly strained.' He patted Delaware's rump as he stood up. 'I would keep icing it and make sure he rests it. If it doesn't improve in a few days, we might get it X-rayed.' He tightened the bandage around the horse's fetlock and returned the packet to his bag. 'How is Jadin?'

James sighed. 'No change this morning.'

Mark shook his head. 'Poor lad. I've always liked him. Give him my best.'

'I'll do that.'

Delaware looked mournful when the other horses were being taken out to warm up and he still had to stay in. 'I'll take him on a little walk while you warm up,' Caitlyn said as James vaulted onto Lacklustre's back. She passed him the reins over the horse's head.

'Okay. Just remember to take it very slowly.'

'I will.'

Lacklustre warmed up easily, his long limbs loosening up as they popped over some small jumps and cavaletti.

He watched some of the earlier competitors, trying to spot the problem jumps. Quite a few horses were failing to clear the water; it was a tight angle into the jump. The final fence, an upright oxer of planks, was also coming down regularly.

Lacklustre felt good, and James felt confident he could pilot him clear. They entered the arena and cantered towards the first obstacle. Lustre jumped well over, his ears pricked forward.

Keeping an eye on his watch, he took a slower, wider line to the water. Lacklustre stretched over it, his rear hooves just missing the white line. Clear. James released a breath.

They were still faultless as they approached the last, tricky oxer. James signalled the takeoff as late as he dared, and thank goodness, Lacklustre kept his feet up. They were clear and - he quickly checked his watch - within the time. He patted Lustre's neck. The horse tossed his head, obviously pleased with himself.

'Remember this, old lad. This is how we want to do it.' He rode out of the saddle as they cantered out of the ring, then slowed to a walk. Caitlyn met them and reached for the reins.'Nice round. I'll take him.'

'No, I will. I've got time.' James walked the horse around the arena and back towards the stables. Lacklustre pranced happily.

He called the hospital before getting on Marksman for the four-star. There was still no change. He glanced at the time as he hung up. He'd be cutting it close to get to Bristol to pick up Tom and Judie.

Caitlyn came over with Marksman's blinkers and slipped them on. 'Cate, can you do me a favour?'

'Of course.'

'Jadin's mum and dad fly into Bristol at four and I'd be cutting it fine. If I'm not out of the ring by three-thirty, can you go and pick them up?'

'Of course. I want to see them too.'

'Thanks. Take the truck. I'll sort the horses.'

Marksman was also in fine fettle, happily popping over the warm-up jumps and clearing them easily. This could be a good afternoon, James thought to himself. If only Jadin was over there warming up Delaware.

They were sitting third, only two points behind the leaders. A fence down would send any of the top eight down several places.

Marksman was giving each fence room to spare, and James again rode him as close to the water as possible before lifting off. Marksman's long legs cleared it easily.

A round like this reminded James why he still loved show jumping in its own right. Marksman was jumping beautifully. They were still clear as they cantered to the last fence, and Marksman cleared it by a foot. They rode out of the arena to a large round of applause.

He led Marksman around to cool him down, keeping an eye on the arena. The second-placed rider dropped a foot in the water, but the leading rider went clear. James was a little relieved. His mind was on other things.

He decided to load the horses and get them home. Delaware's leg didn't seem much better, but it wasn't worse. He would stay at Manorbrook until Jadin could decide what to do next. He swallowed a sudden lump in his throat.

Delaware and Lacklustre loaded without a whimper.

Marksman was hesitant but getting better now he was realising he wouldn't end up on a plane on every trip. James quickly loaded the tack and double-checked it before getting into the rig. Now he couldn't wait to leave the place. Every time he glanced towards the trees, he saw Jadin motionless on the ground.

He sent Caitlyn a text telling her he was taking the horses home, but not to worry about coming to help. He could call Vicky, but he'd rather do it alone. He backed the trailer up his driveway and stopped. All three unloaded with no fuss and he put them in clean stalls with their evening feed. It would be another hour at least before Vicky came in for evening chores, so he left her a note, locked up and headed for the hospital. Caitlyn and Jadin's parents should have got there by now.

He headed down the ICU waiting room, finding Caitlyn sitting by herself.

'Hey, Catie,' he said softly, and she looked up. 'Are they in with Jadin?'

She nodded. 'We haven't been here long.'

James sat down beside her. 'How was the drive, okay?'

'I guess, under the circumstances.' She leaned her head back. 'It's just so depressing, you know?'

'He'll fight this,' James said automatically. 'He's going to be okay.'

She looked at him with sad eyes. 'You don't know that, Uncle Jim.' She twisted her fingers together.

He sighed. 'No, I don't. But I'm choosing to believe it.' He frowned when he got a proper look at her left hand. 'Where's the ring?'

She shrugged. 'It just didn't feel right wearing it with something like this going on. He was supposed to be at the wedding, in the front row with the family.'

James smiled. Jadin had always been the big brother she'd never had, despite the large age gap. 'I'm sure he still will be.'

She sniffed. 'I want to be sure first.'

He patted her shoulder, and they sat in silence for a bit before James asked, 'Has the doctor mentioned any change?'

'No. But then they probably wouldn't tell me anyway.'

James leaned back with a sigh. He was tired and wanted to go home, but he wouldn't go without seeing Jadin and his folks. He looked up when he heard someone entering the room and stood to meet Tom Steele. He looked a lot older than when they had last met, three or four years ago, but a lot of his appearance was probably due to the stress of the last 28 hours. 'Hi, Tom.'

'James.' They shook hands. 'Thank you for all you've done for us and Jadin.'

James smiled ruefully. 'It hasn't been much, I'm afraid. But Jadin's my family.'

'I know.' The greying man sat down. 'Is there anything else the doctor hasn't told us?'

'I don't think so.' James ran a hand through his hair. 'Listen, I don't know what your plans are, but you're welcome to stay at my farm. I have a couple of spare rooms that I hardly use.'

Tom waved his hand. 'We'll be fine, there's a nice hotel not far away.'

'Tom, I'd like you to stay. It's no bother, and I'll be out at the barns most of the time.'

The older man sighed. 'Well, I'll ask Judie.'

Judie didn't want to impose either but finally agreed on the condition that she be allowed to do some of his cooking. James didn't turn that offer down. Judie Steele used to feed the whole Pony Club with her country food.

Caitlyn took them back to Manorbrook, and James went in and sat with Jadin for a while. He studied the monitors to keep from having to watch his expressionless face. 'C'mon, Jade, you gotta wake up, buddy. Your mum and dad are here safe and sound. But they'd like to talk to you and so would I.'

His mind played over thousands of conversations over the years. Jokes and laughter; arguments and a dream or two. 'We still need our Olympic one-two, Jade. But I'm still not going to let you win.' A small smile peeked out.

He made himself look at his friend's face. It was so foreign to the Jadin he knew and unbidden, he felt tears in his eyes. He couldn't remember the last time he'd cried.

'I'm taking care of Del. I brought all three back to Manorbrook. We're keeping an eye on his leg. The vet thinks it's just a sprain.' James picked up his hand. 'I'll keep Del at Manorbrook. He'll be just fine.'

He sat back in the chair, allowing himself, for the first time since the accident, to consider the possibility that Jadin could be paralysed. The adjustment would be staggering. What would he do? He would never be happy in an office job. He knew of racehorse trainers who were wheelchair-bound, so there were possibilities.

He sighed and pushed himself to his feet. 'Hang in there, Jade.' His cellphone rang as he started his car. The caller ID said 'Kelli.'

'Oh, Jimmy, I'm so sorry. I can't believe it. We've just got back from France. Does the rest of the team know?'

'I don't know.' He cleared his throat. 'I told Steve, but I haven't talked to the other riders.'

'You're there with him?'

'He's at St. Michael's in Bristol. I've been visiting him. I took Delaware back to Manorbrook.'

'Oh.' She sounded quite upset. 'How're you holding up?'

'Okay. Just trying to come to terms with it really.' James put the car in reverse. 'His mum and dad have come over. They're staying with me.'

'Oh, okay. I'm coming through Bristol tomorrow, so I might stop in and see him.' He heard her sigh. 'I hope he'll be all right.'

'Me too, Kell.'

'Well, I'd better go. Say hi to his folks for me.' She didn't have the history they had, but the Kiwi eventing circle was tight-knit.

'Will do. Take care.'

He tossed his phone on the passenger seat and backed out. He grinned at the memory of a 15-year-old Caitlyn trying to get him and Kelli together. Kelli was beautiful, smart, and a lovely rider, but they had never been more than friends. She had her life and he had his, and besides, at the time he thought she'd had eyes for Jadin, and vice versa. Judging by her tone during the phone call, close friendship notwithstanding, he may not have been wrong.

He checked again on Delaware before locking up for the night. Again, he wasn't worse, but he didn't seem that much better. He stood and stroked the horse for a few minutes, knowing Del had probably noticed he hadn't seen his owner in a while. He frowned at the realisation it had only been a little more than 24 hours since the accident. It seemed like a fortnight.

He collapsed into bed just after ten. He wasn't usually in bed before eleven, but the last 32 hours had been draining.

He jerked awake. He looked at his clock radio; the red digits showed 1:00. He half sat up, dragging his fingers through his hair. Had someone got to the horses? Had an alarm woken him?

A tiny light flashed, dragging his attention to his bedside stand. His phone. He picked it up and blinked at the bright display, but there was a voicemail message. The buzzing of a call must have disturbed him.

His heart rate picked up as he played the message.

'Hello, is this James Blackman? This is Dr Andrew Borris from St Michael's hospital.' James shot upright in bed. 'I'm calling because you are still listed as medical next of kin for Jadin Steele. He has been waking up. He will still need a lot of rest, so you may not want to come in until the morning, but you can give me a call when you get this message.' He left the direct line for his department.

Thank you, God! Thank you! He threw on his clothes with one hand while dialling the hospital with the other. 'Yes, can I speak to Dr Andrew Borris, please?'

Dr Borris remained cautious, but he said that Jadin had woken up and asked where he was, and seemed to understand what they'd told him of what was going on. 'But he's sleeping again now, so I suggest you do the same and come to see him in the morning.'

James wanted to see him now, but he knew the doctor was right. 'Okay. Thank you, Doc.'

He could hear a smile in the man's voice and it gave him a rush of relief. 'You are welcome.'

He woke Tom and Judie and relayed the news. Only a lot of persuasion kept Judie from walking to Bristol herself right then and there.

Despite the remaining unknowns, James' sleep was easier.

Chapter Eight

A long day and a sick horse. Amy set her keys on her breakfast
bar as if they weighed ten kilograms. Chester had been off his
food again and this time he was also running a fever. The vet
had said it was a virus, which would go away with some TLC
and time, but his forelegs were both badly sprained.

It was getting to the point where she was wondering if this trip
had been worth it. She was getting nowhere. She was still
working the same job, her horse was out of action, she was
missing her friends and felt like she was in limbo - not going
backward but not going forward either.

She checked her messages and dug some two-minute noodles
out of the cupboard. She wondered what she would do if
Chester was going to be out of commission for a while. Should
she turn around and go home again, at least able to say that
she'd given it a go, or should she stick it out and give the
dream a second chance?

She sat down again with the newspaper. She often wished she
still had someone to talk to at the end of a long day, the way
she used to talk to Mickey when they were in the same time
zone.

Or, way back when, how she and Damien Scott would text
each other late into the night.

She sighed and tossed the paper aside. It was no good thinking
about him now. They had gone their separate ways years
earlier, and never kept in touch. Not even on Facebook. It was
a sad paradox that they were both too hurt by the end to want
to remember the good.

A fleeting memory crossed her mind. Damien was sitting
across from her at an unromantic McDonald's table. His

earnest blue eyes tried to show her that despite their differences they could work it out, even if they were both, at that moment, heading in entirely different directions.

'The world is round, Ames. We'd come together again eventually.'

It was poetic, she had to give him that, but she knew it wasn't that easy. Their journeys just weren't compatible unless one of them was willing to change direction.

And neither of them were.

She shrugged. Maybe one day she'd find another friend like him.

Right now, she was busy finding a way to keep her dream plausible.

She decided to go to bed early. The sooner this day was over the better.

James was down at the barn by 5am, riding a couple of horses so he could get to the hospital by eight. No visitors were allowed before then, and he'd go crazy worrying if he didn't do something to pass the time.

But on the other hand, he dreaded going. How could he look into someone's eyes and admit to them they may never walk again?

Patriot was in a foul mood, but James was glad for something to focus on. James finally brought him to a standstill and made him stay for a full 60 seconds. Patriot fidgeted about but soon got the message. James nudged him forward, and this time the horse did obey, albeit with a slash of his tail.

Vicky came in at seven and offered to ride some of the horses if he needed it. Coalie was still in sickbay, so there was less to do, but he got her to ride Clarabelle, who still didn't like him much. He was starting to lean towards selling her to Jadin.

He sighed. Each time he thought something like that, as if Jadin was back in York and everything was normal, the reality stabbed him again.

He cooled down Patriot and put him out in the pasture for the afternoon, hoping to lighten his mood. He glanced at his watch. 7:42; time to take Tom and Judie to Bristol.

He tried to engage in small talk as he drove, but his heart felt like there was a brick in it. He was happy Jadin was awake, of course, and he wanted to talk to him. But what could he say if Jadin asked how bad it was - and he knew he would. Jadin was never one to hide from reality.

James sat in the waiting room, wondering about the prognosis. He was still going on old information, and the fact that Jadin had woken up could only be positive, right?

He looked up as Tom and Judie exited the room. Judie was a little teary-eyed but composed. James stood. 'How is he?'

'He knows who we are and everything, so he seems to have his memory,' Tom said. 'We told him what had happened and of course he wanted to know if Delaware was okay.'

James permitted himself a smile. 'What about - uh - his spine?' Tom shook his head. 'He doesn't know. The doctors are still running tests, and he's still pretty sedated, so it's hard to say.'

James took a breath. He knew Jadin might be asking someone other than his folks, not wanting to upset them. Judie was not a worrier, but she knew that this sport could be dangerous, and she hated her only child getting hurt. Judie touched his arm. 'He's asking for you.'

James tried to smile again but it felt forced. He took a deep breath and slipped in the door. The first thing he saw was Jadin's eyes, and he smiled briefly despite himself. He was awake, and he was talking. 'Hi, Jadin.'

'Hi, yourself.' Jadin smiled, and James felt a sudden wish to hug him. He sat in the chair beside the bed.

'How're you feeling?'

'Not much. I'm a little chemically imbalanced right now.' He indicated the IV and James grinned. The sense of humour hadn't gone anywhere.

'Did your mum and dad tell you about Delaware?'

'Uh-huh. The dumb horse got off darn easier than I did.' Jadin scratched his head with his free hand. James hoped he kept his relief at that simple movement concealed, but Jadin gave him a strange look. 'What?'

'Nothing,' he said quickly. 'Yeah, he's got a sore leg, but he'll be fine. He's safely at Manorbrook, trying to eat me out of house and home.'

Jadin chuckled. 'Glad to hear it.'

'Kelli called me yesterday. She's back from her trip with what's his name and worried about you. Said she might stop in Bristol.'

A strange expression passed over Jadin's face but it was gone quickly. 'Oh, that's nice of her.' The neutral comment seemed somehow odd. Even if there had been no romantic ties, they were close friends.

Does he remember who she is?

Jadin looked at him. 'How're Catie and Vicky?'

'They're upset about you but all right. Did you know Catie is engaged?'

'Yeah, she told me the other morning. The day I - fell.' His tone wavered.

James smiled. 'I should've known she'd tell you first.'

Jadin chuckled. 'I think she was a bit worried about how you'd react.'

James shrugged. 'Well, I gave her the Inquisition, according to her.'

Jadin laughed, then grimaced. 'Ribs,' he explained. 'But I bet she was right.' He repositioned his IV line with his free hand. 'Have you met her fiance?'

'Yeah. Wilson. He's a jockey. Nice enough guy.'

Jadin raised an eyebrow. 'Only 'nice enough'?'

'Well, I don't know him that well. But she says she's happy.'

Jadin nodded. 'That's what matters.' He paused, looking at the ceiling above him. 'So, are we going to talk about the elephant in the room?'

James suddenly felt cold. 'What do you mean?'

Jadin looked at him square in the eye. 'Don't play dumb with me. We've been through too much for that.'

James sighed. 'Sorry.' He rubbed a hand over his face. 'What do you want to know?'

'How bad the spinal damage is.' Jadin's voice was low. 'I know about the concussion and the broken ribs. But they won't tell me about my spine. I know there is damage, but they won't tell me anything else.'

James sighed. 'Well, they don't know much for sure yet.'

Jadin gave him a warning glare. 'But?'

James hated this, but he owed it to their relationship. He forced his gaze to meet Jadin's. 'There is a chance you won't walk again.'

He heard Jadin's deep sigh. 'I thought as much. They wouldn't tell me, but I can't feel my legs, and it has to be more than just the drugs.'

James nodded slowly. 'I'm sorry, man.'

Jadin grimaced. 'It's not your fault.' He shook his head. 'So, distract me. Anything new in the Coalie investigation?'

'I've been doing a little bit of investigation on my own.'

Jadin raised his eyebrows. 'Such as?'

'Well, I did some investigating at the last event.'

'By which you mean snooping?'

'Meh, same difference.' James shrugged. 'I did also decide to talk to Cole Kendrick, but kept it vague - is Clive working out, is everything okay at his stables, etcetera.'

'And?'

'It all checked out. He seemed completely at ease with me.'

'He is an iceman, remember,' Jadin said.

'I know. But he left me alone in his motorhome to go outside and talk to someone. No one who's guilty would do that.'

'So Cole doesn't know, but Clive is involved?'

'I struggle to believe it at times, but that seems to be the case.' James cleared his throat. 'I'm going to call him.'

'Is that a good idea?'

'He can't do anything to me over the phone.' James shrugged. 'I can't sit around and wait forever.'

'Just be careful, okay?'

'I will.'

The next day he went through all his emails looking for any correspondence with Clive. He turned up a handful of emails, all mundane. He racked his brain, trying to think of any alarm bells in the three years he'd worked at Manorbrook. He went through his accounting, which Clive had helped manage. Nothing untoward.

And then he caught a break.

Opening a new tab, he saw Clive had failed to log out of his email inbox. A quick check proved he was the only one currently in the box. He started reading. There were a lot of bills and receipts, personal messages, and promotions. Then at the bottom of the second page, a subject read: "Re: Employing KR". James opened it.

"So, I will contact KR and see how we go. Thanks for the info." It was signed L.

James read through the rest of the chain. There were references to "stopping those against us" and "recouping control", but predictably, nothing identifiable. He downloaded and attached it to an email to the inspector anyway, and made sure he didn't log out.

Then he picked up the phone.

'Hello?'

'Lisa, hi. It's James Blackman. Is Clive around?'

'Oh, hi, James. He's not, I'm afraid. Shall I ask him to call you?'

'Please. How are the kids?' Over the course of the conversation James surmised that, if Clive was involved, he hadn't told his wife.

Lisa promised to get Clive to call and James hung up.

The returned call came three days later. James asked if they could catch up for a drink and Clive agreed.

They chatted amiably about Clive's family and how it was going for him working for Cole Kendrick. Then James asked him point-blank, 'Were you at my stable a couple of weeks ago?'

'No, why?' He looked surprised.

James stared into his eyes. 'Have you heard about what happened to Coalbridge?'

This time, Clive's gaze dropped to the table. 'I did.'

'The cops are saying you are involved.'

Clive didn't answer right away.

'Clive?'

Clive cleared his throat and raised his eyes. There was a haunted expression there. 'I'm so, so sorry, Jimmy.'

James' mouth opened. 'It's true, then?'

Clive blew out a breath. 'About six months ago, I was contacted by a group of people offering me a lot of money to help them take you down. I said no. But they kept coming back, offering more and more money, and said I wouldn't really have to do anything. Then they started threatening Lisa and the kids.' He shuddered. 'These were powerful people. Gang connections. Out to get whatever power they could. So I gave them the gate code.'

He shook his head. 'They told me no real damage would be done, and that was the last I heard of it. I never set foot on your property. Not that that makes it any different.'

They sat in silence. James cleared his throat. 'Well, thank you for being honest, anyway. Do you know how they got a key?' Clive shook his head. 'I got the impression they'd reached out to several people close to you and just kept badgering them all until someone caved. But it wasn't me who gave them the key.'

'So someone else has betrayed me too.' James put his head in his hands.

Clive didn't respond, but he tossed a £10 note on the table.

'I'm sorry, Jimmy. I hope someday you can forgive me.'

'Me too,' James murmured as he walked away.

Coalie was almost completely recovered, but Delaware's leg remained badly swollen. Judging by the frown on Mark Clinton's face, he was concerned.

'If it's not down by tomorrow, I think we'll get him X-rayed. There's a chance he may have a small break in there.'

James butted into the conversation. 'And if there is?'

Mark raised an eyebrow. 'Why, hello to you too, Jimmy.' His grin took any sting from his words. 'Well, it depends on the severity. If it's just a hairline fracture or a small crack, he may recover fully and quickly. If it's any bigger--' He looked sadly at them. 'It may impact or even end his career.'

James let out a long breath.

'Let me know how he is in the morning.' He packed up his kit and headed back to his vehicle, in step with James. 'How's Jadin?'

'Well, he's alive.' James didn't know how else to put it. 'But we don't know a lot about his spinal injury yet. He's taking it pretty hard.'

Mark nodded sympathetically. 'Think he'd be up for a visit?'

James looked at him, a little surprised. 'I think he would, Mark. That's kind of you.'

Mark tossed his gear bag in the back of his van and shut the door. 'Jimmy, you work a lot of hours in this job, and you don't have much of a social life. Most of the people you see are customers…' He opened the driver's door. 'But a few of those turn into friends.'

James smiled. 'I'm sure it's mutual, Doc.'

Mark pointed a finger at him. 'It won't be for long if you keep that up.' He buzzed his window down. 'Take care, all right?'

James watched the truck disappear down the driveway. *Don't let Delaware's leg be broken, please.*

Amy hit her alarm with enough force to knock it off the stand. It was earlier than she usually got up but she wanted some extra time to check on Chester. He had been pretty miserable the day before; she hoped it was only a virus like the vet said. She dashed through the rain to her car and headed for the stable. Chester was looking slightly brighter, and he'd drunk all his water.

She refilled his water and fed him, stroking his neck for a few moments while he ate. He had perked up a lot, but he was still warmer than normal. His forelegs had cooled down, however. Maybe that afternoon she could take him out for a walk.

She drove to work, still wondering about her options. Chester seemed to be on the mend, but now it wasn't just about her horse. It was about her own goals and her desire to stay until she reached them. She had hoped to be further along by now, six months into her relocation.

But there wasn't a lot calling her home.

Tori wasn't well, so she had double work to do. But she didn't mind; it was good to be busy.

The editor eventually came down and shooed her out for a lunch break. She put her jacket on, and the phone rang as she stood up from her desk. She hesitated but decided to grab it.

'Enfield Gazette, you're speaking to Amy.'

'Hi, is Tori Wells there, please?'

'I'm sorry, she's not in today. Can I take a message?'

'Do you know how I can reach her? This is Sergeant Lucas Glenn of the Metropolitan Police. It's an emergency involving her ex-husband.'

Amy's breath caught in her throat. She knew Tori still cared for him, and from memory, he had the boys today since she was sick. 'Um, I can find you her home number. She's off sick today.'

She quickly dug through the directory and relayed the information. The officer thanked her, and she quickly asked, 'Can you tell me what's going on? I'm a friend of hers.'

'I'm sorry, miss, but we can't give out personal information.'

'Right, I understand. I'll call her.'

She stood there a few seconds after hanging up, staring absently at the phone in her hand. She headed out to find some lunch, but she didn't feel particularly hungry. She bought a sandwich and went to a nearby park, nibbling at it. She gave it fifteen minutes and then called Tori's cell. It rang five times and went to voicemail.

'Hi, it's Amy. Just wanted to check up on you because a policeman called me at work trying to contact you. I know it's none of my business but just hoping everything's okay.'

She finished half of her sandwich and decided that was all she wanted, placing the rest in her bag. While walking back to the office she tried Tori's cell again. This time, she picked up, but her 'hello' sounded distraught.

'Tori, it's Amy. I just wanted to check on you after the police called you at work, but if you don't want to say - '

She heard something like a sniff over the line. 'No, it's okay. It's good to talk to someone.' She paused to take a deep breath. 'It's Jack. He had a heart attack while driving the boys…' Her voice trailed off.

'Oh no! Are they okay? Is he okay?'

'They hit the curb and stopped, thank God. Sammy has a minor concussion from banging his head, and Mike a few cuts and bruises, but nothing serious.' She sniffed again. 'Jack is alive, but his heart is weak. They're saying he may need a bypass operation.'

Amy's hand went to her mouth. 'I'm so sorry.'

'Yeah.' She sniffed again. 'Man, I was so mad with him after the break-up and everything, and now all I want to do is kiss him because I'm so glad he's okay.'

'Yeah,' Amy said, not knowing what else to say. 'Is there anything I can do to help?'

'No, I don't think so at the moment, but would you be up for watching the boys if I needed it? Outside of work of course.'

'Sure, I can do that. Just let me know.'

'Thanks, Amy.' She let out a long breath. 'I'd better get up to the hospital. Thanks for checking in with me.'

'You're welcome. Take care.'

She returned to work and got busy, catching up on some of Tori's work so she had less to worry about if she had to take some leave. With Chester unable to be ridden at the moment, she was in no hurry to leave.

She did take him out for a walk when she gave him his evening feed. He didn't favour his legs at all, even though they were still slightly swollen. Maybe in a day or two, he'd be able to go back to a gentle workout.

She wasn't turning tail on her dream just yet.

James was up early the next morning to check on Delaware. To his immense relief, the swelling had gone down and Del was putting weight on the leg.

He was also anxious to ride Coalie again. Mark had suggested giving him some time to recover before resuming training. James sighed.

'I'm still going to find out who did it,' he muttered to Coalie as the big black tucked into his breakfast. 'Don't you worry about that.'

Coalbridge was happy to be out and about. With pricked ears he tugged at the bit, trying to move faster. James kept him at a walk but did allow him to pop over the cavaletti. Even though it was a shadow of what they would usually do, it felt wonderful to ride his favourite horse again.

He decided to get most of the horses done and go into Bristol after lunch. He wondered how much more time it would take before they had a definite diagnosis. It must be hard for Jadin; heck, it was tearing him up, wondering how hard the road ahead would be for his best friend.

He made his way up to Jadin's room and tapped on the doorframe. Jadin looked up with a small smile. 'Hi.'

'Hi yourself.' He went in and sat down. 'How ya doing?'

'Well, my heart's still beating.'

'Anything further on the diagnosis?'

Jadin shook his head. 'But the swelling's going down, and they're going to run tests tomorrow.' He swallowed and looked down at the sheets. 'But I still can't feel my legs, and I can't pretend it's just the drugs.'

James felt a small crack somewhere in the heart region. 'Oh, Jade.'

He shrugged. 'I'm dealing. I don't have much choice.' He looked back up. 'How's Del?'

Well, at least he had some small good news. 'Better. The swelling's going down and he's putting weight on it again.'

'Oh good.'

'Coalie's doing good too. I rode him a bit this morning.'

'Have the cops found anything?'

'Not so far.' James leaned back in his chair. 'I talked to Clive, though.'

'And?'

'He admitted giving the thugs the gate code but said he had nothing to do with the key. So someone else did that.'

'I'm sorry, Jimmy.'

'It is what it is. I'm going to keep looking.' James cleared his throat. 'So, how's Kelli?'

That same strange look came back into Jadin's eyes. 'Fine, as far as I can tell.'

'You want to tell me what the heck is going on with you two?'

Genuine surprise came to Jadin's expression. 'What are you talking about?'

'You're talking like awkward acquaintances.'

Jadin shrugged, then winced a little at the movement. 'Just haven't seen each other in a while, I guess.'

'If you say so.' They talked for a while on the merits of taking different horses to different events before James stood up. 'Anything you need?'

'Not that I can think of.' They both looked up at a tap on the door.

A familiar face appeared in the doorway. 'Hiya strangers, mind if I come in?'

'Get in here, Kyle,' Jadin said with a grin.

Their friend and New Zealand team-mate Kyle Rogers strolled in and shook hands. 'How are you doing, buddy?'

Jadin grinned ruefully. 'I've been better.'

James headed for the door. 'I'll let you two catch up. I'll see you, Kyle.'

He walked slowly towards the elevators, trying not to dwell on the possibilities of what the next day's tests might reveal. They had so much more to do, too many dreams to realise.

Kelli Holmes shut her apartment door, pulled her boots off at the jack and dropped her keys on the table. A tear fell next to them, making a slowly widening circle on the cream tablecloth.

What is wrong with you? She scolded herself. *Bawling over a friend.*

There was a ferocity in the manner with which she made her pasta for dinner. She was hurting for Jadin, whose career may have just bitten the dust. He had always been a good friend. And a year ago, she had been four seconds away from dating him.

Her boyfriend, Troy, was starting to talk about marriage, but she wasn't at all sure, and she hated being pressured. Especially since it felt like a bit of a marriage of convenience. And especially when he wasn't someone she had envisioned marrying.

And since, twelve months ago, Jadin had asked her out. They'd always been close, but in a brother-sister way, and they didn't see each other enough for it to be anything more, anyway. Until one night after a platonic celebratory dinner in Kentucky, where she'd won and he'd come third. As he walked her back to her hotel room, he hesitated, and then blurted, 'Would you consider going on a date with me?'

There were two answers immediately on her lips: no, it would never work because of the lifestyles we lead; and yes, I would love to. She'd opened her mouth, suddenly ready to risk the latter, when her room phone started ringing through the door, and she'd quickly said the former. The safe option.

She'd never forget his disappointment, but he masked it well and said he'd see her tomorrow. The disappointment that was even harder to forget - or forgive - was her own.

They hadn't seen each other for another three or four months, and when they ran into each other at an event, no mention was made of it. Another month later she met Troy, and they'd been seeing each other quite steadily.

But she didn't want to marry him. That much she had come to see. There was still a corner of her heart that wondered about Jadin Steele, and it would never belong to Troy. That wouldn't be fair to either of them.

She sniffed and stirred her sauce. She was pretty sure she'd be in tears if James or Kyle or any of the other riders she was close to were in this predicament. But there was something more at play here, no matter how much she tried to deny it.

The tragedy of it was that she had blown her chance. He thought it would make for an awkward friendship if he brought it up, and she wasn't about to launch herself and ask him out. She was old-fashioned, and shy, that way.

But maybe she owed him the information about the regret she felt for her answer.

She dished up and ate in front of the TV news. She and her number two horse, Kaleido, were flying to the US in a week for some lead-up events to Kentucky. They were flying out of Bristol.

And if he had moved on...well, it was better than never knowing.

James decided he'd take Silver Flint to Kentucky, but only him. Kelli Holmes had agreed to fly him over with her horse, Kaleido, and then he'd fly out closer to the time. Kelli's apprentice would work him in the meantime.

While still at Manorbrook, he had to work on getting Marksman ready for Badminton. He stayed out working horses for a long time, but he knew he was just putting off the inevitable. Even if he stayed at the barns all day and didn't see Jadin until the morning, it wouldn't change the outcome of the tests.

He dismounted and handed Silver Flint over to Vicky. Putting it off any further was only going to make it worse. He turned back to her.

'Would you mind taking Marksman out today? I'd better get to the hospital.'

'Sure.' Her smile was empathetic. 'Give him my love.'

'Will do.'

The drive, short as it was, was an exercise in dread. No traffic and nothing was interesting on the radio. Deep breaths did nothing to calm his swirling mind.

He parked and walked as fast as he could to the correct floor. Now he was here, he didn't want to have time to think until he found out the news. His prayer continued in time with his feet as he climbed the stairs.

He put a hand on the doorframe of Jadin's room and took a deep breath before rounding the corner. The bed was empty. He walked stiffly to the nurse's station. 'Excuse me, do you have any news about Jadin Steele? He's not in his room.'

The matronly nurse looked up at him. 'That the horse riding lad?'

'Yes.'

She nodded. 'I think they took him into traction to see if that would help.'

Hope blossomed like a firework. 'Do you know what the doctors said about his spinal injury?'

She peered at him through her glasses. 'You family?'

'I still have medical power of attorney.'

She squinted as if deciding whether to believe him and then nodded when he produced his ID. 'All right, here's what they know.' She read off her screen a garble of medical terms.

James frowned. 'What does that mean?'

She looked back at him. 'There is still motor function at some level, probably below the neurological level, although the muscles have been damaged. He can't walk, but it may not be permanent. The fact that there is still some motor function is a good sign.'

James tried to comprehend what he'd been told. 'So he can't walk right now, but he may be able to in the future?'

He must have sounded over hopeful because she smiled empathetically at him. 'It's not a hopeless case, but there's a long road ahead if he's to walk again.'

Hope was hope! James felt like he could fly back into Jadin's room. Granted, he couldn't walk right now, but at least there was no 'he'll never walk again'.

He walked back into Jadin's room and sat down in the chair by the bed. No, it wasn't good news, but it wasn't dreadfully bad either. There was still hope he could recover.

Twenty minutes had passed before a therapist pushed Jadin's wheelchair back into the room. 'Hi, Jadin,' he said softly.

Jadin smiled wearily. 'Hi yourself.' The therapist helped him back onto the bed and glanced over what seemed to be a checklist. 'So I'll check in with you tomorrow morning, okay?'

Jadin nodded.

James cautiously slid the chair closer to the chair. 'How are you feeling?'

Jadin's smile came out more of a grimace. 'I've been better.'

James pursed his lips, unsure of how to discuss the diagnosis. 'Have you talked to the doctors again?'

Jadin sighed. 'Yeah, they've made a partial diagnosis.'

James didn't know whether to be thrilled or alarmed that it was 'partial'. He let Jadin talk.

'At the moment, it's an incomplete C - there is still motor function but the muscles are damaged. At least that's how I understand it.'

'But from what the nurse said to me, it's not permanent, right?'

Jadin sighed again. 'It may not be. It's too early to say.'

James scooted closer to lay a hand on his arm. 'Jade, you've got to fight this. I refuse to let you do anything less until there's no hope. And there is hope.'

Jadin's expression remained flat. 'Easy for you to say.'

'I know it is. But you have too much to accomplish.'

Jadin looked him square in the eye. 'And if it is too late?'

'Then we'll cross that bridge when we come to it.'

Jadin stared up at the ceiling. 'Jimmy, regardless of what the doctor says, the fact remains that I can't feel my legs.' He looked him in the eye again, but with tears in his. 'And that scares the life out of me.'

They had never been demonstrative types, but James didn't know what else to do except carefully hug him. So he did.

Jadin sighed as he pulled back. 'Sorry if I'm taking this out on you.'

'It's okay.' James leaned back in his chair. 'So what's the therapist like?'

'A pain in the neck, that's what. Fussing about doing this right and that right.' He allowed a small smile. 'I know that's a good thing, but I hate finicky details.'

'What kind of stuff are you doing?'

'Mostly traction, but a bit of moving around, trying to reawaken the muscles if we can.' He shook his head, looking at James with incredibly sad eyes. 'It's the most awful, weird thing, needing someone else to move your legs around for you, you know?'

James bit his lip. 'I can imagine.'

Jadin frowned a moment, then turned to James. 'Have you heard anything more from Kelli?'

Something in his tone kept James from teasing him. 'No, I haven't.'

'Is she...happy with Troy?'

James frowned. 'I wouldn't know. We haven't talked about him.' He leaned back, wondering where this was going, but when Jadin said no more, he changed tack. 'How's Kyle?'

Jadin raised an eyebrow. 'You don't talk to your friends, do you?'

James grinned. 'Not as much as I should.'

Jadin chuckled. 'He's doing all right. Taking both his top horses to Kentucky, then back to Badminton. It's a five-week break this year, so he thinks they'll be okay with the turnaround. They're both good travellers.'

James shook his head. 'Lucky guy.'

Jadin tried to reposition himself, and the difficulty of the movement sent another pang through James. 'How's Delaware?'

'Doing better. The swelling's gone down a bit.'

'I'm just glad it wasn't broken,' Jadin said. 'It's hard for a horse to come back from that. Although I may never ride him again anyway.'

'You don't know that.' James kept his tone just short of fierce.

Jadin sighed. 'Look, Jimmy...' He paused as if searching for the right words. 'I appreciate your optimism, but it's a bit hard for me to see right now.'

'I know. But you're not going to give up.' James leaned back, offering a slight smile. 'I'll see to that much, anyway.'

Jadin glanced at him speculatively. 'Listen, if I can't ride Delaware again...' He held up a hand to forestall any protest. 'I know, it's early. But if I can't, I want you to have him. Take him to Badminton for me.'

James was touched. 'Thanks, Jade.'

There was a timid knock on the door, and they both turned to see Kelli Holmes, looking like she was going on trial. 'I'm not interrupting, am I?'

"Course not,' James said, standing to go. 'Are you all right, Kell? You look pretty pale.'

She nodded. 'I'm fine. Just came to see how you were.'
James held in a frown but he was suddenly aware of the
tension in the room. Jadin looked overly calm. 'I'm fine, Kelli.
You didn't need to stop by again.'
'Well, I…'
James waited, but when she said nothing else, he took his
leave. Something was going on here and it wouldn't be
resolved with him in the room. 'Well, I'll catch you both later.'

Kelli didn't know whether to be relieved or annoyed that
James Blackman was already in Jadin's room. But he soon left,
and she edged herself into the chair, trying not to sit too close.
Jadin studied her quizzically. 'Are you okay, Kelli?'
She nodded. 'Yeah, fine. Long trip, that's all. I thought I'd call
in and check on you before I take off to the US.'
Jadin smiled, that old, familiar smile from when they were
close friends but nothing more, and nothing was awkward. 'I'm
sure I'd have still been alive when you got back.'
She grinned. 'I'm sure.' She paused, not knowing how to bring
up what she wanted to say. So she started with the facts. 'Troy
and I broke up.'
His sympathy seemed genuine. 'Gosh, I'm sorry.'
She smiled ruefully. 'I'm not sure I am. He wanted me to
marry him, but I don't want that. It's a marriage of
convenience; certainly for me, probably for him too.'
Jadin returned her expression. 'Then I guess it's better this
way.'
'Yeah.' She twisted her hands in her lap. 'Listen, what I wanted
to talk to you about - it was about what happened in Kentucky
last year.'
Jadin waved a hand. 'Don't worry about it. You wanted to go
another way and I respect that. You'll still be my friend.'

'Thanks, but what I wanted to say was,' she looked up at him. 'I wish I'd answered differently.'

Jadin frowned. 'What?'

'I almost said yes, then the phone rang and I was trying to catch it, so I went with the safe option.' She shrugged and looked away. 'But the other reason I broke up with Troy is that there's a part of me that's still wondering about if I'd said yes. And you can't marry someone when there's unfinished business elsewhere.'

She suddenly noticed he was watching her intently. She wished she was articulating this a bit better. 'I guess I'm trying to let you know that the door isn't completely closed.'

Jadin stared at her. 'You're serious.'

She nodded, wondering how far her foot was down her throat.

'Kelli,' his tone was reluctant. 'If you're wondering if it's too late, it isn't for me. I'd still like to get to know you better. But it's too late for you. I'm injured and I may never walk again, let alone ride. The rules of engagement have changed.'

She cleared her throat. 'You're still the same man.'

'Kelli--'

'I mean it. I'm not walking away because you're injured.'

He looked at her, and then reached for her hand. 'Then you're a special girl.'

She smiled shyly, the hint of a blush creeping onto her cheeks. 'Listen, go to Kentucky, knock 'em dead, and we'll talk when you get home. Okay?'

She nodded. 'Okay.' She looked at her watch. 'I'd better go, got a flight to catch. You take care of yourself.'

'Yes ma'am.'

She walked out of the hospital feeling lighter. She knew that nothing still may come of any kind of relationship. But she was no longer dating a man who wanted to marry her for convenience, and even if she didn't date Jadin Steele, at least the questions would have been answered first.'

Amy rose early to ride Chester before work. His bug was gone, and she was gradually easing him back up to a full workload. She was still keeping an eye on his forelegs, but so far they were fine.

Chester was bright-eyed and alert when she led him out to saddle up, despite the early hour. She warmed him up gently, but he was pulling on the bit, eager to get going properly. She chuckled and let him have a canter on the racing track. He pricked his ears and tossed his tail, almost dancing along.

She cooled him down, thinking about entering him in another one-day event the following weekend. He was running well, and she needed to get him back on track.

Tori was back at work and seemed to be coping fine. Her ex-husband had come through his heart surgery, and Amy suspected they may be considering getting back together. She hoped so.

She got stuck into her work, feeling more cheerful than she had in a while. Tori came in a few minutes later, breathing heavily as if she'd run from the car.

'You okay?' Amy asked, not taking her eyes off the document she was typing.

'Yeah, just running late.' She slid into her chair and shouldered off her coat. 'The boys have been edgy since the accident. A bit clingy.'

'Ah.' Amy turned to look at her. 'Not wanting to go to school?'

'Well, they're happy enough when they get there. Just prolonging the goodbyes and stuff, you know.' She sighed and leaned back in her chair. 'I've been worried about them for a while now. The divorce was hard on them, even though they still see their father.'

Amy nodded sympathetically. 'How is your ex-husband?'

'Getting stronger. The doctors think he'll recover completely.'

'Well, that's great.'

'Yeah.' She had a distant, thoughtful look in her eyes, and Amy bit her tongue before she asked how the two of them were getting along.

The phone rang, and Amy answered with her usual greeting, putting the caller through to someone upstairs. She glanced back at Tori. 'You doing okay?'

'Yeah, I'm fine. Dealing with it.' She smiled. 'Thanks.'

'Hey, if the boys are interested, they could come out to an event and help me with Chester. If they're into that sort of thing.'

Tori smiled. 'They love farming. You sure about that?'

'Sure. Chester's easygoing; he doesn't mind kids. You can come too if you like, but there's not a lot to do if you're not competing.'

'A nice day in the country sounds good.' Tori smiled. 'When?'

'Well, we're heading to Epsom this Saturday. I think he's ready to get back into competing. You can meet me at the stables early and we'll go from there.'

It was a beautiful morning when she loaded Chester into the rig that Saturday. Mike, 11, and Sam, 9, were both completely engrossed in the tasks of taking care of a horse. Amy liked them already. They were very gentle with him, not at all brash as she'd feared they might be.

'Thanks, guys.' She showed them how to slide the ramp, and they both helped on the other side. 'Let's roll.'

When they parked at the venue the boys helped her brush and saddle Chester, who watched his new grooms with magnanimous interest. 'All the best,' Tori said, as she mounted and settled her boots in the stirrups.

'Thanks.' She gently nudged Chester forward, and he started walking, head held high as if he knew he looked sharp today. The test was a good one. Chester seemed relaxed and obeyed her well. The only major fault she noticed was an extra step as they went through the flying change. She knew they would lose marks for that but overall she was very happy with him. She smiled when she saw Tori and the boys clapping as she exited the ring. It was a nice feeling, she suddenly realised, having somebody there to cheer you on. She wondered if someday in the future she'd have kids of her own helping her with her horses, cheering her on with their dad.

She suddenly recognised the kids in her daydream; they looked like Damien. She blinked herself back to reality. They'd both made their choices.

She walked Chester back to the trailer to rest before the cross country. Mike and Sam came up to pat him as she dismounted. 'He was good, wasn't he?' Sam asked, wide-eyed.

She grinned and patted his neck firmly. 'He was great. He made a little mistake but overall he did a good job. I'm very proud of him, aren't I, boy?' She patted his nose, and he nosed her fingers, obviously hoping for a reward.

She chuckled and let the boys give him some carrot. He picked it up and chewed happily.

Amy checked Chester's legs one more time before heading out to the cross-country course. No warmth or swelling. She breathed a sigh of relief.

It was a fast track, and she could tell Chester was enjoying himself. Ears pricked forward, he cantered easily around the course, soaring over the jumps as if they weren't there. They got to the end well within the time, with Chester pulling at the bit wanting to keep going. She laughed as she rose in her stirrups to bring him back down to a walk. 'Sorry, Ches. That's the finish line.'

He snorted and tossed his head. She patted his neck. 'Save it for the show-jumping so you can pick your feet up this time.'

'That looks like fun, Amy,' Sam said as she slid from Chester's back.

'It is.' She could feel the sparkle in her eyes reminding her why she was here chasing this dream. She patted Chester's neck. 'How about you guys get up on him and ride around a bit after the show-jumping?'

'Can we? Please!' Sam said, rounding beseechingly on his mother.

Tori looked at her cautiously. 'Is he safe?'

'Safe as a lamb.' She patted the horse again as she removed the saddle. 'They can just walk around on him for a bit if they like. Nothing dangerous.'

Tori nodded. 'All right then. If you're sure,' she added to Amy.

'It's fine.'

She could feel her nerves building as the show-jumping approached. She knew it was only a minor one-day event, but she hoped that his jumping had improved. He'd been good in practice, but the practice wasn't where it mattered.

'You look nervous,' Tori observed as she was saddling Chester.

Amy wrinkled her nose. 'Thanks.'

Tori made a face. 'Sorry.'

Amy chuckled. ' I am. The last time he jumped he went through rather than over most of the jumps.'

'Oh, I see.'

'Yeah.' Amy patted the grey neck affectionately. 'He's been better in training, but this is the Litmus test.'

'I'm sure you'll be fine.'

She trotted into the warm-up ring. Chester felt at ease, which was a good sign. They were within the top twenty, but she was more concerned with their performance than their ranking at the moment.

She warmed Chester up slowly and he seemed happy and ready. Their number rang over the tinny loudspeaker, and they trotted into the ring.

From the first jump, she could tell this would be a better round. Chester leapt with perfect timing, clearing the oxer by a foot.

His canter/jump rhythm felt perfect, and he soared around the course with not a fault. She was sure she looked like the Chesire Cat.

Chester tossed his head in response to her praise as they left the ring. She rode above his withers, letting him have a few extra canter strides before pulling him back to a walk and thumping his neck. 'Good boy, Chester.'

He received more 'good boys' and pats from Mike and Sam. He tossed his head again, clearly enjoying the attention. Amy dismounted and fed him another carrot. He munched happily before slobbering the boys, making them grimace through their giggles.

They drove the short distance back and Tori picked up her car at the stable. 'Thanks, Amy,' she said quietly as the boys got in the car. 'They had an absolute blast.'

'No problem. They're welcome to come again sometime.'

She put Chester away, telling him how good he'd been. He nodded, clearly pleased with himself, and tucked greedily into his dinner. She hoped he remembered this, and that this was how he should perform every week.

She went home happy. There was still a long journey ahead, but they were at least on the right track.

Silver Flint was ready and waiting when Kelli Holmes drove into Manorbrook's long driveway. His gear was all packed and James lugged the transport box to the parking bay.

'Hey, Kelli,' he said when she slid out of the cab. She looked good in her jeans and boots, her long hair braided down her back like a Texas cowgirl. She seemed happier than when he'd last seen her in Jadin's hospital room. 'You look nice.'

'Thank you.' She smiled. 'How're you?'

'Good.' He watched as her assistant rider, a young, thin man, slid out of the other side of the cab. Kelli turned to him.

'Jimmy, this is Henrique. Henrique, this is my friend and colleague, James Blackman.'

They shook hands. 'Nice to meet you.' He waited, expecting her boyfriend to come out and say hello, but no one else was there. 'Troy flying out later?'

Kelli cleared her throat. 'We, uh, aren't together anymore.'

'Oh. I'm sorry, Kell.'

She shrugged. 'It's okay. I didn't love him enough, and he just wanted a glorified housemaid.'

'Well, still, I'm sorry.'

'Thanks.'

James turned his attention to Henrique. He was Latin American and had the look of a man who was perfectly at home with horses. After nearly two decades in eventing circles, you could start to spot who was comfortable and who wasn't.

Watching him with Silver Flint, he knew he was right. Silver seemed to take to him straight away, which put James' mind at ease. 'And you say he's a good rider?' he asked Kelli quietly.

'Very good.' Kelli was watching him fondly. 'He'd be good enough to ride at the top level, but once he's made some money he wants to go home and get back into the racing industry in Puerto Rico.'

Silver Flint walked easily into the trailer, sticking his nose over the divider to investigate Kaleido, Kelli's horse. Kaleido put his ears back, obviously less than thrilled about sharing his territory.

Kelli clipped Flint's lead to the wall and patted his rump. 'Good boy.' She reached over to pat her mount. 'Be nice, Kal.'

James stepped onto the ramp to pat Silver Flint. 'Be good, old lad.' They stepped down and slid the ramp home.

'You shouldn't have any problems with him,' James said. 'He's placid as anything. But if you do need to sedate him or whatever, go for it.'

'Veterinary power of attorney?' She grinned. 'I'm sure he'll be fine. He's a good horse.'

'He is.' James reached out to hug her. 'Have a safe trip.'

She squeezed him back. 'We will.' She stepped back and looked him in the eye. 'Take care of Jadin, okay?'

'You know I will.'

Amy immediately booked Chester into another event the following weekend, but she knew not to get too far ahead of herself.

It was hardly Badminton, but she had been buoyed by Chester's performance. Now that the reason she was here was going better, it put the world in a better light. She caught herself whistling as she walked into work early that Monday.

'You're cheerful for a Monday.' Tori looked up from her keyboard.

'You're early. Everything all right?'

'Yeah. Just wanted to get a head start on everything. I was hoping to sneak away for a school play this afternoon.'

They got busy, and when Amy next looked at the clock, it was nearly eleven. But she'd got a lot done, including clearing her inbox, which was a relief. She headed to the break room, pausing in the doorway. 'You want anything, Tori?'

'Yeah, I'll grab a decaf in a minute.'

Amy raised an eyebrow. 'Decaf on a Monday morning?'

'I'll pretend I didn't hear that.'

Back at her desk, she logged into the supplier's website and set about making the arrangements. If she hurried, she may have it done in time for a late lunch.

She got up and headed to the back room to double-check a few supplies. She heard the front door open and Tori's greeting.

'Hi, can I help you?'

A man's voice. As she counted pens, she thought the voice seemed vaguely familiar. 'Yeah, I'm looking for someone.'
She could hear the patient smile in Tori's tone. 'Someone who works here?'
'I think so. Amy Williams?'
Amy straightened.
'Do you know her?' Tori asked.
'Yes. I'm Lieutenant Commander Damien Scott, Royal New Zealand Navy.'

Chapter Nine

James took Coalbridge out for a full run and he could feel him coming back to his old self. He wouldn't be ready for Badminton, but maybe he could take him to Luhmuhlen in six weeks.

The police had still not uncovered anything concrete about who had sabotaged his horse. The padlock had no unexpected prints, nor had any handles in the building. It looked like a professional job.

Jadin had suggested the day before that maybe one of the wealthy owners behind someone else's horse had instigated it. James didn't think that the eventing world was that sinister, but he had to admit it was a possibility. With the relatively recent development of turning the five-star events into a series, there was big money to be had by winning the Classics.

The fact that it was Coalbridge and not another of his horses would support that theory. Although why hadn't they also poisoned Marksman while they were at it?

He sighed and took Coalie into the jumping ring. They would be found. One day, they'd have to answer for it.

Coalie was happy to be back out doing what he did best. He soared over the small jumps as if scoffing at them, but James wanted him back in top shape before they returned to the competition-standard obstacles.

He cooled Coalie down and walked him back to the hot walker. He dismounted and ran his hands over the horse's back and legs. He was still far from the athlete he'd been but there was nothing new to worry about.

His eyes widened at the sight of the vehicle pulling into his parking bay. It was a police cruiser, and the pretty detective he'd met weeks ago stepped out of the driver's side.

'James Blackman?' She asked as she approached.

'Yes,' he said, frozen in place with Coalie looking - somewhat bemusedly, he suspected - over his shoulder.

'I'm Constable Tessa Martin. My partner and I talked to you several weeks ago?'

'Yes, I remember.'

She cleared her throat. 'We may have found a lead as to who broke into your barn and poisoned your horse.'

The only thing he could think was that they'd better charge the creep with every little law he'd broken. He nodded to Coalbridge. 'Let me put him away and we can talk.'

She followed him towards the stable. 'This is the horse, right? He looks much better.'

'He's getting there.' He unhooked the lead rope and patted Coalie on the rump.

'Okay,' she said as they sat down in the tack room. 'As you know, we weren't able to get any prints off the padlock or door handles. But we also ran a search for anyone who may have been in the area that night. It's a pretty quiet area.'

James shrugged. 'I hardly know my neighbours. So someone could have been around with legitimate reason.'

'Well, we spoke to the occupants in the house to your north. They reported seeing an unfamiliar sedan slow down outside their place before continuing.'

James didn't react. Even he knew that wasn't much.

'They did get the license plate on their security camera. We ran the plates and came up with some interesting info.' She held up a sketch. 'The registered owner is a Colton Everson.'

'Who is that?'

'He's got a record of petty theft and has also been on trial for attempted murder, but he was acquitted.' She looked at him.

'We think he's a hitman. And it wouldn't be too hard to persuade him to take on something like this. Assuming you have no history with him?'

'No.'

'We're in the process of tracking him down. His address records are no longer current. But the bigger issue is who may have been in it with him. We're fairly certain he has no reason to go after you.'

James leaned back. 'But we don't even know for sure it was him, right? All we know is his vehicle was in the vicinity.'

'True. That's why we need to talk to him.'

James kept his view to himself. He knew as much as they were working to solve this, it took second place to crimes involving humans.

'Anything else?'

'Not at this stage. We'll keep at it.' She glanced towards Coalie. 'We'll do all we can.'

'Thank you, Constable Martin.'

'Call me Tess.'

'Okay, thanks, Tess.'

Vicky walked in with a sack of feed and smiled politely. 'Hello, officer.'

'It's Tess,' the redhead said with a smile. 'I'm just leaving. We'll be in touch,' she said to James.

He nodded. 'Thank you.'

He knew Vicky would round on him and demand information as soon as the policewoman left, and he was right. 'So what do they have?'

He grimaced. 'Not a lot. A sedan is seen in the area driven by a suspected hitman. She reckons it wouldn't be much of a stretch for him to branch out into horses.'

Vicky gasped. 'You mean they were trying to kill him?'

'It's a possibility. Anyway, they figure this guy may have been booked to poison Coalie. So they're trying to hunt him down and see who put him up to it.'

Vicky sat on a hay bale. 'So they just think it's sabotage.' She shook her head. 'But if they were trying to kill him, and this guy is an experienced hitman, surely he'd have finished the job? There wasn't enough in his system to kill him.'

'True.' James rubbed a hand through his hair. 'Boy, this is getting heavy.'

'I know.' Vicky picked up Lacklustre's bridle. 'Still want to do him next?'

'Yeah. Thanks, Vick. Do you want to ride Clarabelle?'

'Sure.'

He went to see Jadin that afternoon and they weighed the pros and cons of whether this would lead anywhere. Jadin, ever the optimist, was sure that it would, but James reiterated that there was no way to tell whether this man had even stopped the car. 'He may have been driving straight through to Bristol for all we know.'

'At least it's something, Jimmy.'

'Yeah, but it's no good if it's a dead end.'

Jadin raised an eyebrow at him. 'My, aren't we cheerful this fine evening?'

James sighed and leaned back in the chair. 'Sorry. I'm frustrated about this and I don't want to go to Kentucky.'

Jadin frowned. 'It's not that bad.'

'I know. I've just got a real mental block about it. I didn't want to go at all, but I thought it would be good for Silver Flint.'

'Why? You go every other year.' Jadin paused, then added softly, 'Ah. It was ten years ago this year, wasn't it?'

James had moved to the window and stood staring out, arms crossed over his chest. 'Yeah. I was sure that wasn't it.' He sighed. 'But now I'm not so sure.'

Jadin cleared his throat. 'No one would blame you if you don't go, Jimmy. Heck, I skipped a year before I went back, and she wasn't even my horse.'

James could see the images in his mind's eye as clearly as if it was yesterday. He could see the clouds coming over the hill, the top-notch facilities in the background, Calintha's chestnut mane blowing over his gloves. He heard his boots hit the ground, saw his horse crumble as if her legs couldn't hold her, heard the shouts and the scrambled activity to find a vet. He saw all the pairs of eyes: Jadin's wide with horror, Kelli's filled with tears, his groom Lucy's shut against the sight, the kind sadness in the vet's.

He took a deep breath. 'It's silly to be dwelling on this now.'

Jadin straightened as much as he could. 'No, it isn't. She was your baby, the first one you trained. Besides, everyone loved her.'

'She's just a horse, Jadin. Yes, I loved her, but I shouldn't stay away because of that. It's not like my daughter died there.'

Jadin shook his head, turning back from the window.

Jadin shrugged. 'As I said, it hit me hard. Kelli too. It's only worse for you.'

James shook his head. 'Yeah. But I'm going to go. Silver Flint needs a rider. I don't need to be all sentimental about it.'

Jadin gave him a sad smile. 'She was a wonderful horse.'

'Yeah, she was.' James gave him a small grin. 'Too bad I have yet to find a girl like her.'

Jadin gave him a thoughtful look. 'That pretty redheaded constable seems very nice.'

James rolled his eyes. 'Don't start. She's a cop, for goodness sake.'

'So?'

'Well, I can't marry a cop. She's probably a control freak.'

'And you would know this how?'

James threw his hands in the air. 'I am perfectly capable of handling my own love life.'

'Really,' Jadin snickered.

'Yes really. But while we're on the subject, what is going on with you and Kelli?'

Jadin's face was a mask of seriousness. 'Nothing.'

James squinted at him, but since they were both his friends, he decided to drop the subject. 'If you say so.'

'When do you leave on your trans-Atlantic flight?'

James groaned. 'Don't remind me. I'll be so jet-lagged I won't remember what I'm there for. Thursday morning.'

'Not much time for practice.'

'No. But he's in good hands. All I need is one session with him.'

Jadin sighed. 'I wish I was going.'

James patted his arm. 'Me too. But I have Vicky commissioned to keep an eye on you while I'm gone.'

Jadin groaned. 'Why didn't you just call Mother Superior?'

James laughed. 'I'm going to tell her you said that.'

'Oh do. She'll probably be delighted at my fear.'

Amy froze, her fingers clenched around a handful of pens she'd been counting. What in the world was he doing here? She could tell Tori was trying to decide what to do. 'Well, sir, why don't you have a seat and I'll see if she's available?'

Amy hadn't moved. She was trying to decide if she was available.

Tori came casually walking into the room, closing the door behind her. 'There's a gentleman here to see you, says he knows you. A Lieutenant Commander --'

'Damien Scott.' She released the breath she'd been holding.

'Oh, so you do know him?'

'Tori, he's… the one on the other side of the world.'

Tori's mouth dropped open. 'You're not serious.'

All Amy could do was nod.

'Wow! And he's come over the hill and down dale, all the way to Enfield to sweep you off your feet! How romantic!'

'Shut up, Shakespeare,' Amy hissed. 'I don't even know if I want to see him. What could he possibly want?'

Tori was positively bubbling. 'What do you think?'

Amy rolled her eyes. 'It's not as fairy tale as all that.'

'Prove it,' Tori said smugly, standing over her with her arms crossed like a triumphant warrior. Then she softened slightly. 'Look, Amy, even if he isn't here to take you to the nearest Justice of the Peace, at least talk to him. He found you after all this time. I think you owe him that.'

Amy sagged. She could say she was busy and she'd call him later. But curiosity, and a stubborn desire to see him again, were winning. 'All right. I'll talk to him.'

'Good.' Tori stepped out of her way. 'And Amy,' she added quietly. Amy paused with her hand on the knob. 'Give him a chance.'

Amy pursed her lips and opened the door.

He looked so familiar, standing there in his uniform, despite the extra stripe on his shoulder. She straightened her spine as she approached the desk. 'Hello, Damien.' Her tone was probably cooler than was fair.

'Hi, yourself.' He returned their familiar greeting. 'How are you?'

'I'm good.' She wasn't sure whether to remain prim and proper or to throw her arms around his neck and hug him like the old friend he was. 'You?'

'I'm fine. I wanted to catch up with you and see how you are.'

'How'd you know where to find me?'

'A little bit of research.' He smiled. 'You got time for lunch with an old friend?'

She hesitated, then allowed herself a smile. 'Sure. Give me half an hour?'

'Okay.'

She returned to the office to finish counting supplies, where Tori had been eavesdropping, judging by her guilty expression and the fact she hadn't been doing the sorting she was pretending she was. Amy returned to the desk supplies with Tori hovering over her. 'So?'

'So, what?'

'So how did it go?'

Amy rolled her eyes. 'We're just having lunch as old friends.'

Tori raised an eyebrow. 'Is that all it is?'

'Yes it is, thank you very much.' Amy finished marking her list and stalked good-naturedly back to her computer.

Tori followed her. 'So he didn't sweep you off your feet?'

Amy rolled her eyes. 'No, he did not.'

'Shame. Just give him some more time.'

She tossed a ball of paper at her. Tori ducked and proceeded to concentrate on her work.

Damien reappeared 30 minutes later. Amy introduced Tori, who shook his hand politely. Amy grabbed her coat and followed her friend out to a nice rental car.

'Phew, did you get a pay rise when you became Commander?' She smirked.

'Funny.' He opened the door for her and trotted around to the driver's side. 'I'm here on the Navy's docket.'

'Really?' She buckled in and turned to face him. 'Why?'

'That's partly why I'm here to talk to you.' He kept his eyes on the road. 'We're up here training with the British Royal Navy in Portsmouth.'

She raised her eyebrows. 'That's a long drive.'

He smiled at her. 'It's my day off.'

'So 'we' as in your ship?'

'Yeah. I'm still on the Te Kaha. But I've graduated to being a Navigating Officer now.'

She smiled. 'Congratulations.'

'Thanks. It's good to be back on the sea after the shore training.' He turned onto a side street and parked. 'But we don't usually train in England. There's a special mission coming up, and I wanted to talk to you before we left.'

Amy leaned back in her seat. 'Why? We haven't talked before any other mission. It's been six years.'

He smiled ruefully. 'I know. But I thought you were pretty sure about us going our separate ways.'

'I was.' Amy cleared her throat. 'So why now?'

He sighed. 'Two reasons. One, this mission is a dangerous one. Not a typical exercise. We're going into the war in the Middle East.'

She swallowed but let him continue.

'And I didn't want our relationship to be left where it ended.' He fiddled with the keys, still in the ignition. 'Two, I was wondering if I could convince you to change your mind.' He shrugged. 'I miss you, Ames. Plain and simple.'

She opened her mouth but he held up a hand.

'I'm not asking for anything right now. I just wanted to talk to you and have lunch together like old friends. Repair how it ended.' He reached for her hand. 'Then maybe see where it goes.'

She sighed, but she could agree on one thing. 'I'd like to be friends again, too.'

'Good.' He smiled and opened his door. 'Shall we?'

They walked into the cute cafe and found a window table. They ordered croissant sandwiches and sparkling fruit juice. Amy leaned back and studied him. He'd aged little in the last six and a half years, perhaps because of the military styles he'd had for so long; dark blond hair in the correct cut, clearly still fit enough to ease through his PFTs. There were a few more laugh lines around his blue eyes, but that was the only sign that it had been as long as it had.

'So…' She sipped her juice while they waited for their food. 'Still enjoying it?'

He smiled and nodded. 'As much as ever.'

She returned the smile. 'You always were at home on those boats.' She set down the glass. 'Tell me about this mission.'

He cleared his throat. 'There's a lot I can't say. But we are taking Te Kaha to the Middle East to support the British Navy.' He shrugged. 'We've had a peacekeeping presence in various countries for a long time. But this is more of a show of strength.'

She studied him. 'You don't agree.'

He shrugged. 'I follow my orders.'

'So, you are actually - you know - engaging in battle?'

He pursed his lips. 'Hard to say at this point. Officially, we're going down there to help with the terrorist situation, but there is a chance that we may be called to act. The fact that we're taking the ship down is pretty telling.'

She nodded. 'I guess so.'

'So…' He reached for her hand. 'I guess I want to say I'm sorry for how we parted ways.'

'It wasn't completely your fault. I'm sorry too.'

'I'd like for us to be friends again, to stay in touch. Even if it's not very often.'

She squeezed his hand. 'Me too.'

Their food arrived, and she relaxed a little now they had put the past behind them. She bit into her grilled salmon and capsicum sandwich. 'Mmm, this is good.'

He nodded, his mouth full. 'There's one of these cafes down by the port. I've spent a good portion of my Commander's salary there.'

She chuckled. 'Well, thank you.'

He finished his mouthful and studied her. 'So, what about you?'

'Well, I'm working at the Gazette, as you know. It's an interesting job.' She took another sip. 'But I'm here to try and qualify Chester for some top-level three-day events.'
'How's that going?'
'Well, he was sick for a while, but he had a great outing last weekend. I was very happy with him. Kind of gives me hope that we can keep going, that it's not totally out of reach.'
'That's great.'
They ate the rest of their meal in companionable silence. It felt good, she thought, just to have his company again. 'So when do you leave?'
'For the Middle East?' At her nod, he shrugged. 'Within the next couple of weeks, I think. I don't know the exact day.' He stood to pay for their lunch.
She watched him. All his mannerisms were so familiar, but at the same time, it was strange that it still felt that way after so long. Where would this leave them? He was going to lands of unrest; she was still chasing her dreams in England. Even if she could consider a dating relationship, how could the logistics possibly work?
He came back to the table and smiled at her. 'I'd better get you back to work.'
Amy stood and followed him out to the car. She had half expected him to offer her his arm, but she didn't know if she was disappointed or relieved that he didn't. She was very glad to see him, as a friend, but as anything more? She didn't know. They drove back in silence. She wondered when she'd see him again. It had been nice, seeing her dearest friend. It would be good to stay in more regular contact.
'So...can we do this again before we leave?' Damien asked, pulling on the handbrake.
She smiled. 'Sure. When?'
'I think I have a weekend off at the end of next week. Maybe we could do something nice?'

She pursed her lips. 'I'm taking Chester to Crawley on Saturday.'

'Well, how about Sunday?'

'Sure, I guess.'

'Good. I'll look you up on Facebook and send you a message.' He smiled at her, then hesitated, as if unsure whether he should say the next thing. 'Um -'

'What?'

He cleared his throat. 'As to where we stand… I'm still interested in a relationship. I've never met another girl like you. But I know it's been a long time, so if all you want to be is friends, that's fine. I'd just like to keep in touch more.'

He was looking at her expectantly, and she decided his honesty deserved her own. She cleared her own throat. 'I don't know what I want right now. I do know I want to be friends again, so let's do that for a while, okay?'

He nodded with a sparkle in his eyes, and even all these years later, she could read that reaction. He was happy she hadn't said no.

She picked up her bag. 'Nice to see you, Damien.' She looked into his eyes. 'It really was.'

'You too.' He offered his arm in a hug, and she reciprocated. Regardless of where they went from here, she had her friend back.

'I'll be in touch.' He gave her a small wave as she shut the door.

'Bye.' She waved back and trotted into the building. No, of course, her heart didn't feel lighter than it had in weeks. It was just nice to see a familiar face, that's all.

Tori looked about ready to burst when she walked in. 'Well?'

Amy rolled her eyes. 'All we did was have lunch. Cafe sandwiches, by the way, not the Hilton.'

'Well, seeing as there's no Hilton in Enfield, that would've been something.' Tori grinned at her. 'Was it romantic? Be honest.'

Amy sat down with a sigh. 'No. It was nice, but no, it was not romantic.'

Tori must have heard her sigh because she dropped the teasing badgering. 'You all right?'

Amy shrugged. 'I'm a little mixed up. We've agreed to be friends again, but he wants more than that.'

'And you don't?'

Amy sighed again as she logged in to her computer. 'Right now, I have no idea what I want.'

'Well, it's good you're going to be friends. Then, if something does happen, it does, and if it doesn't, it doesn't.' Tori patted her arm. 'Are you okay if I split for lunch?'

'Sure.'

She picked up her bag. 'Can I make a small observation?'

Amy shrugged. 'If you like.'

Tori gave her a small smile. 'From the way you look at each other, I wouldn't rule out being more than friends.'

James felt a little foolish, but he was glad he'd made the walk. He just wanted to see her resting place. Yes, she was only an animal, but he had loved her.

He looked up at the tree above the stone. She would have liked her grave, had horses had any grasp of such things.

He decided that was enough sentimentality for one morning. He rose and walked back up to the stables. He was glad she'd been able to be buried on his land.

He double-checked he had all his gear packed. Maybe this was another reason he didn't like Kentucky, the feeling of going so far away. If you forgot something, you just had to buy a new one.

Caitlyn walked in looking like she was ready to go to the ball. Her eyes were sparkling and she was bouncing in place. 'Are we ready?'

'Seem to be.' He couldn't help but smile at her exuberance. 'We'll stop in and see Jadin on the way to the airport, okay?'

They got on the road. 'You worried, Uncle James?'

He glanced at his niece. 'No.'

'I thought you believed in telling the truth.'

He gave her a guilty grin. 'Fine, busted.' He slowed the vehicle to make the turn into central Bristol. 'Yeah, I'm not looking forward to Kentucky. I'm a little worried about Jadin. I know I'm not his supervisor or anything but I just like being not too far away.'

She nodded. It felt strange having this sort of conversation with his niece. She'd always been the child; he'd been the adult. But now, she'd caught up with him.

'And I guess I'm a little worried about Vicky doing everything by herself. I know she's capable, but I just don't like doing it.'

'Just pay her extra.'

He gave her a grin. 'I am already.'

'Wow, that's encouraging. I'm the one going halfway around the world with you.' She broke into giggles.

'Yeah, well, she's the senior groom.' He smiled at her.

'Besides, I'm taking you to bluegrass country, aren't I?'

'I can't wait to see those big ranches with the thoroughbreds.'

'Well, I'll let you in on a secret.' He pulled into the hospital car park. 'Kelli and I may be doing a little bit of horse shopping while we're there. Don't screech.'

She stared at him, wide-eyed. 'Really?'

'Well, mostly for her. But I'm probably going to be selling those yearlings. I just don't have the time to train two up from scratch right now. I think I'd prefer one slightly older horse who at least has the basics.'

She grinned. 'Do I get to help pick out the next Coalie?'

He laughed. 'I have veto power.'

'So where?'

'A couple of sport horse farms in Louisville. Kelli bought Kaleido there.'

'He's going to be a star soon.'

James nodded. 'I think so.'

As he figured, the flight was long and tedious, and with his luck, all the movies were chick flicks. Caitlyn had a wonderful time, but he at least caught up on some sleep.

It was another hour's drive from the airport into Louisville. Caitlyn immediately wanted to drive, until James reminded her it was on the wrong side of the road. He drove the rental himself, grateful that he slept on the plane.

'It's beautiful,' Caitlyn said, watching the endless paddocks.

'It is,' James said. 'I wouldn't mind having a farm out here someday. I may have even considered buying property here but England is a better base.'

'I thought you didn't like Kentucky.'

'I don't like the city, but I do like the bluegrass country.'

They drove through Louisville and Caitlyn pointed out the window. 'There's Churchill Downs! Have you ever been?'

James grinned. 'Jadin and I stayed after the event to watch the Kentucky Derby once. It was pretty spectacular.'

'Wow.'

'Maybe Wilson could come and ride here one day,' James suggested.

'Maybe.' She was enchanted with the place. 'I'm going to ask him.'

Several miles later they pulled into the magnificent Kentucky Horse Park and headed for the stables. Two days before the dressage, it was a hive of activity.

James parked close to Barn 47A where the New Zealand horses were stabled, along with the Americans and a couple of the smaller nations. He opened the door and took a deep breath. Calintha had died less than 20 metres away.

'Let's go and check on Silver Flint.'

'You still don't think he's a five-star horse?' she asked as she matched his pace over the sanded walkway.

'Well, I still have my doubts. They may prove to be unfounded.'

Silver Flint nickered at the sight of his owner and favourite groom. 'Hey, old boy.' James stroked his nose. 'How have they been treating you, huh?' Silver Flint nodded into his palm.

'Hey, guys.' He turned at Kelli's greeting. 'Had a good flight?'

'Yeah, well, except for the chick flicks.'

She grinned. 'Poor bloke. How are you, Catie?'

'Fine, ma'am.'

'I'm no ma'am. It's Kelli, remember?' She turned to the horse. 'He's been a very good boy. Henrique's taken a shine to him, I think. He was fine after the flight. He's in good shape, Jimmy.'

'This is his first five-star. You think he's ready?'

'I thought it was. I think he'll be fine. He looks really good. He can handle the atmosphere, too.'

James nodded, patting the horse's neck. 'I need to get my pass before I go; then I'll take over riding him tomorrow morning.'

'Sounds good. You still want to have a look at the farms tomorrow?'

'Yep. I'm pretty sure I'm selling the yearlings.'

She nodded. 'I may be interested in one of them, but I need one more top horse. Max is getting old.'

'He'll be sixteen soon?'

She nodded. 'He'll probably last till he's eighteen, but it's time to start looking to the future. Although I think this one has the makings of a superstar.' She reached over to stroke Kaleido, who was watching proceedings from the stall next door.

'He's a goodie, all right.' James gave Silver Flint one last pat. 'Thanks for taking such good care of him.'

'Oh, you're welcome. He's a doll.'

'See you in the morning,' James said, and he and Caitlyn got back in the vehicle to visit the main office. They would both need their IDs to move freely around the park.

'So, we're going horse shopping tomorrow?' Caitlyn asked as soon as they pulled out of the gate.

James grinned. 'You've been dying to ask that for the last twenty minutes, haven't you?'

'Maybe,' she admitted. 'So?'

'Well, after morning works, there's not a lot else for us to do. The riders' briefings are in the afternoon, and I'll probably give Silver another run. So, yes, probably late morning.'

'It's so exciting. I wish I had the money to buy a top-notch horse.'

'Well, they're still cheaper than racehorses.'

'Yeah.' She looked at the sign. 'Fayette County. That sounds cool. You should name a horse that.'

'Hmm, maybe.'

'So where are we staying?'

'Our favourite hotel.' He winked at her. 'Not the Hilton, sad to relate.'

She made a face. 'Maybe racing is better.'

James chuckled. 'Only in the upper echelons.'

James woke up to rain the next morning. Hopefully, it would blow over by the next day. Silver Flint could handle a wet track, but there was usually some sort of drama at a wet five-star.

Kelli had been right; Silver was in great shape. He was probably in a better place, physically and mentally, than before he left. He was responsive, and his dressage seemed very fluid. He patted his neck and made a mental note to personally thank Henrique.

As he warmed the horse down he watched Kelli on Kaleido. They looked the picture of elegance. He knew the horse wasn't the sturdiest cross-country jumper, but he was slowly learning under Kelli's careful tutelage. And his dressage skills helped make up for it in the meantime.

'He's good, isn't he?' Kelli asked as she left the ring, gesturing with her head.

James glanced where she indicated and saw Cole Kendrick, the British star, on Remover. The duo were clear favourites for the competition, with the Swede Klinsmann not here, and it wasn't hard to see why. 'Yeah, he is. But I was watching Kaleido. He looks poetic.'

She raised her eyebrows and smiled. 'That's a new term, but it's probably apt.' She patted his neck. 'Now he just needs to learn to do a decent jump.'

'He'll get there. He's got the talent. And one of the best teachers.'

She smiled. 'Thanks, if you don't count yourself.'

'Hey, I was trying to be modest.' He grinned at her. He'd missed this, their easy banter. It seemed like a year since they'd last been to an event or team training together.

She walked Kaleido alongside him back to the barn. 'So, you want to leave about eleven?'

'Fine by me. Are we the only Kiwis who made the trip here?'

'No, Kyle came over. He was a late entry after there was a withdrawal, so they put Cetchco in with the Aussie horses.'

James gave her a look of mock horror. 'Poor thing.'

The drizzle had eased when they headed south of the Horse Park towards the farms in central Lexington. First stop: Spy Coast Farm, where Kelli had bought her beloved Kaleido five years before.

A tall thin man met their rental four-wheel-drive at the gate. 'Welcome back, Kelli. How's my boy doing?'

Kelli grinned. 'He's having the time of his life. Just needs to get used to log fences.' She turned to James. 'Jimmy, this is Colton McLean. Colton, James Blackman.'

'Ah, the man himself! How do you do, sir?'

'Very good thank you. By the looks of Kaleido, you've got some special horses here.'

'Well, well, well, we like to think so.' He waved his hand. 'I'm assuming you're looking for something similar to Miss Kelli, Mr Blackman? A young but trained horse?'

'It's James,' he said with a smile. 'But yes, please.'

'Why don't you park up by my barn and have a look around the four and five-year-olds?' He indicated the old-fashioned red building, complete with silo. 'Thank you, sir.'

Colton shook his finger at him. 'If you're James, I ain't sir.'

James had to laugh.

Colton led them to the huge paddock that housed the young horses. There were a dozen of them, and James knew right away they were good stock.

'They're beautiful,' Caitlyn said, leaning on the fence.

'They are,' Kelli said, her eyes following the herd's movements.

'What blood do you have?' James asked.

'A lot of horses are thoroughbred, with splashes of Hanoverian, Holsteiner, Trakehner. Some of them have a little quarter horse and Arabian, for sturdiness.'

James nodded.

'One of our sires, Oldendale, is a son of Stan the Man.'

James whistled. Stan the Man Xx had sired one of the greatest eventers to grace the earth, La Biosthetique Sam, winner of Olympic and World Championship gold with Michael Jung.

'He looks a lot like La Biosthetique Sam. His foals are amazing.'

'Were they full brothers?'

Colton shook his head. 'His dam was a thoroughbred.'

James watched the youngsters grazing in front of him. One pale chestnut had caught his eye. She was tall for a mare and had the distinct grace of warmblood breeding. He liked his horses to be at least half thoroughbred, preferably more - it gave them hardiness - but maybe he would make an exception to the rule if this one wasn't.

He asked Juan, the stable hand hovering nearby, about the chestnut filly. He smiled. 'She's a beauty, that one,' he said in perfect, only slightly accented English. 'Sired by Oldendale. She's got a little thoroughbred, but mostly Hanoverian and German Sporthorse, like La Biosthetique Sam.'

James smiled. He couldn't blame them for maximising that particular point.

James liked her even more after riding her around the arena. She was an athlete, but she was also obedient, even to a strange rider. She was obviously trainable.

'You in love yet?' Caitlyn called from the fence.

James grinned and brought the horse to a stop. She halted perfectly, like the end of a dressage test. 'I think she's a good one.'

They moved on to Bravo Sporthorses, only a few kilometres away. This time it was Kelli who was immediately drawn to a horse, a lovely black gelding. Watching her ride him, James thought he was perfect. He was tall but not too big, and a bold jumper.

They decided to try one more farm before heading back to mull over their decisions over the next couple of days.

They were all good animals, and Kelli seemed pretty sure about her black gelding, but they promised to let them know in a couple of days.

James rode Silver Flint one more time before the riders' meeting and was happy with where he was. He was in good condition, and despite his reservations, he hoped the horse would cope well at the step up.

Riders like he and Jadin and Kelli had sat through so many briefings that they all started to sound the same, but attendance was mandatory. As they left, Kelli rolled her eyes good-naturedly at him. 'We've been doing this for so long, we could sleepwalk through it and get it close to right.'

'You might. I don't sleepwalk.'

'Funny.'

Before going to bed, he messaged Jadin, telling him about Silver Flint and the new horses they'd looked at. Jadin wished him luck, and James laid back on his bed with a sigh. Jadin should be in the next room, and they should be discussing the pros and cons of the new horses over a real American pizza.

He was the 36th to go on dressage day. He felt Silver Flint tense ever so slightly as they entered the ring, but he relaxed as they came to a halt on the centreline. James doffed his hat to the judges and signalled the horse forward.

By the end, he was thrilled with the test. Silver had been soft and responsive, and his flying change was almost perfect. James praised him effusively as they left the arena. They were given a score of 31.2, in fourth place, but there were still forty-odd horses to go.

He grinned down at Caitlyn, who was thumping the horse's neck. Silver stood tall, obviously picking up on their approval. James walked him around the arena to cool down, watching as Cole Kendrick entered the ring on his horse Remover.

The big grey could be accused of being clunky, but Cole was a soft rider. James thought there were very few other riders who could get Remover to do dressage as well as that. He scored 30.8.

Kelli and Kaleido were next. As they passed him James could see Kaleido pulling at the bit, looking less than happy. He bit his lip and watched as Kelli brought him to a stop outside the ring as if trying to get him to listen. She nudged him forward, but he walked into the arena with his ears back.

James dismounted and gave Silver Flint to Caitlyn so he could watch the test. Kelli did an admirable job of keeping him under control, but it wasn't a great test. There were a couple of minor inaccuracies and his flicking tail didn't help. They wouldn't be in the top twenty.

Kelli's face was a calm mask, but she shot James a despairing look. 'He wouldn't pay attention to me,' she lamented. 'He's seldom done that before.'

An image of an ill Coalbridge flickered through James' mind and he felt a small chill. 'Is he feeling okay?'

'I think so, why?' She looked down at him as he walked beside Kaleido back towards the barn. 'What?'

James shook his head. 'Was just hoping someone isn't targeting more than just Coalbridge.'

Kelli's eyes widened fractionally and she dismounted to look the horse over. 'He's seemed okay.'

'I'm probably just being paranoid. The slightest thing makes me wonder.'

She shook her head, her braid slapping from side to side. 'I don't blame you.'

'You just about ready to walk the course?'

'Just let me get this guy settled down. Kyle coming?'

James checked his watch. 'Yeah, he should have time. He's pretty late into the ring.'

He spotted Kyle hanging around the barn, keeping one eye on the scoreboard. His warmblood, Cetchco, was a fine dressage horse and he would likely be in the top quarter by the end of the day. 'Hey, Kyle, you got time to walk the track?'

Kyle glanced at his wrist. 'Yeah, I've still got a couple of hours. Where's Kelli?'

'Just settling Kaleido. He didn't have a happy time.' James leaned on the fence next to him. They had known each other for nearly eight years. They had never been close, but they got on all right. Kyle was somewhat of an outsider; he liked to do things his way, not always going along with the team. But he was a good rider and had his share of successes. 'So how's life been treating you, Kyle?'

Kyle shrugged. 'It's been all right. Cetchco caught a virus a few weeks ago and took him a while to get back on his feet. I almost worried he'd miss this.'

'That's tough.'

'It is. But it gave me a bit of time to focus on my other two. How's Coalbridge?'

'Getting back into shape. They still haven't found the instigator.'

Kyle shook his head. 'Must be hard.'

'Well, I've got all my security alarms and whatnot. I just want him brought to justice really.'

The trio headed out to walk the course, working out angles and distances for the cross-country tomorrow. James couldn't see anything that worried him, apart from the water jump. It was a long, deep pond with two obstacles in the middle. He knew Silver Flint could cope with water, but this one was the trickiest he'd seen for a while.

Kelli was worried about Kaleido. He was still learning, and he wasn't a huge fan of water. She was nervous that he wouldn't get his cadence back after the first jump to be able to get over the second.

'Just take it slow,' James advised. 'It's pretty deep, so it's not going to be fast anyway. And they're not that big.'

'No.' She sighed as she turned to walk away. 'Maybe water jumps are just getting to me right now. I keep thinking of Jadin…'

She trailed off, and James followed her in silence. He hadn't let himself think about it.

Until that night, when he jerked awake gasping for breath. He sighed and sank back against the pillow. The jump at the Horse Park was eerily similar to the one in Portbury. Kelli hadn't seen the accident, and she was still jittery about the water jump. When he closed his eyes, all he could see was Delaware's legs going out from under him, Jadin flying over his head, the flash of the ambulance lights. He shook his head, trying to clear it.

He wondered suddenly just how long the road ahead of Jadin was, not just physically, but mentally. He and Kelli were both in knots and it hadn't even been their fall. He thumbed through a magazine trying to make himself sleepy again.

After an hour, the sun was starting to tint the horizon and he threw back the blanket to get a head start on the day. He went down to the arena and parked, and Cole Kendrick's motorhome caught his eye. The door opened and Cole disappeared on a run.

Should he? He'd spoken to Cole a few weeks ago in the motorhome, but he hadn't had the chance to do any digging. James glanced at his watch. It had just gone 5.30, still too early for most of the eventing world to wake, unlike their racing cousins. He slipped out of the car and tread lightly to the motorhome, to the door that Cole hadn't appeared to lock. It opened, and James slipped in.

He didn't know what he was looking for, but he had to try. He rifled through papers on the bench, opened a briefcase, and ran his finger over the touchpad on the laptop. It didn't wake up. James looked around and spotted Cole's cellphone. He picked it up and it asked for a passcode. He held it up to the light, checked for fingerprints and unlocked it.

He checked the text messages and opened the ones under 'Clive'. He read back as far as it went and nothing suspicious jumped out at him.

James checked his watch and decided not to press his luck. He'd tried. He wiped the mobile on his sweatshirt and left it back on the counter, slipping out the door.

Chapter Ten

'Earth to Amy, come in Amy.' It was Tori's voice.
'Oh, sorry, what?'
'You're in dreamland.'
'I'm not.'
'You're distracted.'
'Fine. Your point?'
Tori rolled her eyes. 'You're still in love with Damien Scott.'
'I am not!'
'So you were thinking about what, what you'll eat on your next
platonic lunch? Do you daydream about what we'll have for
lunch next time we do?'
Amy rolled her eyes back at her. 'What did you say?'
Tori looked back at her computer as if she'd forgotten her
original point. 'Did you order more notepads last week?'
'Of course, why?'
'We only got a dozen.'
Amy shook her head, logging into the paper's store account.
'I'm sure I ordered eight dozen.'
Fixing that little mix-up took most of the morning, to her
annoyance. She bought a sandwich and a caramel latte and
went to sit in her favourite lunch spot. She glanced at her
phone and smiled when she saw a message from Mickey. A
friendly voice - even via text - was just what she needed.
'What are you doing up at your time of night, Mikaela?'
*Ooh my full name. I must be in trouble. FYI I'm finishing up
an assignment. How's your day?*

Amy considered how to word it. 'Wasted a morning fixing an admin error. But guess who I saw a couple of days ago?'
I don't know. Leonardo DiCaprio?
'No.' She smiled to herself as she answered. 'Lieutenant Commander, Royal New Zealand Navy, Damien Scott.'
There was a long pause. Amy chuckled as she bit the other half of her BLT. She could just imagine Mickey, staring open-mouthed at her phone.
You have got to be kidding ME!
Amy laughed outright at that. 'No joke,' she typed. 'He just walked into the office the other day and asked to take me out to lunch.'
Oh my word! Did he kiss you?
'No! It was just a 'let's be friends again' lunch. Although...he does want to see if we can have something more.'
She could almost hear Mickey 'click' from teasing mode to best friend mode. *You're not interested anymore?*
'I don't know right now. It was great to see him and reconnect as friends, but I don't know about more than that.'
Do you love him?
'What kind of question is that?'
Well, do you?
'I honestly don't know. I care about him as a friend. I'm not sure I want to be married to him for the rest of my life.'
Amy, only you can answer that. Think of both options and see which one you don't like the idea of.
'He's going to war.'
He's what?
'Well, not officially. But his ship is going to the Middle East to support Britain. There's a chance they could get involved.'
Oh wow.
Another pause.
So how does this affect things?

'It doesn't. We're just going to be friends. But how could anything possibly work when we're on opposite sides of the world?'

If you love him, you can make it work.

Amy sat back and smiled. 'Thanks, Mickey. I guess I'll just see what happens for now. Better get back to lunch. Love you.'

Bye. Love you and miss you.

She stood and tossed her wrapper in the bin. She looked up at the towering pines above her head as if searching for inspiration.

Did she love Damien Scott?

She glugged the last of her coffee and tossed it after the wrapper. Years ago, when they'd been walking home under a star canopy, not holding hands because they both asserted to all that they were just friends, she would have said yes. He could have dropped to one knee on her front porch, having never been on a date, and she would have said yes.

But that was nearly seven years ago.

Kelli Holmes wasn't used to being this nervous. She had ridden more than 30 five-star events in her career. She had won six of those, an amazing strike rate if she did say so herself. She had ridden 107 different horses in her ten years as a professional rider; she knew because she liked to keep a record of them. But ever since Jadin's accident, she'd had nightmares.

She knew it was a dangerous sport, and she'd fallen off her horse countless times. But she'd never personally known someone who had been seriously injured, and Jadin's fall had shaken her.

She stared at herself in the mirror. She looked tidy enough; she'd never be one of those riders who looked glamorous on the cross-country course. She added her mascara and gave her

plait a quick spray, leaving her room before she had any more
time to brood.

She waited impatiently for Kyle to show up outside. They'd
decided to split a rental car since they were coming and going
from the same places. He appeared a couple of minutes late
and tossed his gear in the back seat.

'You're late,' she said calmly as she put the vehicle into drive.

'Sorry.' He buckled his belt, and in doing so must have seen the
look on her face. 'Hey, you all right?'

Kelli nodded. 'I'm fine. A bit nervous is all.'

Kyle leaned back against the chair. 'You're nervous,' he
repeated quietly. 'I am too. Ever since Jadin fell.'

Kelli sighed. 'I guess we just have to get through this.' She
straightened her shoulders. 'Once we've done it a few times
it'll be easier.'

He didn't answer, and she studied him out of the corner of her
eye. He had always been Mr Cool on the surface, but maybe he
had a heart under there after all.

She felt better once she was mounted and warming up Kaleido.
Even though he still had some learning ahead of him, he knew
his way around a cross-country track. She came across James
warming up Silver Flint, who was only a couple of slots before
her. Silver Flint looked very relaxed and loosened up, James
slightly less so.

'He'll do fine,' she said, nodding to the horse.

James smiled thinly. 'I think I'm more worried about how I'll
do right now.'

'Just go on instinct, Jimmy. You know what to do.'

He nodded tersely.

She gave him an encouraging smile, hoping she concealed her
butterflies. 'Good luck.'

He was soon off, and she kept an eye on the board as she got
Kaleido ready. He was eager, which was a nice change from
the dressage yesterday.

She lined him up in the starting arena, waiting for the signal. She nudged him forward, and he quickly settled into his ground-eating canter. She rode a few inches above the saddle, keeping the reins steady.

He popped over the first oxer and she relaxed a little. He took the ditch in stride, and then she shortened his stride as they approached the in-and-out double. He jumped the first element, got one quick stride in and hopped over the second. She exhaled as she let him back up to a full canter.

The water was her only main worry. She felt her brain lock up for a split second as he approached, but once he jumped into the pond she didn't have time to fear. He jumped the first, cantered on, jumped the second, and cantered out. She patted him.

They got round clear and within the time, and she felt her knees sag a little as she dismounted. She'd made it.

James was waiting for her, holding Silver Flint's reins. 'Good job.'

'Same to you.' They shared a smile, congratulating each other for more than just a clear round. She nodded to Silver Flint. 'How'd he go?'

'He was fine. Seemed to be reaching a little on some of the taller jumps, but he's not a big horse.' He stroked under the metallic-grey mane.

By the end of the day, James was in ninth place on Flint, and she and Kaleido were twentieth, which had been a dramatic improvement from day one. The water had caught out a lot of horses who had refused the second element. It didn't look like there would be a Kiwi win, but they'd done okay, all things considered.

'So, you think you're going to take Flint to another five-star?' She asked James over dinner.

He shrugged, pushing his pasta around on his plate. 'I think he's done enough so far to merit another shot.'

'Are you okay?' She indicated his plate.

He sighed. 'Yeah, just not hungry, really.' He glanced up at her. 'I got a call from Jadin today. He's fielding all my calls and stuff while I'm away. He heard from the cops today.'

Kelli felt her eyes get fractionally wider. 'About Coalbridge?'

'Uh-huh. Anyway, they tracked down that hitman whose van was spotted in the neighbourhood. He was under suspicion for a couple of other things anyway, so they raided his place. They found emails from someone who called himself 'Biff'; they're still working out who that is.'

Kelli nodded.

'Anyway, they found who else he was corresponding with, who was supposed to help him do it.'

'And?'

'Clive Ressler was involved.'

Kelli's hand flew to her mouth. 'Your groom?'

'Ex-groom, but yes.'

Kelli shook her head and reached over to cover his hand with her own. 'I'm sorry, Jimmy.'

He smiled grimly. 'I was happy enough to let him go and work for Cole; it was a big opportunity.' He shook his head. 'But they've traced his address; he is definitely involved somehow.'

'What about Cole? If his groom is involved…'

James shrugged again. 'I guess it's possible. I wouldn't have thought him capable of it. If it is something to do with him, it could be just one of his backers and he knows nothing.' He sipped his water. 'Or they just used Clive because he knows the lay of the land, so to speak.'

'Either way, it's a betrayal to you.'

James shrugged. 'I can take it. I just don't want anyone else getting to my horses.' His jaw tightened. 'And I want them to pay.'

'They will. They'll get them.'

James sighed and leaned back in his chair. 'I'm going to be immature and say this whole thing stinks.'

'I don't blame you. So what now?'

'They try and find out who 'Biff' is, find Clive and see what he has to say, find out who the heck is at the bottom of this.' He looked like he wanted to bang his head on the table. 'What a mess.'

Kelli smiled sadly. 'We'll get to the bottom of it. And you and Coalie will come out of this stronger than ever.'

James gave her a weak grin. 'Did anyone ever tell you you should've been a therapist?'

Kelli laughed. 'No, not exactly.'

His smile seemed genuine. 'Thanks.'

Amy was delighted with Chester's dressage test at the two-star event in Crawley. He was responsive and his final halt was the best he'd ever done. She nodded to the judges, fighting to keep the grin off her face. She rode out of the ring and dismounted, praising him effusively. He stood there looking very pleased with himself, and even more pleased when she offered him a carrot.

She knew not to get too far ahead of herself, but maybe he was ready to move up to three-star. His cross-country wasn't an issue, and his dressage was obviously improving, but the showjumping still worried her. Although, in fairness, she couldn't remember a time he'd been as bad as he had a few weeks ago. It probably wasn't an accurate measure of where he was at.

They were in the top five after dressage, which both stunned and thrilled her. The cross-country was one of the harder ones she'd seen at this level, and she could feel Chester hesitate a few times, but he cleared everything. That put them up to fourth.

Settle down, Amy, she scolded herself for the fifth time as they warmed up for the last phase. It wasn't the Olympic finals, after all. But it meant a lot to her right at this moment.

Chester, darling that he was, jumped clear.

She was immensely proud of him. After walking around for a bit, she dismounted and hugged him, telling him how wonderful he was. They stayed outside the ring, keeping an eye on the contestants negotiating the show jumps. The third-place horse put a foot in the water, but the top two were both clear. They finished in third place, which was still an excellent result. They'd had success within New Zealand, but this was another step up.

'So what do you think, Ches? Ready to tackle a three-star?' She chatted to him as she put him back in his trailer. He was more interested in whether she'd give him another carrot. She obliged since he'd been such a good boy.

She checked her phone as she buckled in. There was a new message from Damien, asking about going to a movie tomorrow. It felt a bit too much like a date, but since it was a daytime screening she finally agreed. It was a film she'd wanted to see for ages.

She double-checked her international clock, which was set to New Zealand time, before sending Mickey a message, telling her they'd come third. She knew she'd get an 'I told you so', because Mickey had been a vociferous supporter of her going to England, but she'd also be happy for her.

She put the rig in gear and eased it forward, driving at snail's pace through the maze of trailers, horses and riders. She decided to look up nearby three-star events when she got home; she thought Chester was ready.

As she turned onto the main road north, she saw a man in military uniform walking down the side street, hand-in-hand with a pretty woman. He must be a British soldier because she knew that any foreign military personnel were discouraged from wearing their uniforms in public. A week ago, she wouldn't have given them a passing glance; today, the image stayed in her mind, forcing her to think. Could she ever be a military wife?

She knew Damien was thinking of marriage; not right away, but that was the only place anything more than friendship would lead. She admired that in him, but at the same time, it scared her to death. Did she want to spend the rest of her days with him? Heck, she didn't even know if she still loved him. She tried to take Mickey's advice: imagine both scenarios. Say 'I do' to Damien Scott, or just stay friends and maybe marry someone else down the road.

Somehow, the second option seemed unappealing.

James warmed Silver Flint up slowly, making sure he was ready for show jumping. The poles would be slightly higher than he'd ever done in competition, and he wasn't the best jumper in the world. For the final round, the riders went in reverse order of standing, so the leaders went last.

He watched Kelli and Kaleido, who jumped a perfect round. She was so far down it didn't affect anything, but it was good for the horse.

Silver Flint felt ready, popping over the practice jumps with ease. James patted his neck and walked him up to the ring. He felt relaxed, which was a good sign.

Until the previous horse exited, and the crowd roared for a clear round. Silver Flint laid his ears back.

'Easy, boy.' He tightened the reins but the horse stomped in place. 'Come on; it's all right.' He squeezed him forward, and the horse obeyed but he wasn't very happy.

James set him to a canter towards the first. And Silver Flint came to an abrupt halt, sending his rider over his head.

James was vaguely aware of a gasp from the crowd as he hit the sand. He felt pain in his shoulder and dust in his mouth as he tucked and rolled.

He scrambled back to his feet before any medical personnel got ideas. Silver Flint hadn't run off, but he wasn't happy. James took the reins and tried to calm him down. Falls were instant elimination, so the only thing left to do was leave.

He led Silver out, one hand on his neck trying to soothe him. He settled down quickly now he wasn't in that amphitheatre. James waited until he was completely calm before heading back to the stables. So much for their first five-star outing.

Kelli met him at the barn and gave him a once-over. 'You all right?'

'Nothing broken,' he said, trying to hide the flinch that surfaced when he tried to take off Silver's bridle.

Kelli carefully pushed him out of the way by his good shoulder and did the bridle herself. 'You should get that looked at.'

'I'm fine. Just a bruise.'

Kelli pinned him with a glare that could melt ice. 'You're probably right, but you can hardly lift your arm. It's better to be sure.' She started on the saddle. 'If you won't go I'll take you myself.'

James sighed. It wasn't worth the energy to argue with her, and his shoulder was starting to throb pretty badly. 'I'll just head over to the medics' tent, then.'

'You okay to get there?'

He returned her glare, then softened. She was only looking out for him. 'I'll be fine.'

James trudged over and they manipulated his shoulder around, which was unpleasant but at least it wasn't broken. It would be stiff and sore for several days, they warned, so they gave him some ibuprofen.

'Do you still feel up to going back to the farms this afternoon?' Kelli inquired when he returned to the barn.

'Yeah, I want to have another look at that filly.' He reached over to pat Silver Flint with his good arm. The grey was now clean and dry and happily chewing on a piece of hay. 'Thanks, Kelli.'

She just smiled. 'So, want to go now or rest for a bit?'

'I'll be fine. If I rest it, it might only seize up more.' He winced slightly as he pushed away from the wall.

She frowned at him. 'You don't want a sling?'

'No. It makes me feel infirm.' He headed for the parking lot, not surprised when she put her arm through his good one to make sure he could walk.

'All right, stubborn. But I'm driving.'

They stopped at Bravo Sporthorses first, where Kelli finalised her deal for the black gelding she'd liked. He would ship to the UK in a couple of weeks.

James could feel Kelli watching him as she buckled her seat belt. 'You sure you're up to this? It's not like you'll never be in Kentucky again.'

He turned to face her, and she whistled. 'Nice shiner.'

He put a hand to his forehead. 'I didn't even know I'd hit my head. It all happened so fast.'

'So I'm assuming you didn't get it checked out?' His expression must have answered her because she rolled her eyes as she put the car into drive. 'James Avery Blackman, what am I going to do with you?'

'How do you know my middle name?'

'Saw it on an entry once.' She pulled onto the motorway. 'You need to start listening to your niece.'

'What's that supposed to mean?'

'You need to find a nice girl to look after you.'

That got the humph it deserved.

Despite her protests, he got on to ride the filly one more time. He liked her a lot; he just wondered if she had the toughness

for a big cross-country track. He looked down at Kelli, who was leaning disapprovingly on the fence. 'What do you think?'
'I think you should get off that horse.'
'Kelli.' Sometimes she took her sister role too far.
She threw up her hands. 'Okay, okay. I think she's a good horse, but I do worry a little about her being able to run around Badminton.'
'Me too.' James brought her to a halt.
Kelli cocked her head. 'Not saying she couldn't be brought to that level.'
'No. But I'm not sure.' He dismounted gingerly. He knew some riders that bought, trained and sold horses alongside the ones they kept for themselves, but he wanted to buy a horse he could take to five-star. Then, if it didn't work out, he'd sell them on.
He thanked Colton Everson but decided he'd opt out this time. By the time they got back on the road his head was throbbing, and he felt Kelli take an unexpected turn.
'Where-?'
'I'm taking you to the emergency room. Don't argue with me.'
He sighed and put his head back against the rest.
The doctor said he'd had a bad bump but he didn't think he had a concussion. James was relieved he didn't have to postpone the flight home. His bruises were sore and he was tired, but he'd live.
Kelli walked him to his door to make sure he didn't keel over on the way. 'Are you sure you're all right?'
'I'll make it,' James grumbled. He turned back to face her.
'Look, Kell, I know I've been a grouch, but-'
'Yeah, you have,' she said cheerfully.
'You didn't have to agree so quickly.' He allowed himself a grin. 'But, well, thanks for looking out for me.'
'Anytime, Oscar. Get yourself settled in your trash can.' She snickered. 'See you in the morning. But if you need anything-'

'I know, I'll just set off the fire alarm. Night, Kelli.'

He was glad to get his head down, but he worried about how stiff his arm would be in the morning. But he had a transatlantic flight the next day, so he opted for rest.

He made it through the night without calling any emergency departments, and his arm wasn't as bad as he'd feared. If he didn't look in the mirror, he wouldn't remember he had a shiner either.

Thank goodness it wasn't any worse, he thought as he checked to make sure he had all his gear. He felt a stab of guilt when he saw Jadin's name pop up on his phone.

It wasn't fair. Jadin had a fall and had to learn to walk again; he had a fall and escaped without even a concussion.

He wrote him back. 'Yep, headed home today. Silver had a refusal in the jumping but overall he seems like he can handle it.' He gritted his teeth, hoping he wouldn't ask for any more details. *Oh yeah, I forgot to say, I took a header and walked away.*

Both horses loaded with no problems, but he noticed Silver Flint favouring his right foreleg, probably from skidding to a stop in front of that oxer. He put some ice on it for the trip to the airport.

Caitlyn was still bubbling about Kentucky and swore she'd come back one day to work at a sport horse farm in bluegrass country. James still wondered if he might set up his breeding farm here after he retired, although England was closer to his target market.

The flight was long but he slept most of the way. They touched down in Bristol just after noon, UK time. Kelli and Kaleido would transfer on to York after a two-hour layover, so she was going to call on Jadin.

'You want to come?' she asked, settling Kaleido in the trailer and checking he had water.

'Uh…' He bit his lip and shook his head. 'No, I'll let you two catch up. I'll stop by in a few days.'

Kelli frowned. 'Why?'

'Well, I'm tired. Besides you two probably need a private conversation.'

She lifted an eyebrow. 'What makes you say that?'

'A gut feeling.'

She shook her head. 'I'm too tired for a deep conversation.' She stepped away and lowered her voice so Caitlyn couldn't overhear. 'Besides, this isn't about our privacy, is it?'

James sighed. 'Darn, Kell. When did you start reading me so well?'

She grinned. 'The first time I met you, at the bottom of a cross-country ditch, if you remember.' He had to grin as well at the thought of that long-ago day. 'So why aren't you going to see your best friend?'

He sighed and indicated the bruise just above his temple.

She frowned. 'What?'

He leaned back against the trailer. 'He'll see I've had a fall.'

Understanding slowly dawned over her face. 'Ah. But Jimmy, it won't matter-'

'Yes, it will.' His tone was quietly final. 'He had a fall and he has to go through all kinds of therapy to be able to walk again. I have a fall and don't even crack a rib. How's he going to feel?'

'It's not your fault.'

He shrugged. 'I know that. But that doesn't make it easy for him to deal with.'

She sighed. 'He'll find out sooner or later.'

'Not if I don't go in until the bruise is gone.'

She looked at him sadly. 'Well, I can see where you're coming from, but I still think you're wrong. Falling is a way of life in this crazy career. If not you, it'll be someone else.'

'True. But I just don't want to face him looking like I've just walked away from a fall. Not yet.'

She sighed again. 'Well, I'm not your boss.' She reached to hug him goodbye.

He quirked an eyebrow. 'You sure about that?'

'Funny. See you at Badminton?'

'Sure thing.' He smiled as she pulled away. They'd grown closer on this trip, probably because of their shared feelings over Jadin's accident. 'Take care of yourself.'

He checked on Silver Flint before getting into the driver's seat for the short stretch to Manorbrook. Caitlyn was already in the passenger seat on her iPod. 'Are you sure about her?'

'Who?' He put the truck in gear.

'Kelli.'

'What about her?'

'That you don't like her.'

He rolled his eyes. 'I thought you left that particular matchmaking project behind when you were sixteen.'

'I did. I was just double-checking.'

'Look, Kelli is a nice girl and a great friend, but that's all we could ever be.'

'Why?'

'We just don't feel that way. She's like a sister. Anything more...well, I just don't love her that way.' He checked over his shoulder before pulling onto the motorway. 'Besides, I think she has an interest in someone else.'

'I thought the boyfriend was history.'

'He is. It's not him.'

'Then who?'

'Look, little miss nosy, if you want to know details about Kelli's personal life you can ask her yourself.'

Caitlyn huffed good-naturedly. 'Fine.'

He heaved an involuntary sigh of relief when he turned into Manorbrook's winding drive. It was a relief to leave Lexington behind him. He didn't know why; he'd hardly thought about Calintha since the first day. But it hadn't been his finest hour. He checked Silver Flint again as he led him into his familiar stall. His knee was slightly swollen, but it wasn't too bad. He headed to the tack room freezer for some more ice.

Vicky looked up from the saddle she was meticulously polishing. 'Hey, welcome back.'

'Hey, yourself. Everything looks great around here. Thank you.'

'No worries.' Her face melted into a frown. 'What happened to you?'

'Silver Flint decided he didn't want to jump the first oxer.' He gingerly touched the bruise. 'It's not bad, just this and a sore arm.'

'The ice for you?' She asked with a grin.

'No. He's hit his knee on said jump, I think.' He filled an ice boot and shut the velcro. 'It's not too bad.'

'Good. Other than that, how did it go?'

'Okay. I think I'll give him another run at five-star. If the crowd hadn't frightened him right before we went in, he might have done quite well.'

She followed him back to Silver's stall. 'So did you find any additions to our midst?'

He cocked his head. 'Not in the end. I liked the look of a filly at Spy Coast Sporthorses, but I wasn't sure if she was tough enough for a five-star cross-country. Kelli agreed with me.'

Vicky leaned against the half-door, patting Silver. 'You still don't want to go into training horses to sell?'

He shook his head. 'I think I've got enough to go on with.'

She nodded. 'Unless you brought Caitlyn on full-time.'

'I could. But I still don't like the idea of training a horse for someone else. If they don't work out for me, that's different.' He shrugged. 'Besides, I don't know how much longer Catie will be here.'

Vicky nodded, a nostalgic look coming into her eyes. 'She's grown up, hasn't she?'

James smiled. Vicky had known Catie since she was a little girl. 'Yeah, she has.'

'Did you see Jadin?'

James shook his head. 'No. I, uh, didn't have time.'

He caught her look of surprise but she didn't elaborate. 'I think everything's in order. Jadin heard from the cops while you were away - '

'I know, he told me.'

She nodded. 'I'm sorry, Jimmy.'

He smiled sadly. 'Not your fault.'

'Clive Ressler was under my training,' she said slowly. 'I still can't believe…'

'Me neither.'

'What kind of punishment can they get for this?' Vicky asked. 'I mean if they're involved but didn't physically administer it…'

'I don't know.' James ran a hand through his hair. 'And there's no way to prove who administered it unless someone confesses to it.' He clicked the stall latch back into place. 'Man, I wish I'd installed cameras sooner.'

'No one could've foreseen this.'

'Yeah, I know.'

It was a beautiful day, almost romantic if one was that way inclined. Amy walked next to Damien, enjoying his company and the view. After this, he'd be gone to the Middle East for who knew how long.

Why was that so hard to think about?

'Penny for your thoughts?' Damien asked.

She shrugged. 'Thinking about you leaving.'

He didn't react.

'Does it worry you?'

He looked out to the sea, the colour seemingly reflecting his eyes. 'A little. In the sense that we don't know what to expect, or what we'll do once we're down there.'

'You still can't say exactly where you'll be.' It was more of a statement than a question. She kicked a pebble, watching as it jittered into a roadside puddle.

'No. It's classified; only a few men on the ship know in advance. I'm one of them since I'm steering us there.' He sighed. 'It may stay classified forever, especially if something less than politically correct goes on.'

'And you think it will?'

'Given the hush-hush, I'm not ruling it out.'

'You ever have second thoughts?' She looked up at him.

'About my job? No. One or two orders, maybe, but never my job.' He looked at her. 'It's my life, and I can't imagine another one.'

See, if nothing else, we'll never work out. You won't give up your life and I won't give up mine. Amy cleared her throat, trying to decide whether to say it.

'And if - heaven forbid - something happens to one of the men over there?' She sat down on a bench. 'The family never gets to know what happened?'

'If it's classified, no.' Damien sat next to her. 'It's rough, I know, but it's a price they are all willing to pay. We're serving our country, Amy.'

'Yeah. Just seems hard to accept. This isn't our war. It's not like the World Wars where it touched everyone.'

Damien gave her a small smile. 'The edict still stands: 'where Britain goes--''

'I know. I support your efforts, the Navy; I do. I just wish the cost wasn't so high.'

'The price of freedom is high. Always has been.'

They sat in silence for a while. She studied his profile. Even in jeans and a Liverpool T-shirt, he looked like a Navy Commander. She sighed. She was starting to hate the idea of his leaving after they'd just found each other again. But he couldn't be anything other than who he was: Commander Scott who was prepared to lay down his life for his country if it came to that.

And she couldn't, or wouldn't, throw away her dreams to be a military wife.

She remembered what he'd said that fateful day nearly seven years ago; that they could find a way to make it work. She didn't think so. But right now that wasn't the issue. The issue was, she wasn't sure she even wanted to marry him.

'So…' He turned to face her, with that same smile she'd known since she was a teenager. 'Where does all this leave us? We won't meet again for months.'

'I know.' She cleared her throat. 'I say we part as friends, and you'd jolly well better come back alive. I don't want to lose my best friend twice.'

He smiled. 'I'll do my best.' He leaned back, his gaze on the view rather than her. 'Ames, is there a chance...down the road when I come back?'

She put her hand into his. 'I loved you when you left, Damien.' She thought he deserved to know that much. 'In some ways, I still do. But I'm not sure if it's the kind of love we both need in the person we'll marry. So I still say we part as friends and leave it there, under no obligations.'

He gave her a grin. 'At least it's not a definite no.' He raised a hand. 'And you don't owe me anything. I was out of your life for years. I half expected to find you married with kids.'

She smiled. 'Nope, just one partly spoiled thoroughbred.'

He chuckled. 'I hope you get to where you want to be.'

'You too.' She smiled into his eyes. 'Wherever that may be.'

He gave her a look, as if she should know where that was, but said nothing, standing and extending his hand. 'You ready to head back?'

She let him pull her up and they headed back to his car.

'You miss New Zealand?' he asked suddenly.

'In some ways, terribly…' She shrugged. 'In other ways, I'm glad to be this far away.'

She caught the flicker of sympathy in his eyes. 'How's Mickey?'

'She's good. She went through the roof when I told her I'd seen you.'

He grinned. 'I miss that girl.'

'Me too.'

He drove her back to her apartment and walked her to her door. As she unlocked she almost wanted to cry. What was the matter with her?

She turned back to face him with a small grin. 'Permission to hug the commander?' she asked, quoting a military show she used to love.

He grinned back. 'Permission granted.'

They embraced tightly, and she wondered fleetingly if they'd ever be able to do this again. *Of course we will,* she admonished herself. *He'll be back.*

He brushed a piece of hair back from her face as she pulled back. The gesture was so like the Damien of old, when they'd been inseparable, that she had to bite her lip. 'Stay safe, Damien.'

He smiled. 'I will. Take care.'

And with that, he was gone.

She locked her door. And she cried.

James decided to have a little faith and book Coalbridge in for Badminton. He was recovering quickly and he should be close to one hundred per cent. He decided that Marksman would be the other one. Badminton was the pinnacle, so Silver Flint and Lacklustre would have to cut their teeth at some of the other five-stars first.

He finally went in and saw Jadin a week after getting back. Jadin looked up from his magazine when he walked in the door. 'Well, it took you long enough to visit your best friend.'

'Sorry.' He probably owed him an explanation, but he didn't know how to say it.

Jadin frowned. 'Is your arm okay?'

'It's fine.'

Jadin frowned at him. 'What's the matter, Jimmy?'

'Nothing.'

He studied him critically. 'You're hiding something from me.'

James bit his lip. 'All right, yeah.'

'Spit it out.'

'I had a fall in Kentucky. When Silver stopped at the first jump.'

'And you didn't tell me this why?' He paused as if it was coming to him. 'You thought I'd hate you because you weren't injured and I was?'

'Not hate me but...well it can't be easy for you.'

'Jimmy, everyone's going to fall off their horses, and most of them will be a lot less injured than me. It's an occupational hazard. I can deal with it.'

James sighed. 'Sorry.'

'No sweat. Now since you're dying to know how I am...'

James grinned. 'Hey, not fair. I am actually.'

'Well, the therapist is encouraged by my progress. Says my likelihood of walking again is improving.'

'That's great!'

'Yeah, I guess. Still a long road, but I'll take all the encouragement I can get.' He looked at him funny. 'Your arm bothering you?'

'Yeah, it was my landing pad.'

'Ouch.'

'Yeah, it's just bruised, but pretty stiff and sore.' He rotated his arm and flinched slightly.

'So have you decided to take Coalie to Badminton?'

'Yeah, got the forms off today. I think he'll be close to 100 per cent.'

Jadin shook his head. 'I still can't believe that it was Clive.'

'Well, there's a lot we still don't know.' James leaned back in his chair. 'But it hit me pretty hard too.'

'I guess some people will do a great deal if it means big money.'

'I guess so.' He sat forward, leaning his elbows on his knees. 'Jade, how are you - really?'

Jadin grimaced. 'I'm dealing. It's not easy though. Sometimes I feel a tingle and it turns out to be nothing. And a lot of it's in my head - trying to realize that my world has changed completely but everyone else just carries on unscathed.'

James nodded in understanding. 'But you should know that not all of us are continuing unscathed.'

Jadin smiled sadly. 'I know.'

Kelli Holmes pulled on her riding boots and trotted the short distance between her house and stables. Her little lifestyle block was nothing like James Blackman's stately Manorbrook, but she was happy with it. It allowed her to do the job she loved.

She was excited about her new horse, a lovely black sport horse gelding with a healthy splash of thoroughbred. Of her three horses, she had Kaleido; Maximus, who was fifteen and probably in his last years of competition, and Chipper, a full Holsteiner who was just graduating to five-star. With Maximus retiring soon, it was time to look to the future.

She saddled him up and took him out to the dressage arena. He had been extremely well trained in the basics, and he had the conformation to be a very good dressage horse. She worked him through his paces, working up to the flying change. He switched canters without missing a beat.

She then rode Maximus over to the neighbour's farm. They had a hillside track that was great for building and maintaining fitness. Maximus was still in great shape, but she knew he would start slowing down soon. He was still enjoying his work, and as soon as he wasn't she'd let him have his retirement. But she would miss him terribly. He wasn't a flashy horse, but he was as reliable as the sun, and he was her friend.

She rose in her stirrups as he cantered up the road. She could hear his grunts as he neared the top, and she gave him his head, letting him dictate how fast he wanted to go. He, of course, decided to gallop full speed ahead, so she just enjoyed the ride. They cantered back down and repeated the process before heading down to pop over a few show jumping poles. He'd always been a little on the clumsy side with his feet - he didn't have the finesse of the finer-bred warmbloods - but he'd jumped a few vital clears in his time. Not least to win New Zealand the team gold at the World Equestrian Games seven years ago. That was still the highlight of her career, and probably most of her team-mates'.

She smiled at the memory. They were never meant to win that event, but they'd dug themselves out of the dressage hole with amazing cross-country rounds on a very difficult track. A then-young Coalbridge had led the way, going all clear in his first five-star. It had melded them together as a team unit, and forged friendships that would last a lifetime.

She warmed Maximus down, taking extra care as she always did with his aging muscles. She figured she'd better go and see Jadin again. She'd only called in once, during her layover between flights in Bristol, and he'd promised they'd talk when she got home.

Maybe that was why she hadn't been back. As much as it excited her, it scared her too.

She'd always liked him as a friend in the decade they'd been acquainted; anything more was a relatively new development, only coming up in the last couple of years.

But was it love? She wasn't sure.

She sighed. She knew it was possible to be an eventing couple; several famous riders had done it. She flashed back to that hotel hallway in Kentucky, a year ago to the day. What if she'd taken the plunge and said yes?

Well, you still have the chance to say yes.

She wasn't looking forward to a stilted, awkward conversation. They'd been friends so long that anything else felt kind of weird. But what if they did get to be happy ever after?

Kelli Steele? *Oh, cut it out! What are you, 14?*

She shook her head and concentrated on Maximus. 'Maybe I'll just stay a horsey spinster. Much less complicated. What do you think?' Maximus nodded and nudged her hand. Kelli laughed and palmed a carrot for him. 'Your advice comes with a price.'

Before she could chicken out, she changed clothes and decided to go for an afternoon drive. They didn't have to talk today. They could just chat like the old friends they were.

Although it did feel a bit like the elephant in the room.

It was two hours to Bristol one way, so she couldn't get up there very often. She wondered if there were any plans for Jadin's long-term care. She shook her head; that sounded so grim. She knew his groom, Sarah, would be taking care of his horses and yard, but what of his recovery?

She shook her head again against the tears that stung the back of her eyes. It wasn't fair.

She parked and walked up to Jadin's floor, rapping on his door. 'Hey, stranger.'
He looked up from his motorsport magazine. 'Hey yourself.'
She sat down. 'How are you feeling?'
'Okay, I guess. The therapy is getting easier as I go. A few little victories make it easier to hope.'
She smiled. 'That's great.'
'Yeah.' He shifted to face her. 'How's your new boy?'
'He's great. He's been perfectly trained in the groundwork. I'm pretty excited about him.'
She thought she saw a shadow pass over his face at the talk of a future he was struggling to regain, but he said nothing.
'Anything new from the doctors?' she asked.
He shrugged. 'They are starting to talk a little more positively, but it's hard to know if there's anything concrete, you know?'
'I guess so.' She leaned forward in her chair. 'So...when can you go home again?'
Jadin shrugged. 'Right now, they are talking in terms of staying here in the rehab centre. But it feels like it makes it real that I am disabled.'
She shook her head. 'No, it's about you getting better. It's just easier in an environment like this where there's everything you need.'
He sighed. 'I guess.'
She reached to take his hand. 'I'm not going anywhere, you know. And neither is Delaware. You can go to the Paralympics. This isn't going to beat you.'
He gave her a tight smile. 'I know that. But you're under no obligation to me, Kelli. When you look at it, all we are is good friends.'
She bit her lip. It wasn't her style to be forward, to be pushing the relationship's direction. But to her relief, he continued. 'But if you are still interested I'd like to see if we could be more.'

She nodded, a little shyly. It felt a bit strange to change from a brother-sister friendship to a relationship.

'So, when we can…' He glanced uncomfortably down at his legs for a second before returning his gaze to her face. 'Would you go out on a date with me?'

She nodded again. 'Okay.'

He smiled. 'Good.'

She leaned back in the chair. 'Is there anything I can do to help with your rehab?'

'Not really. Other than moral support. I have to push through on my own.'

She nodded. 'Yeah, I guess so. But you'll get there. And the doctors talking more positively must be a good sign, right?'

'I hope so.' He resettled in the bed. 'Is James doing okay - after his fall, I mean?'

'Ah, so he did tell you.'

'Yeah, eventually.'

'He'll be fine. A bit bruised and sore but nothing major.'

'Good. Just checking he wasn't glossing over it.'

Amy Williams, you stop this right now! You're acting very immature! She scolded herself as she drove. The HMNZS Te Kaha had been gone from English waters for two days, and she was checking her phone every two minutes like a schoolgirl. She didn't even love him, and this friendly concern was getting over the top. Keeping her eyes on the road, she thrust her phone into the depths of her handbag, resolving not to look at it until the end of the day.

She parked and hurried into work, arriving just on time. Tori looked up from her screen with a raised eyebrow. 'Morning.'

'Hi.'

'Any news?' Tori inquired neutrally.

Amy kept her groan to herself. Everyone asking questions wasn't helping. 'Nope.'

'Well, I assume they don't get much internet time.'

'No.' *Enough time to send a one-sentence message on Facebook or email, though,* she added to herself.

But then, they were only friends; it wasn't like she was the girlfriend expecting a daily update.

Right?

'Anything new going on?' She asked as she glanced through her emails.

'Well, there's some Duke of something or other - first cousin to the Prince of Wales - coming to open a trust, and everyone's pretty busy working out the logistics.'

'Oh, that's pretty exciting.'

Tori raised an eyebrow. 'Oh, I forgot, you're a Kiwi - you're all monarchists.'

'Not all of us. There's quite a movement of republicans now. But I'm one. There's just so much history and tradition, you know?'

Tori shrugged. 'Yeah, I guess. I think I'm a bit ready for a change, though. The concept needs modernising.'

Amy raised her eyebrows. 'I thought all Londoners were royalists.'

'Not this one. I'm not saying get rid of it completely, but maybe upgrade it a bit.'

They got busy with their work, but Amy's mind kept wandering to her communications device at the bottom of her bag. No, she would not check it. She had work to do.

She purposely took only her wallet when she went to grab some lunch.

The whole town was abuzz with the upcoming appearance of Duke Whats-his-name. But Amy was enjoying it. Growing up in Waikato in the far reaches of the Commonwealth, a royal visit of any kind was a major event.

She drove home after checking on Chester and giving him his evening feed. She still hadn't looked at her phone. She was not going to carry on like a teenager with her first crush.

She decided two-minute noodles were on the menu that evening. She was exhausted from all the arrangements they were working out at work, and if she dared admit it to herself, she was a little worried. Even a casual friend would normally have got in touch by now, wouldn't they?

She ate her noodles in front of the TV. There was no mention of Te Kaha's deployment anywhere - not the news, not the internet, not even the Navy web page. There wasn't even a general mention of an assignment. She wondered if even Damien had been entirely truthful.

Her phone beeped from her handbag. Well, this time she had a legitimate cause. She plucked it out.

One new message: Damien Scott.

She swallowed and opened it.

Hi, Amy. We're well underway now and I can't say where, but it's starting to feel real. I think we may be required to get involved, but hopefully not too much. How are you?

She swallowed again and started to type.

'I'm good, busy at work, prepping for the royal visit. So you're going to do more than you thought, huh?'

Looks that way. I have a lot of faith in this crew, but I'm not sure how kindly this will be taken.

Something clenched in her gut. 'Hope you're staying safe over there. It must be tough for all the families, not being able to know what's going on and where you are.'

It is, but it's part of the job. Our families understand.

There was a pause.

Do you?

She smiled sadly to herself. 'Sure, in theory. But I don't want my friend to get hurt.'

I'll be fine. I'm tough.

She had to laugh at that. Some things never change.
'Well, long day, I'd better head to bed. Stay safe.'
We'll do our best. Take care.
She breathed a sigh of relief, unaware of how uptight she'd
been. They were fine, but it seemed things could get murkier in
the coming weeks.
Could she marry a man with this life?
Or, perhaps more importantly, could she not marry him?

James Blackman wasn't sure whether he wanted to throw up or
punch the polite police officer in front of him. But considering
that she was only the messenger, that wouldn't be particularly
fair. He tightened and unclenched his fists under the table
instead. He'd known for a while Clive could be involved, but
to have it staring at him in the face was another matter.
She almost looked nervous, so he tried to power down. 'I'm
afraid it looks that way, yes.'
James turned to stare out the window. He and Clive had been
friends, and his care of the horses had always been exemplary.
How could anyone do that to any horse, let alone one they
knew?
He turned back to the officer when she cleared her throat. 'We
don't have absolute proof yet. But the way it looks from our
inquiries, it would seem that your former groom accompanied
another man onto your property - most likely because he knew
the place and the horses. If this was administered orally, it
would have helped to have a familiarity with the horse. The
second man would be to make sure the deed was done -
sometimes those who turn on people they know can back out at
the last minute because of the guilt.'
He wanted to tell her to spare him the psychobabble, but it was
part of the case. He nodded for her to continue.

'Then, they locked up again and got back in the vehicle, which was seen heading back towards Bristol that same night.'

James didn't move from his spot by the window. 'So what happens now?'

'We need to find any other evidence we can, and then charges will be laid.'

He cleared his throat. 'What kind of charges?'

'Trespassing, breaking and entering, animal cruelty.'

He nodded again. At least that sounded sufficient; he'd feared that the creep would get off with a slap on the wrist. 'And what would the sentence be?'

She cocked her head. 'It depends on a lot of factors, such as how much we can prove and an individual's level of involvement. It may be anything from a fine to a few years in jail.'

'Okay.' That sounded reasonable, but something Vicky had said immediately after he got back from Kentucky came back to his mind. 'And what if - if they'd been trying to kill the horse?'

'Destruction of property is a crime. But since your horse didn't die, it's going to be very hard to prove.'

'Yeah, I realize that.' He decided to sit back down. 'Have you found anything on who the original instigator was?'

'Not so far. We've spoken to Cole Kendrick and some of his associates, and we're fairly convinced that he's innocent. But there's a chance somebody who backs him - one of his owners or sponsors, for instance - may be involved. Or even some kind of betting company.'

James didn't think many people bet on who was going to win Badminton, but he supposed some people must. 'And how do we find this out? Does Cole suspect somebody?'

'I'm afraid I can't divulge that information, Mr Blackman.'

That was probably as good as a yes as he would get. He was pretty certain the Brit wasn't involved, at least not knowingly.

'We are, however, following all leads that come up in our inquiries.'

James nodded. 'Okay. Thank you. Is there anything else?'

'I understand you are planning on taking the horse in question to Badminton?'

James nodded.

'We would recommend not doing so. This appears to be a bigger scheme than we had anticipated, and putting him in the public eye may put you both in danger.'

'I'm sure we'll be fine. The security is very tight.'

'Even so,' her tone was firm, 'we recommend keeping him out of the limelight for a while.'

James frowned. 'But they know where I live. He's one of the most famous horses in the world; he's in the limelight anyway. What difference does it make?'

She hesitated. 'We think there may be a wealthy syndicate behind not only this but other successful riders, not just in eventing but in dressage, show jumping and racing.'

James frowned. 'What do they want?'

'Money, mostly. To prevent likely horses and riders from winning to give the horses they are backing a clearer shot. There appear to be several horse owners caught up in this as well.'

James sat back heavily. Heck, if all this was correct, how did he know that one of his owners wasn't involved? Coalbridge, Lacklustre and one of the yearlings were the only ones he owned himself, and Marksman he part-owned. Clarabelle, Silver Flint and the other yearling were all owned by others. No, they can't be. He'd known them for years.

'Do you know who is involved?'

'We're investigating it, but we can't release any details at the moment.'

He took a deep breath to maintain his calm demeanour. 'Could I take Coalbridge to Badminton if I just hire extra security?'

She paused while gathering her papers and glanced up at him. 'It would be better not to, at least until this case is further along.'

James took another deep breath. He couldn't just put his career on hold while they tried to reel in this betting-extortion ring. He watched television; he knew this kind of thing could take months. And what about all the other riders who weren't directly backed by the syndicate? Surely their horses were in danger too?

This was becoming just like a racing scandal, only worse.

He showed the officer to the door and watched grimly as the police car disappeared down his long driveway. What a mess this had turned out to be.

He decided to go and talk to Jadin. Security or not, he wasn't keeping this from his best friend.

He saw Kelli sitting next to Jadin's bed and paused. 'Sorry, I didn't know that...'

'No worries, come on in.'

He pulled a chair in from outside the door and sat down. He noted they looked quite close but decided against commenting. 'How're you doing, Jade?'

He seemed a little lighter today somehow. 'Not too bad. The therapy went quite well.'

James grinned. 'That's great.'

Kelli frowned at him. 'Are you okay, Jimmy?'

He took a deep breath. 'I had another visit from Constable Martin today.'

Jadin quirked an eyebrow. 'Oh yes, and how is the pretty policewoman?'

James rolled his eyes. 'It wasn't a social visit, I can assure you.'

Jadin sobered. 'Bad news?'

James nodded, letting out a breath slowly. 'She doesn't want me to take Coalie to Badminton. They think he may be targeted again. They think there's a whole syndicate going around trying to clear the path of whatever horse they are backing.'

Kelli's blue eyes were wide. 'You mean they're just attacking horses they think might be in the way?'

James nodded.

'Then aren't we all in danger?'

'Theoretically, yes, but if you're being backed by them, they won't go after you. It's widespread, reaching into racing, dressage and jumping too. And they think some of the owners are involved. That's how it's working.'

'So how do we know who's safe and who isn't?'

James shook his head. 'We don't.'

Kelli sank back against her chair. 'They're sure about all this?'

'They seem to be. But don't spread it around; she didn't even seem to want to tell me.' He ran a hand through his hair. 'They think they're in it for the money. Probably for the power too.'

'Is it gang-related?' Jadin asked.

James shrugged. 'Who would know. They "won't release any details at the moment".' He made quotation marks with his fingers.

'Well, this is just great,' Kelli hissed. 'Our horses are all in danger and they won't even let us know.' She paused. 'Are you going to go to Badminton?'

'I don't know. I don't like the sound of it, but they can't just cut me out of my career like that.' He sighed. 'Maybe I just won't take Coalie. They didn't say I can't go at all.'

'So what now?' Kelli asked.

'I wish I knew.'

Jadin stared at him, and James recognized the expression in his eyes. It was an expression of wow-how-did-we-get-here. He'd seen it once before when they went to the Olympics for the first time. Only now, it was a bad 'wow'.

Jadin turned to Kelli. 'So what are you going to do about Badminton?'

She pursed her lips. 'Well, so far they've only said not to take Coalie, right?' At James' nod, she continued. 'So I think I'll go ahead and go. The security is always tight and they'd have to be mad to try something there.'

'True,' James said. 'But still…'

'Still...the risk is there.' Her nervous gaze met his again, and he could feel the despair of uncertainty pass between them.

'So…' Kelli ran her hand through her blond hair. 'We just have to carry on pretending everything is normal until they spring these guys? Or until someone else's horse gets hurt?'

James sighed. 'I wish there was a better alternative.'

He left soon after, having decided he wouldn't take Coalie to Badminton after all. Yes, the whole thing was outrageous, but he wasn't risking his horse.

But should he take any of them? Just because Marksman or Silver Flint hadn't been targeted yet didn't mean they weren't in danger.

He groaned aloud as he braked in his parking bay. What a horrendous mess.

Kelli Holmes drove back to her little farm with her brain in a bit of a fog, thinking through all the details that James had revealed earlier. There was a syndicate out to win at all costs, to the point of harming other people's horses if need be.

She parked in her yard and instinctively went to check on her horses. Sure, she had security installed, but she just wanted to see that they were okay.

Henrique was saddling Kaleido. Kelli watched as he hooked the bridle over his head, slipping the snaffle bit into his mouth, patting him as he did. But how was one to ever really trust an employee? She'd known Clive Ressler pretty well, and James had known him even better, but he had apparently turned on him all the same.

'Thanks, Henrique.' She took Kaleido's reins and led him out to the mounting block. As they walked towards her small arena to practice jumping, she tried to put all the worry out of her mind and just focus on doing what she enjoyed. Riding, training, feeling the horse respond to her commands; the sheer delight of getting to the end of a big cross-country course clear.

She sent Kaleido over the first jump. He picked up his heels and cleared it easily. She felt herself smile at the feeling of soaring.

Kaleido was in a happy mood and his jumping corresponded. It was a good ride; it reminded her of why she did this. Some small-minded bullies would not take that away.

She handed him over to Henrique and went inside for some lunch. A glance at the calendar reminded her that Badminton was only two weeks away. What was she going to do?

She was pretty sure that James would insist on at least taking Marksman. He wasn't the type to back down from a fight. She liked his attitude but she'd never forgive herself if something happened to one of her horses because she decided to take a risk.

She made herself a sandwich and glanced through her emails. Nothing urgent that she could see. She stood up, and her eyes fell on the framed photograph on her desk. She and her teammates were wearing gold medals.

Jadin's grin was probably the brightest, and she felt a pang somewhere in her heart region. He had to get back. For all the team's success, they had yet to win Olympic gold. James' bronze medal two years ago was the closest they'd come.

Her eyes found Jadin again. He was a gentleman; a good man.

She knew she had feelings for him. She knew, even if he - heaven forbid - never walked again, it wouldn't change anything. But the whole thing was a little scary. Was she ready for that kind of relationship? One that may very well last forever?

She sighed and turned away from the photo. She didn't know why this was so unnerving. This was Jadin, who had seen her at the bottom of a water jump, seen her at the top of the Burghley podium, and stayed her friend through everything in between.

It had nearly been a week since Amy had heard from Damien, and her mood was deteriorating. Mickey informed her it was because she still loved him, but that was ridiculous. And even if it wasn't, they lived in two different worlds. Even if she was madly in love with him, where could it possibly go?

There was a pause at the other end of the phone line. 'Well, maybe you can.'

'Heck, Mickey, if you think he's so great why don't you marry him?'

'Because it wasn't me he came to see before he went away to war.'

Amy rolled her eyes. The girl should be a romance novelist. 'Look, Mickey, so what if I did love him? It doesn't matter. It wouldn't be fair to start something that won't end up anywhere.'

'Aha, progress.'

Amy groaned. 'I didn't realise I'd called the relationship hotline.'

Mickey's chuckle echoed across the miles. 'Fine, sorry. How is Chester?'

'Good. Going to his first three-star this weekend.'

They talked a bit more about their jobs and what was going on in their corners of the world. Not for the first time Amy wished they still lived within a few kilometres of each other. Modern communication was great but it was no substitute for real human contact.

'I'd better get going,' Mickey brought the discussion to an end. 'Take care of yourself. And for goodness' sake, Amy, be honest with yourself.'

Amy sighed. 'It's not that easy.'

'No, it isn't, but it is that simple. Talk to you soon.'

Amy pressed 'end call' and tossed her phone across the bed, where she still lay spread-eagle. Maybe it was that simple; if they loved each other, everything else could be worked out. That was what Damien had said the night they broke up all those years ago.

Her phone blipped again as she locked her back door, and she glanced at it. The name on the screen suddenly made her forget how tired she was.

For goodness' sake, girl, you've got it bad.

So what? A lot I can do about it. She opened the message.

Hi Amy. How's it going?

Oh sorry. Didn't notice how late it would be your time.

She locked the door and changed into something comfortable before flopping onto her bed to reply. She thought about a shower to get the hay out of her hair, but she was too tired. 'No worries. I'm up anyway. Been a busy day. How are you?'

We're good. We are docked at a Middle Eastern port and helping the peacekeeping efforts. So far we have not had to engage, which is great.

Amy breathed a sigh of relief. In truth, she'd had a couple of nightmares of Damien getting caught up in the fighting. 'That's good. How long will you be there?'

Probably at least three months.

She sighed. 'I hope you all stay safe.'

I'd better let you sleep. Take care of yourself.
'You too. Bye.'
She lay back on her bed and stared at the ceiling. She'd started praying more since the HMNZS Te Kaha had deployed.
Please, God, keep them all safe.

Chapter Eleven

Jadin sat up a bit straighter and studied James critically. 'So you're going to go.'

James nodded. 'Yeah.'

'Even Coalie?'

'No. I won't take him, since they've already got to him.' He sat up straighter. 'But I will not let these thugs dictate my life. What next? If this isn't solved, we skip Burghley, Luhmuhlen, Adelaide? The Olympics?' He shook his head. 'In a way, that's only playing into their hands. They've got us out of the way.'

Jadin nodded. 'It's an awful situation to be put in. I don't know what I'd do.'

'I don't know what to do either. I'd hate the thought of anything happening.' He shook his head again.

'Catch 22,' Jadin said softly.

'Exactly. But what is the alternative? Not competing until they sort this out? I'll just have to trust that the security people can do their jobs.'

Jadin nodded. 'I think Kelli's going to just bite the bullet and go. Kyle too.' He paused. 'Have you heard from Debbie lately?'

James shook his head. 'I just assumed we'd catch up at Badminton. We don't talk a lot.'

Jadin cocked his head. 'Why?'

James shrugged. 'It's not personal. We've just never really connected. And she hasn't had the history you and Kelli and I have, being the core of the team for so long and all.'

'True.'

'Why? Have you talked to her?'

'Just in passing, her seeing how I am, that sort of thing. Just wondered. I think sometimes we can be a bit exclusive.'

James nodded. 'Probably. But when you think about it, we only actually compete as a team once a year maximum.'

'True. But the team should stick together anyway.'

'Any particular reason you're bringing this up?'

Jadin sighed. 'I've just been thinking with my abundant spare time.' He smiled wryly. 'Just thinking about who might take my place in the team.'

'Nobody, Jadin.' His friend's tone was firm.

Jadin gave him a sad smile. 'I appreciate your optimism. But the fact is, I still can't walk. It will be a long time before I can ride around Burghley again.'

James sat back in his chair.

'I'm not giving up, Jimmy. I still want the trophies and the thrill and the Olympic gold medal. But it's not going to happen overnight.'

James sighed. 'I know.'

'So in the meantime, someone can take that spot of the number three.'

'I guess Kyle is next in line. Unless we put Kelli there.'

'She's too good at being the first rider out.'

'True. So how's the therapy going, really?'

'Trying to hurry me back, huh?'

'Of course. Who's going to eat the other half of my pizza?'

Jadin chuckled, but then his expression grew serious. 'I've got most of my upper body back. Not that I lost most of it, but it was very weak.' He sighed. 'Same, mostly, with my legs. The nerves aren't completely dysfunctional, but they are very weak, and the muscles aren't great either. But the conditioning is helping.'

'Do you notice any difference?'

'Not a lot, other than feeling a little stronger overall.'

James gave him a sad smile. 'When are you allowed to leave?'

'Probably not for another month or so. All the facilities are here and I need pretty intensive treatment.'

'And the prognosis?' He seemed scared to ask.

Jadin sighed. 'They're still saying it's hard to say. But there is a decent chance I can recover fully.'

James shook his head. 'It's a wonder you're as positive as you are, Jadin. It's a mountain to deal with.'

Jadin grinned wryly. 'Well, I surprise myself sometimes. But I also have my mental health police, Officers Blackman and Holmes.'

James grinned. 'Glad to be of service.'

'So, back to Badminton, are you going to take extra security?'

'I don't know. I want to make sure nothing will happen, but I don't want to slap the organisers in the face. I'm not that regal as to bring all my own stuff.'

'Really?' Jadin smirked.

'Thanks a lot. I just hope they catch these people before they do any more damage.' James stood up. 'You want anything from the cafeteria?'

'Sure, a muffin and the newspaper?'

'You got it.'

When he returned, he nearly walked right into the doorpost.

'You alright there?' Jadin inquired.

Wordlessly he turned the paper around, showing him the headline. "2,000 Guineas Favourite Found Dead." Jadin's jaw dropped open. 'Them?'

'I wouldn't bet against it.'

'What are the cops saying?'

James skimmed the article. 'Next to nothing. The investigation is still ongoing.'

Jadin looked at the full-page photo of the bay thoroughbred, in full flight en route to winning a prior race. 'What a shame. He was a wonderful horse.'

James nodded. 'They'd thought he'd be spectacular.' He sagged back against the back of the chair. 'This is getting out of control.'

'Well, we're assuming a lot.'

'It's a pretty weird coincidence, isn't it?'

'Yeah,' Jadin sighed. 'Well, since I'm out of the way, I'm guessing all my horses are safe.' James got a strange look on his face. 'What's the matter?'

James looked up at him. 'Nothing.'

'Don't lie to me.'

James cleared his throat. 'Just wondering what else they've been involved in. Even months down the track, and even if they've caught them, how do we know they're not involved every time someone's horse gets sick. Or any time there's an accident…'' His voice trailed off.

Jadin shook his head. 'I'm sure they didn't have anything to do with my accident. How could they?'

'I don't know. I just had a sick thought.' James shook his head. 'The worst thing is, no one's going to be able to trust anyone else. We'll all be looking sideways at each other, wondering who's involved.'

Jadin shook his head. 'Let's talk about something else. How's Catie and that beau of hers getting on?'

'Good, I think. Her dad's come around. But they're not rushing into a wedding.'

'That's good. They're still pretty young.'

'Well, she is. He's a bit older.' James shrugged. 'But if she's happy, that's all that matters.'

Jadin grinned. 'Glad you came around.'

'So, while we're on the subject…What about you and Kelli?'

'We're just friends.'

'But hoping to be more?'

'Well…maybe.'

James grinned. 'I thought you two looked pretty close.'

'Nothing is official. It's just a possibility. You need to swear to secrecy.'

'My lips are sealed.' James gave him a grin. 'But if I may say, it's about time.'

Jadin rolled his eyes. 'I thought Catie wanted you to ask her out.'

'She did. But I'm sure this is a tolerable solution.'

Jadin glanced away. 'I just don't feel I have anything to offer her anymore. She deserves better.'

James shook his head. 'Don't talk like that. If she cares for you, nothing else matters.' He cleared his throat. 'But it does prove you're worthy of her.'

Jadin raised an eyebrow. 'Even I'll get the big brother treatment, huh?'

'Count on it. But I meant that. You're a good man.'

Jadin smiled. 'I hope she agrees.'

'So, if I can change the subject,' James said, 'I've been doing a little bit of investigation.'

Jadin raised his eyebrows. 'Such as?'

'Well, I did some investigating in Kentucky.'

'By which you mean snooping?'

'Meh, same difference.' James shrugged. 'I did also decide to talk to Cole, but kept it vague - is Clive working out, is everything okay at his stables, etcetera.'

'And?'

'It all checked out. I even managed to get into his motorhome to do it.'

Jadin grinned at him. 'Nice work, Sherlock.'

'He seemed completely at ease with me.'

'He is an iceman, remember,' Jadin said.

'I know. But he left me alone to go outside and talk to someone. No one who's guilty would do that.'

'So Cole doesn't know, but Clive is involved?'

'I struggle to believe it at times, but that seems to be the case.' James cleared his throat. 'I'm going to call him.'

'Is that a good idea?'

'He can't do anything to me over the phone.' James shrugged. 'I can't sit around and wait forever.'

'Just be careful, okay?'

'I will.'

The next day he went through all his emails looking for any correspondence with Clive. He turned up a handful of emails, all mundane. He racked his brain, trying to think of any alarm bells in the three years he'd worked at Manorbrook. He went through his accounting, which Clive had helped manage. Nothing untoward.

And then he caught a break.

Opening a new tab, he saw Clive had failed to log out of his email inbox. A quick check proved he was the only one currently in the box. He started reading. There were a lot of bills and receipts, personal messages, and promotions. Then at the bottom of the second page, a subject read: "Re: Employing KR". James opened it.

"So, I will contact KR and see how we go. Thanks for the info." It was signed L.

James read through the rest of the chain. There were references to "stopping those against us" and "recouping control", but predictably, nothing identifiable. He downloaded and attached it to an email to the inspector anyway, and made sure he didn't log out.

Then he picked up the phone.

'Hello?'

'Lisa, hi. It's James Blackman. Is Clive around?'

'Oh, hi, James. He's not, I'm afraid. Shall I ask him to call you?'

'Please. How are the kids?' Over the course of the conversation James surmised that, if Clive was involved, he hadn't told his wife.

Lisa promised to get Clive to call and James hung up.

The returned call came three days later. James asked if they could catch up for a drink and Clive agreed.

They chatted amiably about Clive's family and how it was going for him working for Cole Kendrick. Then James asked him point-blank, 'Were you at my stable a couple of weeks ago?'

'No, why?' He looked surprised.

James stared into his eyes. 'Have you heard about what happened to Coalbridge?'

This time, Clive's gaze dropped to the table. 'I did.'

'The cops are saying you are involved.'

Clive didn't answer right away.

'Clive?'

Clive cleared his throat and raised his eyes. There was a haunted expression there. 'I'm so, so sorry, Jimmy.'

James' mouth opened. 'It's true, then?'

Clive blew out a breath. 'About six months ago, I was contacted by a group of people offering me a lot of money to help them take you down. I said no. But they kept coming back, offering more and more money, and said I wouldn't really have to do anything. Then they started threatening Lisa and the kids.' He shuddered. 'These were powerful people. Gang connections. Out to get whatever power they could. So I gave them the gate code.'

He shook his head. 'They told me no real damage would be done, and that was the last I heard of it. I never set foot on your property. Not that that makes it any different.'

They sat in silence. James cleared his throat. 'Well, thank you for being honest, anyway. Do you know how they got a key?'

Clive shook his head. 'I got the impression they'd reached out to several people close to you and just kept badgering them all until someone caved. But it wasn't me who gave them the key.'

'So someone else has betrayed me too.' James put his head in his hands.

Clive didn't respond, but he tossed a £10 note on the table.

'I'm sorry, Jimmy. I hope someday you can forgive me.'

'Me too,' James murmured as he walked away.

Amy trotted up to the paddock to fetch Chester and got him ready for a mock dressage test. Although he would never be a superstar at the discipline, his dressage was very good now. Now they just had to work on making sure he cleared the show jumping poles.

'Good boy.' She patted his neck after bringing him to a halt. Something was working; she was confident she could come out of the ring with a good score.

She got back in her car and heard her phone ding in her bag. She waited until she parked in the garage below her apartment.

Hi Amy, it's Damien. Just wanted to touch base; how are you?

She locked her car and headed up to her apartment, greeting a neighbour on the way. The middle-aged lady smiled benevolently at her. 'Ah, heard from that young man of yours, have you?'

She raised her eyebrows and smiled politely. 'Oh, he's just a friend.'

The lady peered critically at her. 'I wouldn't be so sure about that.'

If it had been Mickey, she would have rolled her eyes, but she didn't want to be disrespectful, so she smiled again and wished her a good day.

No, she wasn't racing inside to answer a text. She was walking slowly, taking her time like a sensible person.

'Hi. I'm doing okay. Chester's training is going well. How are things where you are?'

Well, one of the reasons I'm getting in touch is because I just wanted to talk to you before tomorrow. We'll be going inland and may need to engage with the fighting.

Her heart leapt into her throat. 'But you're on the navigational team. You won't be going ashore, will you?' She scolded herself; that was a selfish thing to say.

Well, I may be called into action, either on the ship or if there's an emergency, on the ground.

Amy slowly sank to the edge of her bed. He's going into a warzone. She swallowed a couple of times. 'So you're going to be fighting?'

Looks like we may have to. But don't worry. This is what we've trained for.

There was no way on earth she wouldn't worry. 'Well, stay safe over there, okay?'

We'll do our best. But Ames, if something was to happen...

She closed her eyes. She didn't want to think about it. When the phone dinged again, she opened them to read the rest of his thought.

...You need to know that I care about you very much and I always will.

Tears sprang into her eyes, and a drop landed on the touchscreen. She wiped the device on her leg. 'I care about you, too, and I'll be waiting to see my best friend again in one piece.'

I'll be in touch as much as I can. Take care.

'You too.' She sniffed and watched as his status changed to "active one minute ago". He was gone, off into battle the following day. He hadn't said I love you, but she could read between the lines. He wanted a relationship with her, but he didn't want to say the critical words if they weren't face to face.

She stared at the ceiling, vaguely aware of a tear trailing down into her ear. She knew now if something did happen, she'd be devastated, more devastated than she'd be for a friend. Underneath it all, she did love him.

She sat up and took a deep breath. He'd be okay, and he'd come back and ask again about developing a relationship. And this time, she would say yes.

She rolled onto her stomach and imagined what it must be like to be sleeping on that warship tonight, going into battle the next day. Her generation had little experience of real war. They'd done all the history, but it was nowhere near the same as living through it. What must it be like, lying on cramped bunks trying to sleep, thinking of wives, girlfriends, or children back home, wondering what fate they would meet the next day?

And, with the secrecy surrounding this operation, would the families ever know what happened, beyond that their lives were laid down for their country in an alien land?

She sat up and went back to her evening routine. Funny, six months ago she had come to England wanting nothing more than to succeed as a three-day event rider. She still wanted that very much, but now there was another hope taking up residence in her heart.

James led Lacklustre out of his stall, patting his neck as he led him into the trailer. Despite the cloud overhanging this year's event, he couldn't deny the excitement hiding somewhere underneath. The familiar thrill of going to Badminton was underway.

He was incredibly fortunate to live only a half-hour drive from the grounds. Most other riders would have to fly at least part of the way. Often, he'd had some of his Kiwi teammates keep their horses with him for a week or so beforehand so they could get the flight out of the way earlier.

But this time it was just his two, Lacklustre and Marksman. They were loading happily enough, even Marksman, who had had a few better experiences since his last plane journey. He hooked his lead rope up and gave each of them a pat. Oh, how he hoped he was doing the right thing.

'Got everything?' Caitlyn asked as he slid the ramp up.

'I think so.' James turned to glance over the landscape as if to jog his memory.

He wasn't thrilled about leaving Caitlyn in charge after what had happened to Coalbridge, but Vicky's husband Brett promised to keep an eye on things. He looked at his niece. 'You sure you're okay with this?'

'Of course, Uncle Jim. All the security's up and everything. I can handle it.'

'If you say so. Thank you, Catie.'

'Sure. Good luck.'

He climbed into the driver's seat and put the rig in gear. 'You ready for this, Vick?'

'Sure.' She pulled her feet off the dashboard as they headed down the drive. 'Those idiots aren't going to win.'

James pulled onto the motorway and settled in for the drive. He glanced over at Vicky, who was already buried in her James Patterson novel. He was grateful she had agreed to come, despite the cloud hanging over the event. He loved his niece, but Vicky was a much more experienced groom, and he wanted the best at Badminton.

'You're sure you want to do this?'

She glanced up at him over her book. 'You've asked me that a dozen times over the last two days.'

'I know. But I don't like dragging you into this mess.'

'First of all, most of the riders and grooms don't even know what's going on. At least I had a choice. Second of all, you're going, and so I'm going with you. And third, I don't think anyone would be stupid enough to try something at Badminton. The security is ridiculous even for the riders themselves.'

'True. But the fact that the police warned me…'

'Yeah, but it's their job to be over-cautious.'

'Well, just as long as you know what you're getting into.'

'Oh, believe me, I'm well aware.' She returned to her book, apparently not noticing his grin. He'd found gold when she joined his team.

He kept one ear on the horses behind him as he watched the traffic. They made quick time to Badminton county. Four days out from the first dressage day, the traffic around the area was okay. It would get impossibly congested once the event was underway. He'd learned that the hard way.

He dug out his ID and showed it to the gate guard, who waved him through. He eased the rig forward and down to the stabling area. He recognized Kelli's posh new truck and eased his old clunker to a stop next to it. He really should upgrade soon.

The New Zealand horses were usually stabled together even though Badminton wasn't technically a team event. It made for a nice atmosphere, a sense of camaraderie. He slid from the cab and made his way to the back of the truck, helping Vicky let down the ramp. Both horses blinked against the bright light.

'Hey, guys, ready to take on the world?' He unsnapped Lacklustre's lead rope and led him down the ramp. He was still not sure how he would go, but it was only fair he had a chance. He let Lacklustre investigate his new surroundings as he led him slowly towards the barn. He sniffed his way along, curious but calm. James patted his neck and led him into an empty stall. He stuck his nose through the wall, trying to say hello to Kaleido, who ignored him.

'Hey, Jimmy.' He turned to see Kelli walk up. 'Good trip?'

'Yeah, fine. How about you?' He checked the water trough in the stall and picked it up to refill.

'Fine.' She leaned against the outside wall, absently patting Kaleido.

James studied her as he shut the half door behind him. 'Everything all right?'

She nodded and leaned closer. 'Everything just feels a bit creepy, you know?'

'Yeah. I'm trying not to think about it.'

Vicky led Marksman into the box on Lustre's other side. He heard the two women exchanging greetings as he made his way to the tap. Kelli was right; there was something of an edgy undercurrent around here. Maybe it was just their knowledge of what was going on that was putting them on alert.

He returned the water to the stall. Lustre had cocked one rear hoof and was nodding off, but Marksman was alert, keenly looking around him. He didn't appear to be getting on too well with the horse on his outside, either.

'Come on, old boy, you should be used to this place by now.' He stepped into the stall and stroked his neck. He glanced up and down the aisle as if looking for something amiss that was unsettling the horse.

He shook his head.

Kelli stuck her head in the door. 'Hey, you coming to the briefing?'

James opened the stall door. 'Do I have a choice?'

'Not really.'

They sat through the typical one-hour session, trying to pay attention. Then the Kiwi team decided to have dinner together at the estate restaurant down the road. James was about to decline but changed his mind. It had been a long time since they'd been together as a unit.

Debbie Mangrove fell into step beside him as they trekked out to Kyle's rental car. 'Haven't seen you in a while.'

'I know. How've you been?'

'Okay. I haven't won anything if that's what you're asking.' She gave him an easy grin.

James smiled. 'Can't say I have either.'

'How's Jadin?'

'He's getting there. The therapists are pleased with his progress, so that's a good sign.'

'It is. Look, James, I know I haven't always fit in with you and Jadin and Kelli --'

James held up a hand. 'It's not like that.'

'Yeah, well, whatever it's like, I know it hasn't always been happy families. But I still consider you my friends, and I can't say how sorry I am about Jadin's accident. I said the same to him.'

James smiled. 'Well, it's not only your fault. We've had our ups and downs. But thanks.'

It was a nice evening. James went with Kelli back to the grounds to unhook his car and drive home. She liked to stay right on the premises in her little motorhome.

'Was it me, or was it just not the same?' Kelli inquired as they approached the gate.

James shook his head, reserving his answer for after they'd been cleared to pass through. 'It wasn't just you. I think not having Jadin there feels wrong for everyone.'

She shook her head. 'Not just that. Yeah, it was partly that, but it's also never been the same since WEG.'

'That isn't your fault, Kelli.'

She parked and turned to him. 'Well, then, whose fault was it?'

'Kell...' They'd talked about this several times over the past two years, but Kelli still blamed herself.

'No, I gave the wrong information, and someone was disqualified. If it had been me, fine, but it wrecked the whole team's chances. And it made everyone believe the big three were the only ones who mattered.' She shook her head. 'And after Kyle was disqualified, they all came out against us and said we got prima donna treatment.'

'You were only giving the information you thought was correct.'

'Well, fine, maybe it wasn't completely my fault, but it messed us up. We used to be a family, Jimmy.'

'I'm sure we'll get back to that. In and of itself, it was hardly an issue, but I think it became the catalyst for all the other little things to come out.' He shrugged. 'And it has to be said the management didn't handle some of the complaints very well.'

Kelli sighed. 'I guess.' She straightened up. 'Well, I'll see you tomorrow.'

'Sure. See ya.' She shut the door and ambled over to the trailer. He and Jadin had never blamed Kelli for the rifts that appeared, and they were probably the only ones who didn't, not even partly. Her course information had led to a disqualification, which sparked cries of it being on purpose and soon insults were flying and the team was split. In some ways that had made the trio grow even closer. *Seems like I might be about to become the third wheel, though.* He grinned to himself.

But no matter how cool and aloof her public persona appeared, Kelli would never hurt a flea. She'd just been in the wrong place at the wrong time to foster wrong perceptions.

He started his ute and headed back to Manorbrook. They were getting back to being a team again.

And they still had a dream waiting.

Chapter Twelve

It was raining.

Kelli sat in front of her mirror French-braiding her hair. She never enjoyed competing in the rain. The sand in the arena was soggy, the cross-country track was muddy, and Maximus always got bad-tempered when he had rain in his face.

But then again this was England.

She stood up and double-checked her bag. Boots, jodhpurs, chest protector, helmet. She hoped she'd remembered to pack her goggles. They were usually only used by race jockeys, but she liked wearing them if they were running on a muddy track.

She took a deep breath and sat back down on the queen bed.

So far, nothing suspicious had shown up, but she felt like she was walking on eggshells, dreading something happening. The death of the racehorse was a chilling reminder of what could happen. Nobody would confirm the reasons behind the death, but it was too weird a coincidence in her mind.

She glanced once more around the room and headed out the door. Kyle was just passing down the hallway. 'Morning, Kelli. Lovely weather, huh?'

'Yeah, delightful.' She shouldered her duffel bag as they entered the lift.

Kyle seemed to be looking at her strangely. 'You all right, K?'

She swallowed. He hadn't called her that in years. 'Sure, why?'

'I don't know. You seem to be all nervous.'

She sighed. Despite all the differences between them, this man had once been her good friend. She thought he deserved to know, but she wasn't sure she was meant to say.

She cleared her throat. 'I'm concerned that whoever went after Coalbridge may go after someone else.'

'Well, I guess it's a possibility, but you'd have to be Houdini to get through security here.'

'Yeah.'

Kyle leaned against the wall. 'How's Jadin?'

'Doing okay. The therapy's going well, but he's pretty impatient.'

Kyle nodded. 'I don't blame him.' He looked down at his feet. 'When he was in that coma, all I could think about was the stuff that came between us, you know?'

'That's in the past. Jadin's not worried about it.'

'I know. I've talked to him. But it just gave me a wake-up call.'

Kelli gave him a sad smile. Under the disagreeability her friend still existed. 'It did for all of us.'

Kyle hesitated, then looked at her, really looked at her. 'I'm sorry, Kelli. For what I accused you of and all that came between us.'

She met his gaze, reading his sincerity. 'Me too.'

He held out his hand. 'Friends?'

She studied him a second before reaching out and hugging him with her free arm. She thought absently she probably hadn't done that since he'd won Luhmuhlen, four years ago. 'Friends.'

She had to turn the window wipers to maximum speed. It was raining cats and dogs now. It wasn't going to be a pleasant day.

The traffic, predictably, was horrific. She drummed her fingers on the wheel along to the radio, thankful that she had a later start. She wondered momentarily why so many people wanted to go in the rain.

She pulled into the gate and showed her pass. The guard waved her through, and she eased the vehicle towards the barn. Heck, the visibility was getting pretty bad.

She parked as close to the barn as she could and pulled her poncho from the back seat, dashing the door. She shook her plait from side to side.

'Hey, we don't need showers inside, too.' James walked past her.

'Oh, sorry.' She grinned at him.

'And Marksman's going to be in a foul mood.' He nodded to the stall, where the big bay was poking his nose through the bars, trying to harass Lacklustre.

'Yeah, I'm glad Max's test is tomorrow.' She glanced at him and lowered her voice. 'Thankfully there's been no trouble yet.'

'No. I'm kind of thinking there won't be. It will be hard to pull off.'

Not impossible, though, she added to herself, but decided against saying it.

She slipped into Kaleido's stall and patted him good morning. He was bright and looking for more food, so hopefully, his mood would hold until the dressage arena. She checked her wristwatch. There were still a couple of hours to go, but she decided to give him a light workout before the warm-up.

She saddled up, keeping her poncho over her shirt and helmet. It was still raining pretty hard. Kaleido took one step out the barn door and jerked his nose back.

'I know, fusspot, but we don't have a lot of choice, so come on.' She led him forward, and he obliged, albeit stiffly. She vaulted onto his back and walked him towards one of the back arenas. She watched Debbie Mangrove putting her lovely Arab/thoroughbred, Mazumo, through his paces. His Arab blood made him feisty, but he was a little machine when he wanted to be. Debbie guided him towards the exit and over to the main ring. 'Good luck,' Kelli offered.

'You too.'

She waved and walked Kaleido on, warming up to practice a few important passages. She and Debbie had been close when Mazumo was first selected for the New Zealand trials. She'd been excited to finally have another girl in the squad, but they'd drifted apart over the years. Ever since the discontent and the them-versus-us fiasco that followed WEG.

Kaleido was not happy, and the hesitation in his movements reflected it. She feared this may not be a great test. She could only hope that a few other horses would also be affected by the rain and it wouldn't be totally hopeless.

They exited the ring just as James fought Marksman into the arena. Well, one other horse was affected at any rate. 'He okay?'

James shook his head. 'Nope, he's throwing a right royal tantrum.' His words were punctuated by Marksman's rear hooves leaving the ground. James clamped both his knees and the reins. 'Easy, boy.'

Kelli frowned. 'It's just the rain?'

'I think so. That and he appears to have got up on the wrong side of the stall.' He pulled Marksman's nose to his chest, forcing him to stand still.

'Okay, I'll leave you to it. Good luck.'

She walked Kaleido back towards the barn. He still had another hour before they had to warm up for the test itself. She hoped the rain might ease by then.

She settled Kaleido down and went back out to watch Marksman's test. James had succeeded in calming him down, and while he was still a little stiff, it was a decent test, placing them in the top ten.

'Well done,' she offered as he left the arena.

'Thanks.' He dismounted and patted Marksman's wet neck. 'It wasn't great, but it wasn't the disaster I thought I was heading for.'

Forty-five minutes later she was mounted on Kaleido, who was quite cross and unresponsive. She walked him through a few easier passages, hoping to lighten his mood. He relaxed a little, but he was still rather unhappy with the elements. She kept up a running monologue, trying to keep him calm. His ears flicked back and forth, so he was listening.

At their number, she trotted him into the ring and eased him to a halt. To her surprise, he did it perfectly, and for the rest of the test, he was the picture of obedience. She was thrilled. They scored 27.4, for first place.

'Good boy,' she enthused after they exited the ring. She patted his neck, tiny droplets flying. 'Well done, Kaleido.'

He tossed his head, his ears forward, obviously pleased with himself. She dismounted and led him back into the barn, where he got two horse cookies for his efforts.

By the end of the day, they were second, with only Cole Kendrick and his top horse, Remover, ahead of them. But there was still the second day of dressage to go, and many of the top combinations would compete on day two.

Thankfully, the sun was shining when she headed down to breakfast the next morning. Maximus was cheerful and relaxed when she warmed him up, so she hoped he'd do a good test. He had never been a flashy dressage horse, but he held his own. James was immediately before her on Lacklustre, and she kept an eye on the ring as she got Max ready. Lustre looked good, especially considering this was his first five-star. They scored 39.00, which put them fifth overall with two-thirds of the field gone. She and Kaleido were still second.

Maximus could have been dancing, the way he performed in the test. He was almost graceful - as elegant as a New Zealand thoroughbred probably could be. A couple of minor errors marked them down a bit, and she kicked herself because Max had been perfect. They scored 31.8 for eleventh place. Only five points separated the top twelve riders.

She cooled Maximus down, patting his neck and telling him what a good boy he was. He nodded as if he understood every word.

So at the end of the dressage, New Zealanders were placed third, seventh, nineteenth, twenty-fifth, and thirty-second. All the others were probably too far back for a top ten finish, but the scores were so close that even moving up multiple places was a possibility.

Especially after walking the course. It was enormous. This would be her eighth Badminton and she'd never seen a course like this. It reminded her of the pictures she'd seen of the 80s Badminton winners. She wondered how some of the finer warmbloods would go. They had been bred for more finesse in the dressage ring; but this was built for the tough, hardy jumpers. It was a throwback to an earlier era of three-day eventing.

'A bit confronting, isn't it?' James said as they looked over the water jump. It was a long complex; a jump in, four strides to the centre obstacle, then another five strides to the exit jump.

'A bit,' Kelli muttered. 'I'm pretty sure Max will handle it, but I'm a bit worried about Kaleido. He's not used to this kind of bold course, and not built for it, either.'

'He's pretty tough. I think he should be okay.'

They trekked towards the next element, a big log triple. It was tough, coming immediately after the water. 'You ever ridden a course this big, Jimmy?'

James cocked his head. 'One or two have been close. Burghley last year was pretty big.' He gave the log a tap. 'There seems to be a bit of a trend towards bigger, bolder courses at the moment.'

Kelli shook her head. 'But the whole sport changed to be shorter and easier and better for the warmbloods. Why change it back?'

'Well, they're not going completely back. Not like when they did the roads and tracks as part of the cross-country.' James shrugged. 'But I think we do need to have a reasonable challenge. Some courses I've done hardly qualify as five-star.'

By the time they got to the end, she was sure both her horses would get around. But it was tougher than most of the tracks they'd seen.

Thank heaven, it was fine the next morning.

The horses ran in the same order as their dressage test, so Kaleido was her first to go. He was enthusiastic and tugging at the bit, which was a good thing. She took him to the start gate, and at the smallest relaxation of the reins, they were off.

His big gait ate up the distance, and she knew time, at least, would not be a factor. The first part of the course didn't trouble her; it was the point of the water complex onwards that made her nervous.

She eased him back to a slow canter as they approached. He popped over the first jump easily, but she felt him stumble as he landed. She held the reins firm, trying to get him to regain his footing. He gathered his feet under him but he had no momentum, and he tried to leap over the centre jump anyway. His back legs caught the log but somehow they made it over. He stumbled again on landing but got over the last jump and out. Kelli slowly loosened her grip and let herself breathe again. She patted his neck as they accelerated away. He'd scrambled through that on his own; she'd just held on for dear life.

Kaleido cleared the big treble easily, and from then on he never put a hoof wrong. They cleared the last oxer and her heart slowly returned to its normal location as they cantered down to the finish.

'You all right, Miss Holmes?' One of the officials asked as she dismounted.

'Yeah, I'm fine, thanks.' She dropped Kaleido's reins to the ground and checked his legs. There was no obvious bruising but she'd ice them just in case.

She led him back to the stables, checking for any sign of a limp but found none. She could feel her calves starting to ache from the tense trip through the water obstacle. She filled a couple of ice boots and strapped them onto his rear legs, giving him a gentle slap on the rump. 'Good boy.'

Kyle's head appeared around the door. 'You guys okay?'

She sighed and nodded as she let herself out of the stall. 'A bit sore, but okay.'

She wandered down to Max's stall. She clipped the gate to the side of the stall. 'Come on, old man, your turn.'

She warmed Max up slowly, keeping an eye on the board. James and Marksman had gone clear, and so had Debbie and Mazumo. But there were plenty of rounds with faults.

She felt Maximus falter and caught herself before she fell. She stopped him and immediately vaulted to the ground. He stood still, touching only the tip of his left front hoof to the dirt.

'What happened, Max?' She murmured to him as she felt down his leg, seeing him flinch as she ran her hand over his forelock. There was no obvious heat or swelling, but something was wrong. She looked up to see Mark Clinton and the New Zealand Chef d'Equipe, Steve, coming their way.

'Everything okay, Kelli?'

She shook her head. 'I felt him stumble, and now he's not putting weight on it.' She straightened up, holding on to Max's bridle as Mark ran his hands over the leg.

The vet had a frown on his face as he stood back up. 'Nothing obvious yet, but he's not happy. Try leading him, and if he can't put weight on it we'll get the ambulance.'

'Come on, Max.' She took a couple of steps and he followed but kept his weight off his leg as much as he could.

Mark studied him with his arms folded. 'Keep it slow, and I think we should get him X-rayed.'

She nodded. 'Okay.'

'Sorry, Kelli,' Steve offered. 'I'll let the organisers know.'

She nodded her thanks and led Max slowly back to the stable. He could walk, but he was hobbling. She took off the saddle and looped it over her free arm, trying to give him less weight to carry.

'Here, I've got it.' James materialized at her side and took the saddle.

She gave him a slightly alarmed look. 'Shouldn't you be warming up Lustre?'

'Nope, got heaps of time. What happened?' He nodded to Max.

'I don't know. He just stumbled, and now he's struggling to walk on it.'

'Sorry, Kell.'

She shrugged. 'It happens. I just hope it's not too serious, especially at his age.'

He nodded and continued to the tack room as she tried to settle Max in his stall. She wondered if she should ice it, but decided to wait for Mark. She removed the rest of his tack and rubbed him down.

James reappeared at the door and took the bridle and blanket. She turned to look at him. 'I can handle it, Jimmy.'

'I know. Just thought you could use a hand.'

Mark returned with the portable X-ray. 'I didn't really want him trekking all the way over there.' He set it up in the stall, Max watching with calm interest. 'Hold his head.'

She gripped the halter as he ran the device, but Max held perfectly still. She ran her hand over his mane. He didn't seem to be in pain if he wasn't walking, for which she was grateful. Mark stood back up and removed the machine. 'I'll take these and develop them. I'm pretty sure we're not dealing with a break, but this will confirm it.'

She nodded. 'Thanks, Mark.'

'Sure.'

She stroked his nose and offered him a mouthful of hay, which he munched quietly. James found her a few minutes later, leaning against the horse's good shoulder. 'You okay?'

She glanced up at him wearily. 'Yeah, I guess. Just not having the best weekend.'

He smiled sympathetically. 'We all have them.'

'I know.' She shook her head. 'This is silly. Sorry.'

'It's fine. How's Kaleido?'

'Okay, last I checked. Doesn't seem to have done any damage but I'll keep an eye on him.'

James checked his watch. 'I'd better saddle up. Catch ya later, Tiger.'

She smiled at the nickname. 'Good luck.'

Mark reappeared a few minutes later, several images in his hands. 'It's not broken,' he reassured her. 'I'm thinking he's pulled a muscle.'

'How bad is it?' She asked quietly.

'It's only a small tear which should heal on its own if he rests it. We might get him a bootie to help it heal faster.'

She nodded. 'How long?'

'I'd say he needs to stay off it as much as possible for a few days. Then just start him back gently, and keep an eye on it.'

'Okay. Thanks, Mark.'

He applied the moon boot, and Max just stood there, looking dignified. Mark patted his shoulder. 'Get better, old lad.'

Kelli thanked the vet again and checked on Kaleido. There was still no heat or swelling, but she'd check him again in the evening. She hoped she wouldn't be leaving Badminton with two lame horses.

By the end of cross-country day, Cole Kendrick and Remover were leading. Kelli and Kaleido were third, followed by Australian Martin Keats and Matchmaker. James and Lustre were ninth, and Debbie and Mazumo twelfth. All of those riders had a chance to get in the money, with only five points separating first and fourteenth. One fence down would cost four points.

She had never won Badminton. She'd come close once, on Max, five years ago. She'd had a fence in hand, but Max had dropped a foot in the water before knocking down the last fence. That had given the crown to Coalbridge, his first five-star.

Now, if she jumped clear and the Brits both had a fence down, Kaleido could win the biggest event in the sport. She knew it was unlikely - both leading horses were good show jumpers. But one always had to dream.

She checked Kaleido's legs one more time before heading back to the hotel. He was still fine. She'd look again first thing in the morning.

She gave both her boys one more pat and headed for her rental. She couldn't quite work out why she was so tired. Must be all the excitement today.

She texted Jadin an update before eating a toastie and going straight to bed. Tomorrow, a top-three place beckoned.

'So, how is Lieutenant Commander Damien Scott, New Zealand Navy?' Tori inquired mildly.

Amy rolled her eyes at the use of his full title. 'Fine, last I heard.'

'Which was when?'

'Nine days ago.' She could feel Tori's raised eyebrow even though she refused to look.

'That long?'

Amy shrugged. 'He's in a war.'

She saw her friend's nod in her peripheral vision. 'It's pretty sobering when you think about it.'

'Yeah. I try not to dwell on it too much.' She kept typing as she spoke. The truth was, she found it hard not to think about it. Just because her generation had no firsthand knowledge of war, it didn't mean she was naive.

'So, have you thought any more about your relationship?'
Amy cleared her throat. 'Some. But everything's in limbo right now.'
'Yeah, I guess so.'
Amy was glad Tori dropped the subject. She didn't want to talk about it. She didn't need to be reminded that the man she'd finally admitted she loved was entangled in a tense conflict. She picked up the phone. 'Enfield Gazette.'
She transferred the caller and returned to her billing. She heard her phone beep in her bag but ignored it. She had heard it go off several times over the past week and hoped it was Damien. And it wasn't. It was a Facebook comment or an eBay notification or a message from her mobile provider.
She heard Tori sigh. 'They've scheduled Jack's surgery.'
Amy turned to face her, feeling a little remorse at her impatience with her friend. She wished she hadn't been too introspective to ask before now. 'Are you okay with it?'
Tori sighed. 'No, I'm worried about it. But I know there's no choice.'
'The prognosis is good, right?'
'Yeah. But there's always a risk in the operating room.' She looked down at her keyboard. 'My aunt died during heart surgery. I was only seven but I remember it.'
Amy reached across to pat Tori's arm. 'I'm sorry. I didn't know.'
'I know.' She shook her head. 'But I'm not particularly rational about all this.'
Amy grimaced. 'Not many people would be.'
'I mean, we're not even married anymore. I shouldn't be so worried.'
'But he's still the boys' father.'
'Yes. And yesterday…' Tori turned to face her. 'He said to me yesterday that the divorce was a mistake, and after the operation, he'd like another chance.'

Amy nodded. 'And you still care for him,' she observed gently.
She sighed. 'Yeah, I do.'
Amy patted her arm again. 'It'll be okay, Tori.'
She sighed again. 'I hope so.'
'I can keep on top of things here if you need time off.'
'Thanks. I think I'll be okay, but I may just take an afternoon,
so I can take the boys up there after the operation. Once they
get out of school.'
Amy nodded. 'Sure.' She ran her eyes over her billing sheets
again. Seeing an error, she logged in to fix it.
Her phone beeped again. She checked the time in the corner of
her monitor and decided she'd deal with it at lunch.
At twelve, she decided things were under control and headed
out. She'd packed a lunch today but she still needed a hot
coffee. She took her cappuccino out to the same bench where
she'd sat with Damien that first day he reappeared out of her
long-lost memories.
Her messages were from eBay and Mickey. At least one was
worth her interest. She opened it.
*Hey stranger. How's everything going? Heard from
Damien?*
She sipped her drink and typed back. 'It's okay. No, haven't
heard. But he won't have much spare time. I just worry it's
more than that.'
Well, stop worrying. He'll be fine.
She just wished someone could guarantee that. 'I hope so. To
be perfectly honest, I miss him.'
She could almost hear Mickey's triumphant smile. *That's a
good sign.*
She snorted. She was sorry Mickey wasn't physically present
to hear it. 'If you say so. I'd better get back to work. Ttyl.'
She tossed out her coffee cup and headed back to the
newspaper building.

Kelli Holmes glared down at one of her best friends, who was trying to tell her to calm down. 'It's the final round of Badminton, James Avery Blackman. How am I supposed to calm down?'

He smiled sweetly up at her. 'Taking a breath would be a start.' He ducked away as she threatened to flick him with the end of the reins. 'Seriously, Kelli. Take a deep breath. You'll be fine.'

She leaned forward and patted Kaleido's neck. He'd been raring to go this morning, showing no ill effects from his collision with the water jump yesterday.

She lowered her heels and straightened her back. After all these years, she was still a basket case before a big round. James patted her knee. 'Just do what you do.' It was the quote he'd picked up from his favourite NFL coach, Tony Dungy, and it had become one of their mottos.

'Thanks.' She touched her heels into Kaleido's sides. 'Let's go, old boy.'

He was ready, judging by his pricked ears. She had no fences in hand between her and fourth place, but she could still move up if one of the riders ahead of her dropped a rail.

She piloted him towards the first obstacle and he leapt enthusiastically, clearing it easily. She held him back a little, controlling his gait as they navigated the obstacles. Fences two, three and four were no problem. He jumped the water, his back feet just clearing the white line. The only sound was his hooves in the sawdust.

They were clear with only the difficult treble to go. She loosened the reins, allowing him to judge the jump. He popped over the first, got a quick stride in, over the second, another stride and over the third. The clack of a hoof against the pole sounded like a gunshot in the stadium, but there was no thud of it hitting the ground. She glanced back, and only then released the breath she was holding. It stayed up, and they were clear, third at Badminton.

She thumped Kaleido's sweaty neck as they cantered out of the ring. She had thought he would be a star when she first bought him, and here he was, only nine, and already another prestigious result.

She dismounted and received the congratulations of her teammates and the extended Kiwi crew. Kaleido stood tall, proudly accepting the attention. He'd done well and he knew it.

She left him with Kyle and wandered back to the edge of the ring to watch the two local lads who were ahead of her. She wasn't expecting either of them to falter, but one could always hope.

The second-placed rider dropped a pole. Kelli allowed herself a discrete smile as she clapped with the rest. Kaleido was up to second.

But the man ahead of them was one of the all time greats, and his horse, Remover, was a star on the scale of Mark Todd's Charisma. He had won Olympic and team gold medals, each of the five-star events around the globe, and this would be his second Badminton.

She watched Remover as they cantered into the ring. The big Dutch warmblood looked a little on the tense side, but Cole Kendrick was a picture of relaxation on his back. They negotiated the obstacles with a rhythm that was almost poetic. They cleared the water, the double, and approached the treble on a perfect line. Remover jumped once, twice, and a third time, his hooves never coming within six inches of the poles. The crowd erupted. They were the clear champions, but Kelli was happy. Second at Badminton was an achievement in itself. She congratulated Cole, patted Remover and made her way back to her impromptu supporters' huddle. She was thrilled with her horse, and it wouldn't hurt her bank account or her Classics points either.

She took Kaleido's reins and vaulted back up for the customary parade and presentation. She could see a few Kiwi flags in the bleachers, and she grinned and gave them a wave. She loved adding to her country's rich history in the sport. After the ceremonies she walked Kaleido back to the barns, pausing to let a few young fans pat him over the fence. She dismounted and led him the rest of the way, patting his neck and telling him what a good boy he was.

She put him back in his stall and removed the tack. Max stuck his nose over the divider, looking a little forlorn at having missed all the excitement. She gave him a quick pat and returned to rubbing Kaleido down. 'I think you deserve a treat tonight, don't you?' Kaleido nodded his approval.

She carried the tack and put it away, ready to head out in the morning. She planned on taking Max back to James' farm for the time being so he wouldn't have to travel far on his leg, but she and Kaleido would head straight home tomorrow.

She drove back to the hotel, too tired for a celebratory dinner. So she ordered room service and read through all the messages of congratulations on her phone. She was asleep before nine, with a smile on her face.

James was very happy with Lacklustre's seventh place at Badminton. This event was the truest test of a horse's mettle, and Lustre had passed with flying colours.

He loaded his horses and hit the road early on Monday morning. It was a short drive but he was still keen to get back and get everything settled. Luhmuhlen was in five weeks, and he wanted to be able to take his horses and just compete without threats hanging over his head.

Vicky broke the silence about halfway back to Long Ashton. 'Did you talk to Cole?'

James kept his eyes on the road. 'No more than to say congratulations.'

'And he just carried on like everything was fine?' He could feel her bristling.

'I don't think he knows anything, Vick. Which is stupid, but I'm sure they haven't told him.' He slowed the ute to make a turn. 'I don't know him that well, but we've run into each other a lot over the years. If he knew, he wouldn't just ignore it.'

'Unless he's involved.'

James shook his head. 'I don't think he is. He's competitive, but he's as honest as the day is long. No way would he endorse something like this.'

Vicky's expression was sceptical. 'Normally, I'd agree with you, but after Clive Ressler being implicated, how can you know for sure someone's innocent?'

James shrugged. 'Point taken.'

He heard her sigh. 'When will this fiasco be resolved?'

'As soon as possible, I hope. I don't want to be going to Luhmuhlen or Burghley with it still up in the air.'

He turned into his driveway and let out a sigh as he turned the vehicle off. As much as he loved Badminton, he was relieved to be home. He was thankful that no one else had been hurt, horse or human. He was unconvinced that this group would draw the line at harming just the horses.

He and Vicky let down the trailer ramp and he led Lacklustre out to the paddock. Vicky followed with Marksman, but he saw her pause at the bottom of the ramp and run her hand down his left forelock. 'Everything okay?'

She straightened up. 'I don't think so. He's limping. A bit of swelling there.'

James watched her lead the horse away, and sure enough, he was favouring that left foreleg. 'He did knock that pole down in the show-jumping, but I didn't think he hit it that hard. He seemed fine afterwards.' He turned back to the stable. 'I'll get some ice for it.'

He headed for the tack room, wondering why Caitlyn hadn't come out yet to greet them. He glanced at his watch. It was just after nine; she should be here.

He scooped some ice out of the small freezer and put it in the boot, glancing around the premises as he did so. Everything seemed in order. He checked on his horses on the way back out to the paddock, and they all seemed fine. He patted Coalbridge and went back out to the pasture.

'You seen Catie yet?' He asked Vicky as he shut the gate behind him.

She shook her head. 'I guess she's running late today.'

'Yeah.' He crouched in front of Marksman and strapped the boot in place. 'There we go. We'll keep an eye on it and make sure he takes it easy.'

They unloaded the tack and he parked the trailer in its usual spot behind the barn. It was now almost ten and there was still no sign of Catie, or Brett, who was the fill-in.

He texted his sister. 'Has Catie left yet?'

He was brushing Coalie for a workout when his phone beeped. *Yep, she left ages ago. She's not there?*

He felt a sudden inexplicable chill. He dialled Catie's cell. The phone rang seven times before it went to voicemail.

He shook his head and told himself to calm down; she was probably running errands or something. Still, he sent her a message. 'We're back. Can you check in?'

He saddled Coalie, then dialled her mobile again. Still just went to voicemail.

He shook off his worry and mounted Coalie. She'd obviously been working him while they were away; he was still in excellent condition. He patted the shiny black neck. 'Let's hope we can take you to Germany, huh, old man?'

He warmed the horse down and stripped off the tack by the hot walker. 'Vick,' he called into the barn, where she was saddling Lacklustre. 'Did Catie call me back?'

'Not that I heard.' He heard her walk a few paces as if going to pick up his phone. 'Nothing new.'

'Where the heck is she?' He muttered as he clipped the big black to the exerciser. 'She should have got in touch by now.' He dialled her number again.

'Hello?'

'Catie, for goodness' sake, where are you? Why haven't you -'

'This ain't Catie.'

James froze. Instinctively, he pulled the phone away from his ear to check the number. He'd dialled Catie's phone. 'Who is this?'

The voice was gravelly. 'Let's just say it's someone who knows that you know that we exist.'

James felt fear ripple through him like a slow wave. Vicky must have seen his expression, because she came to stand beside him, wide-eyed. 'What are you talking about?'

'Don't play dumb. You know perfectly well what I'm talking about.' The voice released a dirty chuckle that made him sick to his stomach. 'No need to worry, your little niece is fine. She's just having a nice sleep.'

James was not a man given to profanity, but the words coursing through his brain were less than complimentary. It was all he could do to keep from losing it, but he knew that wouldn't do any good.

'However, we need you and your little police friends to stop trying to find us. It is a futile exercise, in any case, so we are only saving you unnecessary trouble.'

I'll give you trouble all right!

'But, we will talk to the police and work this little problem out. Then, upon payment of the ransom and promise of silence, you can have your pretty little niece back. By then, our work will be done, so even if you break your promise, no harm will be done, except perhaps to your quality of life.'

James stood ramrod straight, unsure whether to scream or cry or destroy something. He was vaguely aware of Vicky's hand on his arm, trying to keep him from going off the wall.

'We will be in touch.' The line clicked off.

James stared at the mobile, suddenly aware his hands were shaking, but whether it was from rage or terror, he wasn't sure. Probably both. He met Vicky's horrified gaze. 'They have Caitlyn.'

'I know.' She put her arm through his. 'First things first, call the police. Then we'll deal with everything else.'

James nodded and managed to get put through to Inspector Willbrook. He gave the man a rundown of everything, and the man said he'd be there in ten minutes. Catie was likely snatched from Manorbrook since she'd long since left home. It made James want to throw up.

He suddenly realised he'd have to call his sister Susan. That made him feel worse, and he tried to concentrate on what the officer was saying.

'We will need a copy of your security tape...' Ah yes, security tape. Thank God for something to go on. 'And we'll need to contact any other family or close friends; they may be targets too.'

James' mind started racing...Susan and Mark...his folks back in New Zealand...Vicky and Brett...Jadin and Kelli...what about his other teammates? And surely he was not the only target, which could mean hundreds of people were in danger.

He shook his head, dragging his brain back to the conversation. Inspector Willbrook reiterated that they'd be there as soon as they could and hung up.

James sagged against the wall. 'So now what? Sit on our hands and wait for the cops? I need to find Catie!'

Vicky shook her head. 'You have no idea where to start. I know it's hard, but we have to let them do their jobs or you'll be running blind.'

'And what if it's my fault?' He could feel himself starting to panic. 'Crikey, Vicky, what if me snooping around led to this?'

'No. You couldn't have known.'

He ran a hand through his hair. 'You should go home. They said any other family or close friends might be targets.'

Vicky shook her head. 'Not right now.'

'Victoria…'

'Don't 'Victoria' me. I'm not leaving you alone here right now and that's final.'

He wanted to give her a glare, but he didn't have the energy. 'At least call Brett.'

'Fine, I will. But you know he'll agree with me.'

This time he did give her a glare, but underneath he was grateful. 'Probably, but at least he'll know what's going on.'

'We should call the hospital and let Jadin know. The police may even want to put security in there, but I think he should hear it from us first,' Vicky said.

'Yeah, true. I'd go up there but I need to be here.' He ran his fingers through his hair in aggravation. 'I just feel so helpless. I need to find Catie but there's nothing I can do. I swear if they so much as lay a finger on her…'

Vicky took hold of his forearms. 'Don't think about that now. It will only make it worse. I've been praying since you got that call.'

James pulled his phone out and dialled the hospital, then the extension for Jadin's room in rehab. 'Jadin…it's me.' He cleared his throat, suddenly wondering if he should upset Jadin this much. 'Look, uh, something's happened, and you need to keep an eye out for anything suspicious, okay? The police are saying anyone close to me may be at risk…' He flinched at Jadin's tirade, demanding to know immediately what was going on. He looked helplessly at Vicky, who lifted her hands as if to say, *What can you do?*

He took a deep breath. 'Catie's missing. We don't know anything; the police are on their way.'

'Missing? Someone took her?'

He took another deep breath, not sure if he was trying to calm Jadin or himself. 'It looks that way, yes.'

'Someone from this syndicate we're chasing?' He sounded ready to personally initiate World War III.

'It looks that way.'

'There's something you're not telling me.' Jadin's tone was matter-of-fact, but he'd seldom heard him angrier.

'I don't know much right now. Just that I want to go after them and...' He let the thought trail off.

He heard Jadin sigh. 'Sorry, Jimmy. I know this is killing you too. Are you okay? Safe, I mean?'

'We're waiting for the cops, but I don't think I'm in much physical danger right now. Vicky's here and refusing to leave.'

'Good. Call me as soon as you can, okay?'

'I will. Be careful, Jade.'

'They can't do much with me. But I'll stay aware.'

He hung up and sank back against the wall, wishing someone would come along and wake him up from this nightmare.

Police vehicles rolled up his driveway.

The two officers flashed their IDs and James tried to offer a polite smile, but nothing was forthcoming. He wondered uselessly if he looked as shell-shocked as he felt.

'We're sorry this has happened,' Inspector Willbrook began.

James pasted on a neutral expression and nodded.

The Inspector asked for the full story, and James gave it to him, as much as he knew.

'Anything else suspicious gone on that could have been this syndicate?' Constable Martin looked up from her notebook.

He wanted to tear the notebooks out of their hands, throw them in the nearest trough and scream at them to go and find his niece. Instead, he took a deep breath and responded evenly. 'Well, we saw the story about the racehorse which seemed like it was them. But nothing around here that I know of. But I've been at Badminton.' He felt another chill, wondering if something had happened and Catie hadn't wanted to bother him with it?

Darn you, Catie, if you didn't tell me... He shook his head and tried to pay attention. Why hadn't he told Catie he loved her the last time they spoke? They'd never been demonstrative in their family, but that was no excuse.

Vicky's gentle squeeze of his elbow brought him back to reality. 'I'm sorry, Officer?'

'Did your niece mention anything that had been amiss while you were away?'

He shook his head. 'No, she never did.'

'Did you notice anything going on at Badminton that was suspicious?'

James shook his head again. 'Not that I remember.'

The officers looked around his stable. He hadn't noticed any signs of a struggle or anything out of place, but maybe their trained eyes would pick something up. He leaned against the outer door, hating every second of inaction.

'We've taken some fingerprints, and we'll run them through our database,' the officer said. James doubted there would be any; they'd been so thorough last time. 'Can we also see your security tape, please.'

James produced the file. 'Have you got any idea where Caitlyn might be?'

The officers looked at them, looking so official and correct that James wanted to scream. This wasn't finding his niece. 'We'll review the evidence and see where that leads us. But right now, we don't know where to look.'

'Couldn't you trace my call?'

'Not after you've hung up. But I think you should come down to the station and we'll try calling again. He'll recognize your number so he should pick up. They probably know how much time they have, but it's worth a shot.'

James nodded numbly and headed for the house to get his keys.

'I'll stay here,' came Vicky's voice from behind him, 'and keep an eye on things.'

James turned to face her. 'I'm not so sure that's a good idea.'

She gave him a look. 'I'll manage.'

'No. I'm putting my foot down. I'm your boss and I'm pulling rank.' He took his jacket off the hook and slipped into it as he spoke. 'Either get Brett to stay here with you or go home.'

She put her hands on her hips but appeared to think better of arguing. 'All right.'

'And be careful.'

Her demeanour softened, just a fraction. 'I will. You'd better too.'

James reached out to hug her. 'Thanks, Vick.'

She seemed surprised at his unusual display of emotion but hugged him back. 'It's what friends do.'

He followed the police cruiser to the station and sat grumpily in the lobby while they went through the evidence. Then they tried calling Caitlyn's phone. He held his breath as the gruff voice answered. 'Yeah.'

He knew he had to keep him on the line for at least thirty seconds. 'Hi, I'm looking for Caitlyn. You a new boyfriend I don't know about?'

The reply was a snarl. 'Don't play cute with me. I've got caller ID.'

'Okay, fine. What do you want?'

'Isn't it obvious? I want success and the money that comes with that success.'

'And you want me out of the way to do so.'

'Oh, don't take it personally. Or as a compliment, heaven forbid. We have many people who are an obstruction to our path.'

He was quite articulate for a greedy thug, James thought. 'And what path is that? Getting everyone out of your way so that you can win?'

'More or less. We are a business, and we are competitive like everyone else.'

James saw Constable Martin hold up ten fingers. He bit his lip. 'But why can't you compete like everyone else? Invest in the best horses--'

'I'm not here to listen to your drivel. For your information, your niece is unharmed, and will remain so as long as our requests are met.' The line went dead, and James swore. Inspector Willbrook indicated his computer screen. 'However, we were able to get a general area. She's still in Long Ashton. If I had to guess, I'd say they're in the downtown area, among the warehouses and factories. Some of those are empty. Or they may use a building that's still in use as cover.'

'I think we should wait before we go in,' another officer piped up. 'Sounds as though the girl's okay for now, and we have the time to pinpoint their location.'

'Are you nuts?' James snapped. 'That's a teenage girl in there with a bunch of cruel thugs, and you're going to take more time?'

'Mr Blackman, we have to look at it logically. You know the girl and your judgement is clouded. But looking at the situation from a purely analytical standpoint, it makes sense to narrow the location.'

James took a deep breath. 'So what are we looking for?'

'I agree that it's somewhere among the industrial buildings.' The officer - Jenkins, according to his nameplate - turned his computer screen. 'We have traces of mill scale found at your stables. It's a thin oxide coating that forms when steel comes into contact with air while it's hot. Then it flakes off later.' He turned the screen back around. 'If they are in a building where there is or has been steel production, they are probably carrying it on their shoes or clothing.'

'So how many steel factories are there?' James asked, a small ray of hope starting to dawn.

'Well, it's not necessarily a steel-only factory; it can happen in other places that use steel in their products. But given the concentration of the particles - there's a reasonably thick amount, so to speak - it would seem more likely to have come from a steel factory itself. Of which there are two.'

Thank you, God.

Officer Willbrook stood up. Despite his methodical way of operating, James was starting to like the man. 'How quickly can we get a team together?'

Officer Jenkins checked his watch. 'Give me ten minutes.'

James could have kissed him.

He was not allowed to follow, despite his temper tantrum, so he waited in the station. He suddenly realized he hadn't replied to Susan's 'isn't she there yet?' hours before. He dug out his phone, and read the new message. It, too, was hours old. *I'm assuming she showed up. Let me know if there's any problem.* He put the phone back down, deciding it was safer to text once it was all over.

He paced up and down. His hands clenched and unclenched.

Please God, please God...

The minutes seemed to take hours. He wondered if he'd internally combust. He snatched up his phone on the first ring. 'Yes?'

'This is Willbrook. We've got her.'

James' knees gave out, and he choked back tears.

'She appears to be fine,' the cop said. 'Shaken up but no apparent injuries.'

'Thank heaven. Can I talk to her?' He heard the phone change hands. 'Catie, sweetheart, are you all right?'

'I'm okay. Freaked out, but fine. They just came in and said I needed to go with them. Then grabbed me when I said no.'

James shook his head. 'I'm so sorry, honey.'

'It's not your fault, Uncle Jim.'

Half an hour later, she walked into the station. She looked bedraggled but otherwise okay. James wrapped her in a hug. 'I'm so, so sorry.'

She shook her head. 'It's not your fault.' He brushed his hand over her hair. 'Are you really all right? Did they hurt you?'

She shook her head again. 'No. Other than a bit of rough-housing to get me in the truck.'

Over James' protests, she agreed to answer the police's questions. 'The sooner we can work on this, the better. Have you talked to Mum?'

'Not yet.'

'Can we wait until Dad's home? Please? She'll go through the roof.'

'Honey -'

'Please, Uncle James. There's nothing more that needs to be done right now.'

James sighed. 'All right.'

They sat in the police station for another hour, answering questions and trying to provide pieces to the puzzle. They had caught several men but none were very high in the syndicate's pecking order.

They called in to see Jadin, to calm him down, before heading back to the farm. James decided that they should make sure no one was alone at the stables. He wasn't so worried about being alone in a locked house overnight.

James pulled up the drive and parked in front of the stable, turning to his niece. 'You okay?'

She nodded. 'Yeah. I just want to go back there and remind myself this is where I grew up; not where a crime happened.'
His heart went out to her. 'There's no rush, Catie. If you want some time off, that's okay.'
She shook her head. 'No, I want to get this done.'
He waited until she was out of the vehicle before hitting his fist against the steering wheel. He hated that this had happened to her, and he hated even more that it had happened on his land, in a job he had her doing.
He took her home later, so they could both talk to Susan and Mark. Susan was beside herself. 'My daughter was kidnapped today and I'm only finding out now?'
'I'm sorry, Sue. But in the rush to find whatever we could, I forgot to text you until I was in the station.'
She was fuming. 'And what about all this time after?'
'Mum, I'm an adult now,' Caitlyn interjected. 'Yes, you deserve to know, but it's not necessarily the first thing to be done. They were trying to get me out. And then, I wanted him to wait and we'd tell you later.'
Mark put an arm around his wife. 'They may have not dealt with it exactly as you'd like, hon, but what matters is Catie's safe now.'
Sue nodded. 'I know.' She reached for her daughter. 'So what happens now?'
'They arrested the men at the scene,' James said, 'but there's more of them out there.'
'Well, I think you should stay away until this is resolved.'
Caitlyn shook her head. 'I can't, Mum. It's my job. We're going to make sure there's always at least two of us.'
James cleared his throat. 'Maybe you should stay away for a bit, at least to deal with this, Catie.'
She shot him a glare, but he wasn't so worried about being the unpopular uncle at the moment. 'Even if it's just a week or two.'

'That'll only make it hard to come back.' Catie shook her head. 'I'm all right; they didn't do anything to me. I was just collateral.'

'All the same, I'd feel better if you at least took a couple of days off,' James said.

She seemed to want to roll her eyes, but she didn't. 'Okay, if you insist. But I'm not letting these creeps win.'

'You're not. You're just giving yourself a bit of a break.'

She nodded. 'You and Vicky stay safe, okay?'

'We'll be fine. She's gone into chaperone mode.' He smiled and gave his niece another hug before she left the room.

He sighed deeply when the hall door shut behind her. 'I'm so sorry, Sue, Mark.'

Mark crossed his arms. 'For not contacting us sooner?'

'Yes, and for the whole thing happening at all. She was at my place.'

His brother-in-law cleared his throat. 'For not contacting us, apology accepted. The main thing is that she's safe. But the rest wasn't your fault. You had no way of knowing this would happen.'

'I'm still responsible.'

Sue put a hand on his arm. 'As angry as I may be with you, I agree. Someone should have called me sooner. But this wasn't your fault.'

'It was my property, and my work she was doing!'

Sue shook her head. 'It could have happened anywhere, to anyone. What if you'd taken her to Badminton instead, and they'd decided to go after someone there? It was out of your control.'

James took a deep breath and let it out slowly. 'Today just about gave me a heart attack.'

Mark leaned against the edge of the wooden table. 'What are the cops saying?'

'They apprehended a handful of the group, but they don't think they're the big fish.' James rubbed the back of his neck. 'This whole thing is hideous. We're all living in fear of what may happen next. That's why I didn't take Coalie to Badminton; they thought he could still be a target.' He threw up his hands. 'But if we continue doing things this way we can barely do anything for fear of being attacked.'

'What's their objective?' Mark asked. 'Just money?'

James shrugged. 'Money and power. They want their horses to win.'

'Why can't they catch these people?'

'It's a lot bigger than we first thought. When Coalie was first poisoned, they just thought it could be a rival. Now it seems to be a big, well-organised group.' He shrugged. 'Now that they've figured out how big it is, and they've gone beyond horses, it may be a greater priority. I felt they weren't putting a lot of time into it at first.'

Sue nodded. 'But you're still in limbo until they shut it down.'

'Yeah. I mean, we went to Badminton and it was fine. But the constant threat of trouble is hard to deal with.'

Sue nodded. 'Who else knows about this syndicate?'

'As far as I know, only Jadin and Kelli. I had to tell them. But the police are keeping it quiet.' James shook his head. 'In a way, if everyone knew, it would hamper finding who the instigators are, especially since they think some owners are involved.'

'So that racehorse that died…?'

'I presume so, but there's nothing official.'

Mark studied him. 'You want to stay here tonight?'

James shook his head. 'Thanks, but I'll be fine. I've got security and I'll just lock up. I'd prefer to be closer to the horses.'

Sue smiled. 'Despite everything, thank you for doing what you did to get her back.'

'It wasn't anything.'

He drove home, the dark roads appearing more eerie than usual due to his state of mind. He frowned when his lights illuminated Vicky's car still in his driveway. He parked, locked the ute and headed down to the stables. He found Vicky still mucking out a stall. 'What're you still doing here? And where's Brett?'

'My job, and in the tack room.' She straightened and wiped the back of her glove across her forehead. 'Chores still need doing.'

James sighed. 'I know, and thank you. But you should get home.'

She shook her head. 'I don't like the idea of you being here alone.'

'I'm in a locked house, and I have security alarms. I'll be fine.' He leaned against the door, facing away from her. 'Catie's taking a couple of days off, so I'll help you in the morning.'

He heard Vicky clear her throat. 'It's not your fault, Jimmy.'

He sighed. 'So I've heard. But it doesn't change the fact that if it wasn't for me, this wouldn't have happened.'

Vicky walked up behind him. 'I'm not saying what happened wasn't awful, but at the end of the day, she's unhurt and she's going to be okay. We can't control everything. She could have been working for Kelli or Cole and the same thing might have happened.'

James sighed. 'I know, but it doesn't make it any easier.'

'She's right, you know.' Brett came around the corner. 'You can't blame yourself for everything.'

'My head agrees, but my heart doesn't.'

Brett slapped him on the back. 'Get some rest. We'll start again in the morning.'

'Okay, okay.'

He checked the horses one more time before locking up and heading up to the house. He thought about throwing a frozen pizza in the oven but decided he just wanted to sleep.

He made sure the door was locked before going to bed.

Chapter Thirteen

Kelli Holmes was relieved to get a call from James' groom Vicky letting her know Caitlyn had been found and was now safely at home. She'd arrived with Max about 11 am, only to find James' trailer parked askew in the drive, Lacklustre standing half-saddled in his stall and Vicky and Brett looking somewhat shell-shocked as they went about doing chores. She'd reluctantly left Max in their care, not wanting to add to their burdens, but they insisted. She'd then had to leave for the airport, glad for the busy roads giving her something else to think about. That poor girl; poor Jimmy. This situation with this gang was getting very serious. How long would it be before they started killing people to reach their objectives? She shook her head and returned the phone to the charging cradle. Thank God it ended okay. But where did it leave them now?

An alarm went off, and she was immediately up and into her study. It was only a deer, setting off the motion sensor. She put a hand over her heart, trying to still the racing.

She made some two-minute noodles and settled in front of the TV. There was nothing about the abduction anywhere in the news; at least they'd managed to keep it under wraps.

There was another blip from the motion sensor. Wearily she launched to her feet and padded into the study. This time, the picture on the monitor made her stop cold.

Two figures were walking slowly up her driveway. She waited, wondering if they were coming to her door, even if it was eight o'clock at night. They didn't. One approached the camera and covered it.

She stood completely still for two seconds before launching into action. She switched to the second camera, hidden above the main door to the barn. She gasped; they were trying to get in.

She dialled 999. The operator told her someone was on the way. He also cautioned her to stay indoors and not approach the perpetrators, but she wasn't sure she could. Those were her horses in there.

She watched the camera, her fingers tightening and loosening around the door handle. She wasn't about to just let them waltz in there and kill one of her horses, but since they had resorted to kidnapping, they wouldn't hesitate to get her out of their way.

She wished she'd bought a pistol when she had been thinking about it a couple of years ago. At least then she'd have a point in her favour. She saw red and blue lights reflecting off the barn, and heaved a sigh of relief.

She ran to the front door and down to where the cruiser had stopped, directly in front of the open barn door.

'This is your barn?' One of the cops barked.

She nodded, squinting against the flashing red and blue. 'A couple of guys have just broken in.'

The cops walked right in, the first one yelling, 'Police! Freeze!' Kelli tried to follow them in and see what was happening, but one of the officers held up an arm to block her.

She hung back and waited, feeling very small in the eerie illumination.

'Are you all right, Miss?'

She wiped the back of her hand across her cheek. 'Yes, I'm fine. What's wrong?'

'There's no one in the barn, Ma'am. It looks as though they have broken a window at the far end of the building to escape. Two of our team are searching the paddocks now.'

Kelli held in a swear word. 'Are my horses okay?'

'Seem to be, Ma'am. But you may want to get them checked just in case.'

She nodded. She hated calling her vet out this late, but she had to make sure. 'Is it okay if I go up to the house to make a call, then?'

The cop nodded. 'Just let one of us go with you to make sure it's secure.'

Kelli called her local vet and explained the situation. He promised he'd come right over.

She set the phone back down in its cradle. 'You into eventing, then? I don't usually get recognised unless I'm in one of the big event cities.'

Lisa nodded. 'Loved it since I was a kid. My dad rode as a hobby.'

Kelli nodded. Her phone rang, and she excused herself. 'This is Kelli.'

'Kell, hi, just wanted to tell you Max is doing fine. He's eating and settled in fine.'

She sighed. 'Thanks.'

She could almost hear James frown. 'You okay?'

She sighed again. 'Uh...had a break-in tonight.'

'A break-in? What happened? Is everything all right?'

She sighed again, inaudibly. 'Yeah. I don't think they got to the horses before the police arrived.'

'Are you okay? Do you want me to come over?'

She managed a smile at that. Ever the big brother. 'No, I'm fine. The cops are checking where they've gone. They got out the back. Smashed a window.'

'I'm sorry, Kell. Are you sure you're okay there?'

'Yeah, I'm fine. The cops are securing everything.'

'Okay. This is them again?'

She let out a long breath. 'I don't see what else it would be. Too much of a coincidence.' She saw another set of headlights come up the drive. 'I'd better go; the vet's here to check the horses over. Stay safe up there, okay?'

'Yeah. Heck, this is starting to feel like a warzone, and we're the only ones who know it exists.'

She met the vet outside, and they were allowed in to look at the horses. To her relief, they all seemed to be fine.

The cops tested the pane of the smashed window for any fibres or prints before taping it up. 'You have insurance?' One of them asked.

She nodded.

'Just hold off getting it repaired until we can come back and look at it in daylight tomorrow. This should suffice in the time being.' He turned back to face her. 'You said they covered a camera?'

'Yeah, as soon as they arrived.' She indicated the concealed lens.

The cop pulled down some kind of beanie. 'It'll be just about impossible to get anything out of this, but we'll do what we can.'

'We'll be back in the morning to see if we can find anything else. Call us if there's anything else, all right?' The lead cop handed her his card.

'Inspector, I think this may be connected to some other crimes closer to Bristol. Could you please get a message to Inspector Willbrook?'

She watched the cruisers reversing onto the street and trudged wearily up to the house, locking the door behind her. She was grateful the authorities had arrived before any of her horses had been harmed. But she was so tired of the constant fear. No matter how careful they were, they couldn't prevent - or preempt - everything.

She didn't sleep well that night. Every little country sound that she'd usually never notice made her toss and turn. She gave up about 4am and decided to get an early start to the day's workouts.

Mounted on Kaleido, she rode towards the hillside track. Something about the cool, dark morning, with light just kissing the eastern horizon, was calming. She posted in time to Kaleido's even grunts as they scaled the incline. She patted his neck as she turned him around, pausing to survey her little block of land. She only hoped it, and she, would come through this rocky path unscathed.

Kaleido was in good form, and she wanted to take him straight to Luhmuhlen in five weeks. She thought she might save Max for Burghley, giving him time for his tendon to heal. She was loosely planning to take her new horse down to Adelaide in October.

She'd thought of a name for him at the top of the hill: New Morning. It would remind her of the hope present in the crisp blackness of a new day.

She cooled Kaleido down, checking him carefully to make sure he had no after-effects from the hard track at Badminton. He seemed fine.

After riding New Morning, she went up for breakfast before hitting the gym. She cracked a couple of eggs into the skillet and watched the news as she buttered her toast. A reporter stood in front of the Badminton cross-country course, saying something about a hint as to James Blackman's top horse's 'inexplicable absence' from the event.

'Sky News understands a threat to the safety of Blackman's horse Coalbridge may have been the reason behind the horse's absence. Coalbridge is one of the most successful horses of the last decade and has already won two Badmintons. Sources say blackmail may have been the reason why the horse was not entered, rather than injury or illness.'

Kelli groaned inwardly. She spooned her scrambled eggs onto her toast and texted James. 'Seen the news? They're talking about blackmail being why Coalie wasn't at Badminton. Just so you know.'

She watched the football updates with mild interest until her phone beeped again. *Oh great :-/. Thx for the heads up. How're you?*

'Okay. The cops are coming back soon to look at things in the daylight. Don't know much yet.'

Hang in there, Kell.

She smiled. 'Sure. You too.'

She finished her breakfast, flicked off the TV and went to find her gym gear. She pulled on her shoes and grabbed her car keys, but the two police cruisers stopping in her driveway halted her.

She straightened up the entryway, not out of politeness as much as nerves. She watched the officers approach the front door through the louvre glass to the side of the doorframe, feeling like a spy.

She opened it at their knock. 'Good morning, Miss Holmes.'

'Morning.' She unconsciously tightened her workout jacket around herself. 'Come in.'

'We'd like to look at the stable again,' the inspector began, 'but we'd like to go over a few things first. We think we have one possible suspect for last night, based on a partial print.'

She nodded. 'Who?'

'Are you acquainted with Clive Ressler?'

She wondered if her face looked as cold as it suddenly felt. She cleared her throat. 'I know of him, yes.'

'Are you friends?'

She shook her head. 'No. I saw him around; not much more than that.'

'Where did you see him?'

She wondered why they were making her spell it out when they knew clearly who Ressler was. 'He was a groom for a friend of mine, but he's since moved on.'

'James Blackman?'

'Yes.'

'How well do you know Mr Blackman, Miss Holmes?'

She cleared her throat. 'We're friends.'

'Good friends?'

She straightened her spine. 'I'd say so, yes.'

'Are you and Mr Blackman romantically involved?'

'No.'

'Has he been acting differently lately? Have you noticed anything suspicious?'

'No, nothing like that.'

The inspector nodded somberly as he took notes. 'I take it you are aware of a similar attack on James Blackman's property in Long Ashton?'

'Yes.'

'We have reason to believe the two incidents are connected. Ressler is also under suspicion for that incident.'

She nodded. 'Yes, I am aware of some of the background.'

'We have a few leads but there is nothing concrete yet. We have been in contact with our colleagues in Bristol. Is it all right to have another look at your barn?'

'Sure.'

Kelli dropped to the floor to do a few warm-ups while she waited for the cops to finish. She wondered if James knew the cops were asking questions about him. Although, with the owners being involved, she guessed no one was exempt from suspicion.

They came back to her door and said they would be in touch, and if she saw or thought of anything else, to contact them immediately. She thanked them and watched them go.

She double-checked the barn was locked but then decided not to go out leaving only tape over the broken window. She was no handyman but she could nail a board up. That would do until she could call the glass company.

But right now, she needed a gym workout, mentally even more than physically.

Amy Williams held Chester to a trot as they warmed up for the show-jumping. It was a trick she had learned from a Pony Club instructor who had ridden for New Zealand. If the horse learned to pick up his feet to clear the obstacle at a trot, it would be a piece of cake at a canter.

After another clear cross-country round, they were placed in the top three of the Southgate three-star. It was one of the more quality events in the area, so she was thrilled with Chester. Days like these made her believe that Badminton was more than a pipe dream.

After he'd negotiated the poles at a trot, she let him canter for the final warm-up. He kept picking his feet up and cleared them with ease. There were only three points between the leader and Chester in third place. Any fences down would cost them their position.

They were clear when she aimed him for the final fence, a wide oxer. She felt a back hoof tap the rail and held her breath, but gravity ignored them and it stayed put. They were clear - and at least third.

She patted Chester's grey neck as they cantered out of the arena. He had been improving in leaps and bounds over the past several weeks. She dismounted and led him around the area, to cool him down while still keeping an eye on the ring. The second-placed horse dropped a foot in the water.

'Good boy, Ches. You're second,' she spoke to him as they walked around. He nodded as if he understood every word.

She watched as the lead horse, a flashy bay, entered the ring. She'd seen the young rider around at several events, and he was pretty good.

He was riding a well-bred horse, but the bay appeared quite edgy as they approached the first fence. He jumped - and the rail clattered to the ground as he hit it with both front shins. Amy tried not to be too outwardly delighted, but she couldn't completely hide her grin. Chester had won!

The rest of the round was clear, but the damage was done. Amy remounted to receive her ribbon. The steward clipped it to Chester's bridle and congratulated her. Chester pranced out of the ring as if he was wearing a World Championship rosette. She praised him the whole way back to the trailer and received a few well wishes along the way. She dismounted and stripped off the saddle before giving him a couple of horse cookies. He nickered happily as he munched the treat. She chuckled to herself; he was probably performing solely for the cookies.

She loaded the tack and then led Chester up the ramp. She slid into the cab and turned the key before briefly checking her phone. There was a missed call from a number she didn't recognise, but it was a New Zealand prefix. She knew Mickey would text as well if it was urgent, and she didn't feel like talking about her parents' problems right now.

She got on the road, singing to the radio and enjoying the wind in her hair. She'd finally won something. Maybe this adventure would turn out to be more than just chasing rainbows after all. It was a short drive back to Enfield, and she pulled into the stable yard just as the sun was setting. After leading Chester to his stall, she proudly stuck the ribbon on the 'achievement board' in the aisle. They pinned all the horses' awards up here, from the smallest Pony Club ribbon to a replica of the Burghley trophy that one of owner Karen Brown's horses had won with the Kiwi rider Kelli Holmes.

'You'll get up there one day.' Amy turned to see the manager standing there, indicating her Burghley cup.

Amy grinned. 'I hope so.' She studied the ribbon. 'At least I feel like I'm moving in the right direction now.'

Karen smiled. 'It's a long journey and hard work. So enjoy all the good days.'

Amy turned back to the stalls and checked Chester was all bedded down before heading for her car. As she turned the key, her phone rang, and she hauled her handbag off the passenger side floor.

It was the same New Zealand number.

She frowned but decided to answer it. 'Hi, this is Amy.'

'Amy?' The voice on the other end sounded strained, almost in tears, if she had to guess. 'Amy Williams?'

'Speaking.'

'Amy, it's Anne Scott. Damien Scott's mother.'

'Hi.' A sudden, terrible fear crawled between her shoulder blades.

'Damien gave us your number, so we could get in touch with you if something happened.'

She clenched her fists around the steering wheel. 'Is everything okay?'

'Not really. No, it's not.'

Amy tried to remember to breathe.

'I got a call from Damien's commanding officer this morning. He was in-country, he and his men, dealing with a few spots of trouble. They didn't think it was a very dangerous operation. But one of the rebels took out a grenade. They didn't see it coming. They couldn't get out of the way in time.'

Amy closed her eyes, fighting tears. *Don't say he's dead. He can't be dead!*

'Damien's still alive, but he is in critical condition. They flew him to a hospital somewhere in Egypt, I think. He had shrapnel in his abdomen. He'd lost a lot of blood.'

Amy wondered if this was what a broken heart felt like. Her eyes were unseeing but dry. All she could see was Damien...her best friend...that 'hang loose' grin, the easy laugh, the crinkling blue eyes…

...Closed, in a white face, barely breathing, a team of doctors scrambling, blood, shiny metal instruments.

No!

She'd seen that picture before, in a nightmare the week he left.

'Amy?'

The sound in her ear brought her back to reality. 'I'm here, Mrs Scott. I'm sorry...so sorry to hear that.'

'Well, from what I understand, you and Damien were very close. I'm sure this is a shock for you, too. We asked about going over to see him but no civilians are allowed in that military hospital. Too dangerous. Once they have him stabilised, they'll move him to a hospital in Germany.'

The information swirled around her head. It was like a merry-go-round she couldn't quite catch up to. 'But what if…?'

She realised too late she should not have voiced that fear, but Mrs Scott seemed to be on the same wavelength. 'I know, dear. The commander is going to see what can be done to get us in, but he can't make any promises.'

Amy nodded numbly. 'So what happens now?'

'We will tell you if we hear anything more -'

'Oh, no, you don't have to do that. I'm not family or anything -'

'Well, dear, from what I understand you and Damien were headed that way, so that makes you a part of this too. Please call if you need anything.'

'Okay. Thank you,' she said, trying and failing to keep the croak out of her voice.

The call clicked off, and Amy sat back against her seat. She was in shock; she didn't know what to think, how to react. She was vaguely aware of the crack spreading through her heart.

Oh, Damien. Why did I not tell you sooner?

She could see his blue eyes, crinkled in a grin, often teasing, sometimes tender. He'd always been good to her, a close friend even before they started officially dating. That didn't last long as they split to opposite ends of the earth, but she couldn't deny seeing him again had changed her mind, made her aware of how much he still meant to her.

By the time she got home, her cheeks were wet. She called Mickey, but it went to voicemail. She threw her phone across the room and sobbed into the bedspread.

She didn't know how much time had passed before she heard her mobile buzzing. She scraped herself up and crossed the room. Seeing it was Mickey's number, she answered it.

'Crikey, girl, what's the matter? You sound terrible.'

She sank back onto the bed. 'Damien's been injured,' she managed.

She heard Mickey gasp. 'Oh, my word. How bad?'

'It's bad, Mickey. They don't...don't know if he's going to make it.' The tears came back.

'Oh, honey.'

'I don't know what's wrong with me, Mickey,' she sobbed. 'I didn't even have a relationship with the guy and...' Her voice trailed off.

'Well, he was your friend,' Mickey offered gently. 'You cared for him. It's natural.'

Amy wiped her eyes. 'And what if this is it, Mickey? What if he dies and this is how it ends?'

There was a pause as if her friend was carefully weighing her words. 'You knew you cared for each other. And he'll be happy to have known that.'

Amy took a deep breath which caught on a hiccup. 'But he doesn't know I loved him.'

'Oh, I think he would have had an idea, even if you didn't feel sure enough to say the words.'

'What was wrong with me, Mickey? Why did I keep pushing him away?'

'You had your reasons. And I don't blame you for them, and neither would he. Besides, if you weren't 100 per cent sure, you were right to not say it. There is a difference between liking someone a lot and loving them, especially when we're talking about marriage.'

Amy cleared her throat. 'I did love him, back when we were together. But things had changed.'

'Exactly.'

'But if it was real love, it wouldn't have, would it?'

'Yes and no. You probably still loved him, but whether a marriage was the right thing was another matter.'

Amy laughed humourlessly. 'I can't believe we're sitting here talking about the ins and outs of love when Damien's fighting for his life in the middle of a war zone.'

'Well, sometimes talking about what you're thinking helps. Even if it's slightly off-topic.'

'His mother said she was trying to find out if they could go and see him. I don't even know if I want to even if I could. I don't have the right to.'

'Ames, he would want you to.'

She took another deep breath. 'Thanks, Mickey.'

'Anytime, honeypie. Have you eaten dinner?'

'Not hungry.'

'You need to eat. Grief is exhausting.'

'Yes, Florence Nightingale.'

'Funny. Get some rest, Amy, but call me if you need it.'

'Thank you, Michaela. You know I do appreciate you.'

'Right back at ya.'

Amy hung up the phone and let it drop on the bedspread. She decided she did need a decent meal, so she got up and made stir fry. Then she went to bed, dreaming of happier times when she and Damien were inseparable.

Chapter Fourteen

Kelli Holmes hadn't heard from the police for a few days, and she was starting to get irritable. She hated this waiting in limbo, unsure of making her next move. Unsure of who might be the next unlucky person to have their horse drop dead. Luhmuhlen was a week away, and she was deciding what to do. Having just run Kaleido at Badminton, she usually didn't take her top horse to Luhmuhlen a month later, but he had been sprightly and she thought he was probably good to go for another event. Especially since Burghley, the second-biggest event of the Classics, was not until mid-September this year. As she warmed up Maximus for a four-star in Bramham, she tried not to think about the other thing making her irritable. That being her friendship-maybe-something-more with Jadin. He hadn't talked any more about them, and she was torn between wanting him to move things along -- beyond a vague future date -- and not wanting to discuss it at all.

What was she afraid of, she wondered. She had always liked Jadin, and the more time they spent together and the closer they got as friends, the more she started wondering what it would be like if they took it further. She knew that some more-than-platonic feelings had developed over the last year. Jadin had been hesitant – not wanting to burden her with the results of his injury. To her it didn't matter – he was still the same man. And with time, he may well be able to walk again. The muscles were damaged and weak – not broken.

She patted Maximus' neck and vaulted to the ground. *You teenager, Kelli, thinking about your love life while you're trying to get ready for cross-country.* She shook her head and walked Maximus around to keep his muscles warm while she waited for the start.

The last horse in front of them cantered off, and she boosted herself into the saddle. Maximus danced in place, making her smile. Nearly sixteen but still with plenty of enthusiasm. She was going to hate it when she had to retire him.

The starter signalled them and they were off. She rode above his withers, letting him dictate the pace for the first few hundred metres. He was a pro and knew how to handle himself, especially on this fairly mild four-star track.

He was jumping well but his grunts were getting heavier as they got towards the end. She eased back on the reins, knowing they were well inside the time. He cleared the final hurdle and cantered towards the finish line.

Until he suddenly fell.

It all seemed to be over before she could blink. She tried to hold his head up while not being crushed under him as he went down on his right side. She vaulted free just as he landed and lay there unmoving.

She scrambled to her feet and knelt beside him. 'Max, Max, come on, boy.' She put a hand under his jaw. His pulse was there but he looked like he was frozen, eyes closed and still as a stone. She fought the tears rising in her throat. 'Come on, Max, you're okay. Wake up, Max.'

The horse ambulance pulled up alongside and the vet roughly pulled her away. What was wrong with him? His heart was beating – but he looked so lifeless it was terrifying.

Someone put a hand on her shoulder, and she vaguely registered that Kyle had appeared at her side. She pushed him away impatiently and tried to get closer to Max. He was starting to tremble, and the vet had strapped some sort of cable to his neck. 'What's happening? What's going on?'

The vet shook his head at her to shut her up and she felt Kyle take her arm. 'Let them work,' he said as he steered her back a few metres.

She wanted to yank her arm free but she knew he was only trying to help. She took a deep breath and glanced at him. 'Sorry.'

'It's okay.'

'Do you know what's wrong with him?' She was trying not to sound frantic.

'I don't know, but it looks like it might be a seizure.'

She turned wide eyes to his face. 'Is that fatal?'

He hesitated. 'I don't know.'

'Tell me.'

'In about half of cases, they can be. But it depends on all sorts of things and what sort of seizure it is.'

Kelli put her face in her hands. As the vets' movements slowed, she edged forward, trying to tell how he was. His blinking eyes sent a wave of relief through her heart.

'Is he okay?'

The vet stood up and turned to face her. 'Miss Holmes, it looks like your horse has suffered a seizure. Does he have a history of epilepsy?'

Kelli shook her head. 'No.'

'What about any other neurological disorders?'

'No, he's always been fine. Is he okay?'

The vet took a breath. 'We have to get him back to the hospital and run tests, but the fact that the seizure stopped is a good sign.'

Kelli nodded numbly. 'Can I come with him?'

'If you like.' The vet motioned her back so they could try and get Max to his feet and into the rig. He looked unsteady, but he stood.

The ambulance parked a few metres away and they guided the thoroughbred to the ramp. Kelli took a deep breath and climbed into the back of the rig, making her way to Maximus' head. He looked droopy but he was awake and looking at her. She ducked under his lead rope and rubbed his nose. 'You all right, old lad?'

He blinked at her, and she continued to stroke him as the assistant climbed in and checked his vitals. 'He's looking good.' The young woman looked at her with a reassuring smile.

'Hope so.' Kelli continued to pat his neck, resting her head against his shoulder. He was her baby; the first mount she had trained from the ground up. He was sweet-natured and obedient but could jump a massive cross-country course with the best of them.

Had he run his last track?

Her cell phone buzzed in her jodhpurs, and she plucked it out. A message from Henrique, telling her he'd get New Morning ready in case she was back in time.

Kelli sighed. His run was still a couple of hours away and she supposed she'd better make an effort to get back. New Morning was developing at the speed of light and she needed to continue the momentum.

Maximus unloaded at the clinic without a hitch and Kelli stayed nearby as they ran tests. Whatever the outcome for his life, she knew he would probably never compete again. She blinked back the sting at the back of her eyes.

The vet came out to talk to her, pulling off his rubber gloves. 'Well, he seems to be okay for now, but we've noticed some neurological anomalies in his brain. Some of the pulses are erratic. It looks like a form of epilepsy.'

'Epilepsy?' She blinked again. 'How bad is he?'

'He's settled for now, but these things are unpredictable. He could have another seizure at any time, more or less.'

'So now what?' Her voice came out more like a croak.

The vet sighed. 'I don't think you should compete him again. Even riding around the dressage arena would be a risk to both of you. If it gets worse, you may need to consider having him put down.'

She bit her lip hard. 'So I just need to put him out to pasture?'

'It's probably the best option, Miss Holmes. I'm sorry.'

She nodded brusquely. 'Can I see him now?'

The vet nodded. 'We're going to keep him overnight for some more observation, but you should be able to collect him in the morning.'

Kelli walked stiffly into the small stall. Maximus was quietly munching a mouthful of hay. She ran her palm along his neck and down over his shoulder. Max turned to look at her with his big dark eyes.

'Oh, Max.' Her voice broke. She sniffed and put her arms around his neck, hugging him. He snuffled in her ear. No, he wasn't just an animal; he was her friend.

'Well done, Jadin.' The grin on his therapist's face told Jadin what he already knew. The muscles were slowly getting stronger. He hadn't been able to put all his weight on them, but he'd been able to stay upright with the help of the balance beam.

He couldn't wipe the grin off his face as he settled back into his room. After all this time he could finally start to believe he was getting better.

A timid knock made him look up, and he sobered somewhat when he saw the blonde on the other side of the door. He cleared his throat. 'Hey, Kelli, come on in.'

She did, and he frowned when he noticed her red eyes. 'Hey, what's wrong?'

She sank into a chair opposite him. 'Maximus has epilepsy.'

He felt his eyes go wide. 'What?'

'We were less than 50 metres from the finish line at Brabham yesterday and he just dropped like a stone and started seizing.'

She cleared her throat. 'The vets ran tests and said he has epilepsy and there's no way to cure it. Just a shot to give if he seizes again. But they are saying it would be best not to ride him again because they don't know when it could happen.' Her voice broke.

'Gosh, I'm sorry. That must be rough.' He eyed her carefully.

She nodded, her eyes tearing up again. 'I keep telling myself he's just a horse, but Jade, he's my horse. My baby.' She hid her face in her hands.

'Hey, we get attached to our horses. It's what makes us good at what we do.'

She nodded but gave no reply. Her shoulders trembled.

Jadin bit his lip. He opened his mouth, but nothing came out. He cleared his throat. 'C'mere, Kell.'

She glanced up, her big eyes asking a question.

He grinned nervously. 'I can't come over and give you a hug, so you're going to have to come to me.'

He saw her swallow before she slowly stood. He scooted over and patted the spot next to him on the couch. She edged her way closer and sat down.

He grinned again. 'Hey, I won't bite.'

A faint pink tinted her cheeks before she moved over and Jadin put an arm around her, rubbing her shoulder. 'It'll be okay, Kell.'

He felt her shoulders go up and down in a heavy sigh as she leaned back against the couch. 'I hope so.'

He kept his arm in place. 'I'm not saying to just get on with it. But at least your horse is still here, and he was going to retire in a while anyway, most likely.'

She sighed again, a wisp of hair lifting on the exhalation.

'Yeah, I know. It was just such a horrible shock.'

'I can imagine.' He thought back to Lexington 10 years ago and James' horse Callista just collapsing under him. 'But he'll be okay. Not perfect, but okay.'

She nodded again, her head stopping against his shoulder. He bit his lip at how comfortable this was, just the two of them sitting here. Two friends...oh, who was he kidding?

He glanced down at her, surprised to see her eyes closed. And rather stunned to see how close her face was to his.

And to realise how much he wanted to kiss her.

He cleared his throat and went for the brotherly peck on the side of her hair. 'Hang in there.'

She sighed and straightened up. 'It just shook me up, you know?' She leaned her elbows on her knees and twisted to look at him. 'How're you?'

'Making progress. Today was good. It feels like I can start to see the light at the end of the tunnel now.'

She smiled at him. 'I'm glad.'

He returned her smile. Something seemed to tingle in his heart region. 'So, any updates on this syndicate?'

Kelli shook her head. 'James has been trying not to fight against the cops' handling of it. There's still a lot they won't tell us. They got close to someone after Caitlyn was abducted, but not close enough.'

'Did I hear my name?' James stuck his head around the door with a grin. Jadin caught the quirk of an eyebrow before his friend straightened his expression and entered the room. 'Hey, guys.'

'Hey, yourself.' Jadin leaned back. 'Yeah, we were just gossiping behind your back, as usual.'

'Nice to hear.' James stared at Kelli. 'You alright, Kell?'

She nodded with a sign. 'Maximus fell under me yesterday. Vets say he has epilepsy.'

'Heck, I'm sorry,' James said. 'Is he okay?'

She nodded. 'More or less. But they're telling me not to ride him again.'

'Oh, Kell,' James said softly. 'What are you going to do?'

'I don't see what I can do other than give him his retirement.'
She ran a hand through her hair. 'It wouldn't have been long till
I put him out to pasture anyway. It just came as such a shock.'
She straightened up and put a hand on Jadin's arm. 'I'd better
split. See you guys later.'
'See ya.' Jadin watched her leave, pretending not to notice
James' stare.
'So, you want to tell me what I just walked in on?'
Jadin rolled his eyes. 'Nothing.'
'I'm not blind.'
'She was upset; I hugged her. Nothing you haven't done a
dozen times.'
James quirked an eyebrow. 'If you say so.'
That deserved another eye roll. 'We were hardly making out in
the backseat.'
James put his hands up in surrender. 'I just meant you looked
pretty cosy. I'm not saying it's scandalous.'
Jadin looked him in the eye. Underneath the banter, he was
still his best friend. 'I wanted to kiss her.'
'Why didn't you?'
'Well, it was just a friendly hug. Plus she was upset. I didn't
want to take advantage of that.'
James smiled at him. 'You're a good man, Jadin Steele.'
'Plus this thing between us is kind of undefined.'
'Well, perhaps you need to define it.'
Jadin shrugged heavily. 'She doesn't need a cripple for a
partner, Jimmy.'
'Jade, we've been over this.' James cocked his head and studied
him. Jadin met his stare.
'You two have discussed a relationship, right?'
'Kind of...we said we'd go out sometime, but we haven't yet,
obviously.'
James crossed his arms and raised an eyebrow.

'Look, I don't know how to proceed. I don't know if I can be good enough for her.'

'Well, then you're not going to get anywhere. Kelli'll wait for you to make a move.'

Jadin sighed. 'I know.'

'How do you feel about her?' The question was quiet.

Jadin took a deep breath. 'I'm falling in love with her.'

James grinned. 'Then tell her.'

Jadin exhaled slowly. 'And if she doesn't feel the same?'

'Part of the risk, I'm afraid. But I'm pretty sure she does. You guys have talked about this.'

'Not in any detail.'

'Quit making excuses, Jadin. Take a chance to be happy.'

Amy fumbled in the dark for the phone. 'Ow.' She pillowed her hand on her duvet and scooped it up with the other. 'Hi, this is Amy.'

'Amy, dear, it's Anne Scott.' There was a tremble in her voice. She sat upright. 'Hello. How are things?'

'They've decided to move Damien to Germany. He's not as stable as they would like but the tensions are rising and they had to get him out.'

Amy sank back against her pillows, her heart pounding against her ribcage. 'What does this mean?'

'We should be able to go and visit him. He's still critical, but they thought it was better to get him out.' There was a soft noise as if her breath shuddered. 'I thought you might like to come and see him.'

She swallowed against the lump in her throat. 'That's very kind of you but I'm not sure that....well, I mean we weren't dating or anything.'

'Amy, dear, you have been the only girl in his life for some time now. Official or not, you're the one he'd want to see.'

Amy took a deep breath. She still felt like it wasn't her place, but she also knew that this whole tragedy had made her realise how she felt about this man who had never completely left her life.

'Okay, I'd like that,' she admitted quietly. 'I'll book some flights in the morning. Where is he going to be?'

'On a US military base in Ansbach. We're getting on a plane tonight. Tell us when you arrive and we will pick you up.'

'I don't want you to go to any trouble.'

'Amy, dear, you have been part of Damien's life for a long time, and it is not any trouble. It gives us something else to think about.'

'Okay. Thank you. I'll let you know.' She took a breath as they hung up, collapsing back onto the bed.

She could see him behind her eyelids, years ago, sitting across the table from her, fiddling with his Big Mac lettuce. Telling her he'd been accepted into the Navy.

She could still feel the annoyance, which was unfair, really, given that she'd always known it was his dream. 'And when were you going to tell me you'd applied?'

'I was. But I knew you'd react like this.'

'Can you blame me?'

'Amy, this doesn't have to change anything.'

'You going halfway around the world? No, of course not.'

'Don't be sarcastic.'

She took a deep breath. 'Sorry.' She took another bite of her cheeseburger to gather her thoughts. 'I can't say I'm happy. I am happy for you because this is what you've always wanted. But I'm also scared for you, and not happy about what this means for me. Although I know that is selfish of me.'

Damien took her hand, those ocean eyes saying more than any words. 'This doesn't have to change things - not forever. I'll do my training, then come back. And if I get posted overseas, you can come with me. We can make this work.'

She shook her head. 'I don't see how it can.'

'Amy, you've been the only one for me for a long time. This only needs to be a temporary separation; not a permanent break-up. We can make it work.'

She hung her head. 'I still want to try my luck in eventing in England.'

'Who says I won't be based there?' Damien took a breath. 'If you care for someone as much and as long as we have, you make it work.'

She looked into his eyes. 'And if you can't?'

He sighed. 'It seems to me you're not very committed to this.'

'I don't know what to think. The laws of engagement have changed.'

'So you're just going to walk away?'

'No. But I'm not committing myself to the unknown, either.'

She took her hand away. 'I think we need to take a break and work out what we want.'

He stared at her, incredulous. 'You're breaking up with me?'

'Yes. I can't commit to something that's up in the air.'

He stared at her. 'Not even someone who is committed to you?'

'No. I'm sorry.'

She blinked and stared at the ceiling. It hadn't exactly ended ugly, but it hadn't been sunshine and rainbows, either.

And then he'd reappeared - out of the blue, turning up at her work, and asked her whether they could be friends again and whether they could, in the future, be something more.

And she'd shot him down.

Tears trickled into her ears. Now Damien was fighting for his life in a German hospital.

The least she could do was be there.

Kelli Holmes leaned on the stall door, watching Maximus eat. He was always cheerful when food was around, so he was quite relaxed about it all. Kelli sighed.

Her pocket buzzed, and she pulled out her Motorola. It was Jadin.

Hey Kell. Just checking that you're doing ok. J.

She smiled and typed back. 'Yeah, I'm good. Max is happily eating so that's the main thing.'

Good. Lemme know if you need a listening ear.

She smiled again. She, Jadin and Jimmy had been something like the three musketeers for several years now. She was lucky to have them in a world that often became a tangle of getting from one competition to the next, trying to win as many points and as much money as you could. Around and around and around.

She had no doubts about the path she'd taken. It was where she wanted to be. But it wasn't everything she'd ever wanted. Someday, she'd like to find a good man to make a life with - and maybe some pony-mad kiddies somewhere along the way.

That was why she had ultimately broken up with her boyfriend, Troy. He'd proposed and she'd taken the ring - but as soon as she started thinking of a wedding, she just couldn't find the blushing bride in her heart. She was a career woman - but she still had dreams of princesses and knights and happily-ever-after.

With Jadin?

He was interested. They'd been friends for a long time. There was something else there.

But was it going to go anywhere?

Jadin was fighting to walk again and didn't want to burden her. But she didn't care. If he loved her, that was all she needed.

But wow, love was a big thing - and it wasn't something she would usually associate with 'her buddy' Jadin. But the funny thing was, she was more comfortable with him than she'd ever been with Troy.

She took a deep breath and pushed off the stall door. Why couldn't life and love just work themselves out?

This was the longest flight Amy had been on since her haul to the motherland. She wasn't a huge fan of flying but she wasn't about to drive to Germany. She crossed and uncrossed her fingers. She had to see him - had to make sure he was okay.

It had been a long time since she'd seen Damien's mum and dad. But they hadn't appeared to have aged. Worry lines were evident, but they still seemed to be calm.

'Amy, dear.' Mrs Scott opened her arms as she stumbled into the terminal. Amy considered briefly that Damien mustn't have told them details of the breakup - otherwise, she wouldn't be treating her this nicely.

She tried to engage in the conversation around her as they drove towards the hospital. But her brain was stuck on a loop: *Please let him be all right. Please let him be all right.*

The taxi let them out and Mr Scott took his wife's arm as the sad little group made their way towards the main doors. Amy followed along, not paying attention until they arrived outside a ward room.

'You go - I'll come in soon.' She retreated to a nearby chair, letting them have time with their son.

Please let him be all right.

She stared at her knees, struggling to fathom where she found herself. She wasn't sure how much time had passed, but at the shuffle of feet, she looked up. Their faces were sad, but not devastated, she registered fleetingly. 'How is he?'

Mrs Scott dabbed at her eyes. 'The doctors say he's hanging in there. He's got some broken bones and a concussion. He hasn't --' her voice quivered -- 'he hasn't woken up yet.'

Amy nodded. 'I can wait out here if you'd rather--'

'No, no. He'd want to see you. He'd be happy to know you're here.'

She slowly rose and made her way into the room. Not long ago, she'd told Damien that they'd have to go their separate ways, and yet here she was, dashing across Europe to his bedside.

The man in the bed looked like Damien, but he was very still. Not like the Damien she knew, who always tackled life with both hands.

There were bruises on his face and a thin streak of blood in his hair, but otherwise, he didn't look too beaten up. She sank slowly into the chair beside his bed. She wanted to take his hand, but she didn't think she had the right. His parents may think they were still bordering on boyfriend and girlfriend, but she didn't have the right to act like one.

Apart from the fact that the thought of him dying was enough to break her heart.

Tentatively, she touched his hand. 'I'm sorry, Damien,' she said softly. 'I know I probably shouldn't be here, but I had to know you were okay.' She ran her thumb over his knuckles, which were sporting a few scrapes.

'I wasn't sure how I felt, before, when you surprised me,' she went on softly. 'I didn't realise how much I still felt for you until there was a chance I'd lost you for good.' She cleared her throat, wondering if he could hear any of this. 'Anyway, I just wanted you to know I do care. Very much.' She pressed a kiss to her fingers and laid them on his hand before slowly rising. His mother wanted to stay, so his father also decided to wait around the hospital. Amy took a cab back to the nearest hotel she could find and collapsed on the bed, suddenly realising she was alone in a foreign country.

She dug her phone out of her bag, wondering what the extra cost would be using her phone across the channel. She decided to turn on roaming and hope for the best.

'Hello.'

'Hi, Mickey.'

'Where are you? You don't sound good. Are you at the hospital? How is he?'

'I'm now lying on my bed in a hotel with a name I can't pronounce, thinking about what a hypocrite I am to be impersonating the sad girlfriend.'

'What? What brought this on? You're not impersonating anything.'

'I shouldn't be here. This is for his family to deal with.'

'Did they say something?'

'No. But that's just it, Mick. They think he'd want me here as if some connection qualifies me. But there isn't - I sent him away.'

'Amy, listen to me. You were honest with him. You cared for him, but you didn't know if there was more there. Correct? So if you didn't care, sure you should not have bothered to go. But you do care - the two of you have a special connection, regardless of whether or not you're officially a couple.'

'But -'

'Let me ask you this. If this was reversed - if you were lying in a hospital bed - would you want Damien there?'

Amy's silence apparently gave her the answer.

'I thought so. So keep going back there and looking after your friend.'

Chapter Fifteen

Kelli laid her head against the wall of Jadin's hospital room, waiting for him to return from therapy. They'd gotten closer over the last few weeks. She knew he was hesitant about the next step because of his injury.

But his ability to walk, or not, didn't matter to her.

'Hey.'

She lifted her head. 'Hey, back.' She watched him as the male nurse helped him back into bed. 'How'd it go?'

Jadin grimaced. 'Okay, I guess.'

She waited until the nurse left the room, then scooted forward. 'You look terrible. How was it really?'

Jadin laid his head back and sighed. 'It was pretty tough, Kell. They made me walk as well as I could, my weight on my arms. I thought I would be further along by now, but my legs are still so weak.'

Kelli slipped her hand into his. 'You'll get there. Weak is better than non-functional.'

'True. They said I could probably go home next week.'

'That's great news, Jadin.' She couldn't help but grin.

'I'll need a wheelchair, and probably some help.' He smiled back at her. 'But I'd give a lot to get out of here.'

'I'll bet.'

'It begs the question, though…' He threaded his fingers through hers. 'What does this mean for us?'

She raised her eyebrows. 'Does it have to mean anything?'

'Well...it might.' He took a deep breath, squeezed her hand. 'Kelli - you know how I feel about you - and how I feel about my injury.'

Kelli lifted their joined hands and rested her chin on them. 'I also know that makes no difference to me, and I have told you as such. I'd also like to support your recovery at home if I can.'
'Kell, I can't ask -'
'You didn't. And I'm not inviting myself to move in together.' She grinned. 'I still have my horses. But I want to help where I can.'
Jadin lifted their hands and brushed a kiss on her knuckles. 'Well then, yes. Thank you.' He paused. 'And in a week or two - once things have settled a bit -I believe I owe you a date.'
Kelli smiled. 'Why thank you, kind senor.'

Damien tried to work out where he was. It was dark, and he was swimming or something. His head was clouded.
Something hurt. No, most things hurt.
'Hi, Damien.' He knew that voice. It was familiar, comforting.
'You're going to be okay, honey. I'm sure of it. The doctors say everything is looking good.'
Amy. She was there. A weight lifted.
She was telling him about Chester; how his mum and dad were visiting and worried about him; how the flight had been; that she was sure one of the nurses had a secret crush on him.
Damien tried to open his eyes.
'Am-y?'
He felt her brush back his hair, the way she would do when they were best friends as teens -- before the Navy, and moving to England, and trying to navigate friendship or maybe more. Before anything was complicated.
'Hi, Damien. How're you feeling? I'll go, and get your mum and dad.'
'No!' It came out more forcefully than expected. 'No. Please...stay.'

He forced his eyes open. She wore no makeup, and her dark hair was in a scruffy ponytail. Her eyes looked tired, concerned. She was beautiful, he thought.

'How're you feeling?' she asked softly again.

'Like I'm in a dungeon, trying to find my way out.' He blinked, and his vision slowly cleared. 'You're beautiful.' It was the kind of thing he would not normally say, as they danced between being friends and more, and saw her cheeks turn dusty rose.

'Thank you. You're looking a lot better than you did last night.' He felt for her hand. 'I'm glad you're here.'

Her smile was timid. 'Are you really?'

He raised his eyebrows, as much as he could under the bandages. 'Of course I am.'

'Damien - when you're better, we need to talk.'

This was it, then. The end of their connection. 'Tell me now.'

'I think -'

'Please.' If she was going to not be there from here on, he'd rather be prepared.

'Okay.' She took a breath. 'I'm sorry that I pushed you away. I realized, once I heard you'd been hurt, that the thought of losing you would break my heart. I still care very much for you.'

'But you don't love me. It's okay. I understand.'

'No, Damien -' she hesitated. 'I wasn't going to say it this way, but you need to know - I do love you. I just didn't realise before that it was more than friendship love.'

He squeezed her hand. 'Isn't that the best kind?'

The moment was interrupted by a nurse. 'Oh good, Mr Scott. You're awake.' She checked his vitals and nodded. 'Dr Henderson will be in to see you shortly.'

The doctor was also pleased and said he was well on the way to turning a corner. After a few more days in the hospital, making sure his breaks were healing, he could go home.

Damien had to grin. 'I'm afraid home is a warship right now.'
'Well, that won't do. Can you stay with someone nearby?'
'I don't know anyone, doc. Can I fly? Back to my base housing in England?'
'In a few days, as long as there are no complications.'
Damien nodded. 'Okay. Thank you.'
The doctor left, and Damien grinned up at Amy. 'Will you have dinner with me tonight?'
Amy raised an eyebrow. 'You're not allowed out of bed, mister.'
'I know. Therefore, you'll have to go down to the cafeteria and bring us back dinner.'
Amy laughed. 'Yes, dear.'

New Morning didn't like horse trucks.
Kelli rubbed the young stallion's thick mane and offered him more oats. He turned up his white nose.
He was a handsome horse, black as black except for his white muzzle, and no cross-country course was too big and no jump too scary. But getting him into a horse truck was like getting him to walk on hot coals.
Kelli sighed. 'Molasses it is, then.'
That worked, and Kaleido walked in without a hitch. She checked her watch. She had 45 minutes to get to James' ranch and pick up him and his horses. They had decided to drive to Luhmulen this time - neither New Morning nor Marksman appreciated flying.
She drove past what looked like a flash Audi on the street and parked by James' house. Sometimes the extra walk from the stables calmed the horses before they had to get into the truck. She vaulted the still-locked gate and followed the voices down towards the stables. She was just entering the main door when a sound stopped her in her tracks.

'I said, drop the cellphone! Now!'

Kelli held her breath. It sounded like heavy footsteps followed by the smack of a hand and presumably the phone hitting the ground.

'Now, as I was saying. We are not here to hurt you. We are simply here to make sure you do not take your horse Coalbridge to Burghley.'

Oh no. They must have James in there with them. She plastered herself against the wall.

'Now, if you will just let us take your horse, you can get on your way.'

'No.' James' tone was non-negotiable.

Kelli strained to hear the response as she pulled out her phone and called the police, whispering as clearly as she could. They told her to stay on the line and stay in a place of safety.

'Okay,' she said, as she pulled off her boots and crept closer. Keeping out of sight, moving soundlessly in her socks, she entered the stable from the other end. She could see two men in one of the stalls, gesticulating. She moved and saw James against the wall. She caught her breath at the glint of metal against his throat.

She racked her brain. Rocking up and trying to distract them wouldn't help anyone. She looked around, futilely trying to find inspiration.

She ducked into the tack room, looking around frantically. Her eyes stopped on James' hunting rifle.

She snatched it off the wall, grabbed the key to his safe from its hidey-hole and dug out the ammunition. With three quick clicks, it was loaded and she inched towards the stall, holding her breath.

She could hear the voices getting louder. There was a noise like a slap and a muffled curse. She stopped about two metres away from the stall door, back plastered against the stall, splinters digging into her back.

'Give us the gate code, now!' A voice snarled.

Kelli rolled away from the wall, the rifle raised against her shoulder. Her eyes took in two men, one holding James' hands behind his back, and a second, larger man holding a knife against his throat. 'Drop the knife, now!' she barked.

The larger man turned. He sized Kelli up and let out a bark of laughter. 'You think your pretty little girlfriend is going to save you?' He sneered, presumably at James.

Pretty little girlfriend will show you, Kelli thought, but she had no time to get offended. Was that the distant wail of a siren? James' eyes were telling her to run, but there was no way. 'I said drop it!' She snapped, lowering the rifle and shooting. Hay and dust scattered. Whinnies rang out from the startled horses.

'Hey, whoa, take it easy, missy,' thug number two said, withdrawing from behind James' back. Thug number one looked unimpressed with his colleague backing down, but he was starting to fidget, too.

'I'm warning you, back away,' she growled. 'I know how to use it.' She aimed at his right shoulder.

Thug number one looked indecisive, but when she took a step closer, he raised his hands and stepped back, knife still in hand.

'I said put it down,' Kelli hissed, this time stepping much closer. She could hear sirens.

The knife clattered to the floor, and both men stepped back against the wall.

'That's better.' She glanced at James out of the corner of her eye. His throat was red, but he didn't see any bleeding. Her right shoulder was starting to ache, but she kept the rifle raised.

'Police! Drop your weapon!' came from behind her. Blue and red patterns danced on the wall.

'It's self-defence,' Kelli said, reaching into her pocket and handing back the phone, which was still on the line with the now rather frantic operator. She lowered the rifle. 'I walked in here to see these two with a knife to my friend's throat.'

'Hands up anyway,' barked a young female cop. Kelli recognised her as Constable Martin, the one who had been involved in the Coalbridge investigation. Kelli put the gun on the floor and did as she was told. The woman quickly patted her down.

The cops moved in and handcuffed Thug one and Thug two. They were protesting vehemently, but the knife at their feet would be hard to argue with. One checked James over for injuries, and he brushed them off. Kelli pushed herself off the wall and threw her arms around his neck.

'Whoa, easy,' he said, hugging her back. One hand brushed over her hair. 'You probably saved my life today.'

She stepped back, suddenly realising it was his neck that had been injured. 'Sorry.' She inspected the area. 'You okay?'

'I'll bruise, but I'm fine.' He squeezed her around the shoulders. 'Thank you, Kell.'

'Not so fast, we have to prove what happened here,' one of the cops said.

James kept his arm around Kelli. 'I have CCTV,' he said, indicating the newly installed camera.

It was another hour before they were released and told they would be kept up to date. Charges were likely, at least for assault, but linking the thugs to the poisoning syndicate would be tricky if they didn't confess.

Kelli had been allowed to call her groom to come and take care of her horses. They had been bedded in for the night. They hadn't even talked about whether or not they were still going to Luhmuhlen.

After cleaning up, James ordered takeaway and they ate their Chinese in his living room. The stable had been well locked up and the camera running. James had said he felt a lot safer after the arrests, but there was no way to tell if the pair had been working with others.

'You okay?' James rubbed Kelli's shoulder where she sat on the floor, her back against the couch, picking through the last of the takeaway containers.

She let out a sigh for the ages. 'I will be. Just one of those days, you could say.' She could feel her rueful smile getting watery.

'Hey now.' James slid down onto the floor next to her. 'I'm fine. You were wonder woman. What's wrong?'

'Probably stress release. And the fact that I'm stress-eating so I'll be fat tomorrow.' She wiped her eyes.

James gave her a one-arm hug. 'We're all going to be okay, thanks to you.'

Kelli let her head fall to his shoulder. 'I was terrified. Terrified I'd mess it up, and terrified you would die in front of my eyes.'

'I know.' He rubbed her shoulder. 'But I didn't. I've got a lot more takeaway Chinese dinners left in me yet.'

She chuckled and sniffed. 'I'm glad my dad made me learn to shoot.'

James laughed. 'Me too.'

Kelli took a deep breath and let it all out. She half-turned, putting her arms around James. 'I'm so glad you're okay.'

He squeezed her back. 'Thanks to you.'

She slept in his spare room that night and didn't set an alarm. She slept like a log and was nightmare-free, thank God.

It was sunny when she grabbed an apple from the fruit bowl and trotted down to the stables. James' whistle made her smile.

'Hey, sleepyhead.' James leaned on his pitchfork. 'How ya doing?'

'I'm okay. You?' She stepped up next to him to rub Coalbridge's nose. The big horse wuffled at her.

'I was surprised how well I slept.' He picked up his bucket to move along and Caitlyn came bursting in.

'Ooooh!' She dropped her mucking gear and put her hands on her hips, grinning at the pair of them. 'You two look cosy.'
The subtle shake of James' head told her he hadn't said anything to his niece. Kelli drummed up a smile. 'Nothing to report, I'm afraid. Just a tough day yesterday and my horses were here, so I crashed in the spare room.'
Caitlyn wriggled her eyebrows but her uncle hurried her along with his rake. 'Sorry,' he said.
Kelli waved him off. 'We do need to talk about where we go from here.'
'We do. Are you going to ride your boys this morning?'
Kelli scrunched her nose. 'I'll give New Morning a bit of a dressage run, I think.'
'Okay. Let's talk at lunch. Better yet, I'll get the rest of the team on a conference call. We need to let them know what happened.'
'Okay.' Kelli stretched and threw her shoulders back. 'Let's do this.'
New Morning was in a gentle mood as if he sensed his mistress was upset. His dressage was improving, but he still needed plenty of work, particularly with flow and speed of moving from one motion to the next.
She could feel herself getting into the familiar rhythm, with the events of yesterday fading from her mind. The patter of hooves, the snuffling of her horse (New Morningtely a snuffler) and the movements of dressage. This was who she was.
She was a rider. A darned good one at that. She was a woman. She was a daughter, a friend. She was an ex-fiance. She didn't regret ending it with Troy. It was part of her tapestry, but she'd made the right call.
At lunchtime, they had a conference call with Jadin, chef d'equipe Steve, and the other two leading Kiwis, Debbie and Kyle. Kelli could see the shock in their eyes.

'As scary as it was, I'm not asking you all to put your lives on hold,' James said firmly. 'Even if I have to lie low for a bit, which I don't want to do, you guys shouldn't have to.'

'Luhmuhlen isn't the most secure event in the world,' Steve noted wryly. 'And then, of course, there's Burghley in a month.'

'You should all go as normal,' James insisted. 'I won't be risking taking Coalie, but I'm certainly planning to run Marksman at Luhmuhlen.'

Steve didn't look convinced. 'What do the cops say?'

'I'm meant to get an update today. But it's Coalie they're after. My only guess, from how they were talking, is that someone stands to lose a lot of money if Coalie wins more five-stars. So if I'm not riding Coalie, it's not an issue.'

'Unless they just get to you instead,' Kelli said.

James shot her a look.

'Look, I'm sorry, but did you really think, if you'd handed over the gate key yesterday, they would have just walked away and let you carry on with your life?'

James sighed. 'Probably not. But I refuse to let them win.'

Kelli opened her mouth to say 'at what cost?' but thought better of it. She'd argue with him later.

'I'll let you know what I get back from the cops,' James said. 'But, apart from being security-conscious, you need to just continue.'

'All right. Keep us in the loop,' Steve said.

When the call bleeped to an end, Kelli folded her arms and turned to James. 'At what cost are you going to do this?'

'Do what?'

'Keep going as if nothing is wrong. I understand you not wanting to let fear rule your life, but you can't just carry on as normal. If this is some big nasty syndicate, they could kill you, Jimmy.'

'I'm not being flippant, Kell. But I can't put my life on hold forever. You or I could die on the motorway driving to Germany.'
'Yeah, but…'
'I know. I don't like it, but there's not much else I can do.'
Kelli sighed. 'I know. I just...be careful, okay?'
He patted her knee. 'You got it.'

Amy and her new flatmate, a 40ish motherly type, had insisted Damien stay with them until he was back on his feet. Jude seemed to have cast him into the role of her son. Did he want tea? Did he want some fruit? Did he want more water? Did he need help to get anywhere? Amy suspected he was relieved when she also went to work. He was able to start doing some admin-type work for his job remotely, in between physio appointments.
Their relationship was on her mind. They loved each other, but that didn't sweep logistics under the carpet. He was based in England about six months out of the year and on deployment the other six, depending on the year. They were in distant parts of the country to each other - and he could be reassigned at any time.
He saw this ending in marriage. Amy thought that sounded fine in principle, but she wasn't going to be a full-time Navy wife. And did they want kids? How would that work if he was out of the country for months at a time?
Damien tentatively raised the topic that evening as they cleaned up after dinner. 'So, you and I?'
Amy raised her eyebrows. 'What about us?'
He cleared his throat and put down the frying pan. 'Long-term, how are we going to do this?'
Amy smiled. 'You're the only man in the world who is initiating the commitment conversation.'

Damien grinned. 'You know me.'

'I do.' Her face turned serious, and she pulled out the plug. 'I want this to work, Damien. I want the happily-ever-after. The wedding. The pregnancy announcements. The kids and the dog.' She folded her arms and leaned against the bench. 'But I also want my career. I also want to win Badminton.' She turned to face him. 'How do you feel about that?'

'I want you to have what you want. I don't want a barefoot and pregnant wife. I just want you.'

Amy smiled. 'And you're still here, all these years later.'

Damien brushed a strand of hair behind her ear. 'Love tends to do that.'

'So how do we work this out, logistically?'

'Are you going to be happy as a military wife?'

She shrugged. 'I'm asking you to accept my dream. It's only fair that I accept yours. We compromise. Find a location that works for us both.'

Damien looked right at her. 'So then, will you?'

She felt her eyes get wide. 'Will I what?'

'Will you marry me?'

She threw her arms around his neck. 'Yes!'

In some ways, it had been what she'd wanted all her life, she realised later, as she was lying in bed. Not necessarily the fairytale white wedding - just to never lose Damien Scott. She hadn't grown up witnessing a good marriage, and that scared her. Most days, she still had to work on forgiving her parents. But she also knew she wanted to make Damien happy for the rest of his life.

He hadn't had a ring for her, but that didn't matter. She had his promise. He had sworn to take her ring shopping the next day, and she would have been happy with the simplest one in the world.

She stared at the ceiling above her, thinking of the man lying in the spare room downstairs. They both wanted to wait until after the wedding for anything more intimate than a chaste kiss. She'd never been a girly girl, dreaming of princesses and fairies, but Damien made her feel like one, and that was enough for her.

She looked at the time. 10.30pm meant mid-morning in New Zealand. She had to call Mickey.

After three rings, her best friend picked up. 'Hey, chickadee.'

'I'm engaged!'

'What in the wild world? To whom?'

Amy had to laugh. 'Who do you think?'

'So just like that? Prince Charming Damien just got down on one knee out of the blue?'

She laughed again. 'He didn't! Are you going to congratulate me or what?'

It was Mickey's turn to laugh. 'Congratulations! I always knew you two would end up together. Tell me every detail. He didn't get down on one knee? You should have refused him!'

'Yes, Emma Woodhouse. I'll bear that in mind next time someone proposes to me.'

'Details!'

'We were just doing dishes-'

'Crikey, Damien, that's romantic.'

Amy cleared her throat pointedly. 'He started talking about how we would make this work long-term. I said he's the only guy in the world to bring up the commitment conversation. He asked if I'd be happy as a military wife, and I said it's not fair for me to want eventing but say he can't have the Navy. And then he just asked me, there and then.'

'Oh, my word,' Mickey gushed. 'Not at all romantic, but hey. If you're happy, that's all that matters.'

Amy chuckled. 'I am. We're going ring-shopping tomorrow.'

'Wow, another points deduction.'

'Who are you, Dear Abby?'

'Sorry. I know you're happy; I can tell by how you sound. Congratulations, I'm very happy for you. Have you set a date?'
'We're not in a rush, but we're not delaying, either. We will probably come back to New Zealand for it.'
'Interesting.'
'Why? All our friends are there.'
'No, I mean, you said come back to New Zealand. You didn't say come home.'
The next morning, arm in arm, they visited jewellery stores. Damien told her to choose whatever she wanted, but she was looking for something simple and not expensive. 'I don't care about the ring,' she said. 'That's how I know you're the one.' She finally saw one, immediately fell in love, and serendipitously, it was not expensive. It was a simple white gold ring with a small, but somehow prominent diamond, and two small sapphires.
Damien paid for the ring, took her to her favourite lake spot, and proposed again on one knee. She said yes, and they kissed and bought coffee. And that, Amy thought to herself as they sipped their drinks, summed up their whole relationship. Happiness in the little things.

And then it was on to the next big one - Burghley. Despite all the rise of new, rich events around the world, there was nothing to beat the tradition of the English classics.
Here, as at Badminton, had the greats of the sport run their horses. Here many a tear has been shed and a victory has been celebrated in the spirit of the love of the chase and of the animals that made it possible.
Kelli rolled out of bed and hit the floor with 10 push-ups. There was something about the first day of Burghley. Her country's horses had such a rich history here. A quick shower

and muesli bar later, she was heading down to the stables to give her boys an early morning warm-up.

After getting through the security, she let herself into the big stable. The 10 Kiwi horses were stabled together to give a united feel even though Burghley was an individual event. But eventing, in general, had a sense of camaraderie, riders united in their love of the sport and their horses.

'Morning, Kyle,' she called to her teammate, who appeared to be patting Coalie. 'You're up early.'

Kyle turned quickly, then smiled at her. 'Yeah, I'm just hoping to try and get some semblance of grace into Cetchco.'

Kelli grinned. Kyle's horse could jump the Berlin Wall but he was not a dressage horse. Kyle had once told her if Cetchco was 'clunky but accurate' that was a decent test.

She let herself into Kaleido's stall and gave him a quick brush. 'Good luck,' she called as Kyle led his horse out.

'You too.'

Kaleido was in a jittery mood, which was not a good omen for dressage day, which was his strength. Kelli loved all her horses, but Kaleido was the one who had the characteristics of a star if he could only learn that big jumps were well within his ability.

Kelli took a deep breath of the cool English air as she set Kaleido through some basic dressage steps. He was pulling a bit but he was doing as he was told. She kept it short, knowing he would over-tire if he fought her all morning.

She dismounted and led the horse back towards the stables. And there, she paused.

Two strangers stood at Coalie's stall. She glanced at her watch - it had only just gone 6.30, which was too early for most riders, let alone any sponsors.

Kyle was with them, so it must be above board, she surmised. She felt a wave of relief - and the next second, she wanted to throw up.

James was getting in the shower when the phone rang. He hesitated, then picked it up.

It said Clive Ressler.

You've got some nerve, he thought, but he answered it.

'Hi. I know you are upset with me but you need to listen. Someone's planning an attack on Coalie.'

'What?'

'Get down to the stable. Now. Call 999. They're planning something this morning.'

James threw on the nearest set of clothes, ran downstairs and slammed his rental into drive.

Chapter Sixteen

Kelli caught her breath. One of the group was wielding a large needle.

She tied Kaleido to the nearest pole, prayed it would hold him and broke into a run. 'What are you doing?'

All three turned, and in surprise, something clattered to the ground. Kyle looked faint. 'We were just --' he started, and then, for the second time in far too short a period, Kelli saw a gun.

'Back off now, lady, and this all goes quietly,' a burly man snarled.

'Mitchell, don't--' came from Kyle, but Mitchell wasn't listening. 'I said back off!'

Kelli stopped, but she didn't move. 'You are going to shoot one of the leading riders in the world at Burghley? Are you nuts?' That sounded all right, she thought.

She heard footsteps. They kept walking.

'If that's what it takes.' Burly Man didn't look sure of himself, she noticed. A mark in her favour.

'What are you giving him?' She snapped.

'None of your business, little lady. Now, move.'

She knew better. They couldn't let her get away, now. She lifted her hands and inched towards Kyle. He might be a traitor, but he wouldn't kill her.

'How could you?' She hissed through clenched teeth.

Kyle looked sick but said nothing.

'Do this and get out,' Burly Man snapped.

His assistant collected the needle that had fallen and slipped into Coalie's stall. Kelli wanted to tackle him, but should she risk her life? What were the odds Burly Man wouldn't shoot to kill?

'All right, stop.' Kelli jumped at Kyle's voice and the swipe that knocked the needle to the ground.

'Excuse me?' The assistant said.

'We can't do this. I'll get your money another way. I'll--'

Gunshot. He must have a silencer. Kelli held in a scream as Kyle dropped behind her. She spun around, and Kyle was clutching at his arm. Thank God, he hadn't seemed to be hit anywhere life-threatening.

The assistant put the needle back to Coalie's neck and injected it. The horse, used only to kindness and good treatment, barely moved a muscle. Kelli wanted to cry.

More footsteps. Kelli held her breath.

'Drop your weapon, now!'

Thank you, God.

Burly Man went to shoot, but he must have thought better of it. Three armed guards closed in, repeating the order to drop the weapon. The pistol fell to the floor. Kelli immediately dropped to her knees beside Kyle.

'Nobody move!' a guard barked, but Kelli raised her hands again. 'I'm unarmed. I'm just checking on him. He's bleeding.' The guard nodded at her, and she reached for Kyle's arm. He was bleeding, but not dreadfully. 'Here, let me see.'

Kyle looked pained. 'Leave me alone.'

She ignored him and gently pulled his hand away, wrapping the wound over top of his shirt with her sweatshirt. He looked like he was fighting tears, or the urge to throw up, or both.

'Kelli, I can't even begin to say how sorry I am.'

'It's not me you need to apologise to,' she said simply before the guards interfered.

The next hour was a blur. An ambulance, the police and the vet were called. James came rushing down half crazy with worry.

Kyle, probably thankfully, was on the way to the hospital before he got there.

'Oh my word, Kelli.' James hugged her tightly. She could feel the tears swimming - tension release, the relief it was over, the pain at Kyle's actions. *Later,* she told herself sternly.

'You're really all right?' James held her by the shoulders.

She nodded. 'I'm fine. Shaken, but fine.'

'I'll bet. I'm so sorry.'

She shook her head. 'It's not your fault.'

The vet arrived and immediately treated Coalie to try and minimise the effects of the drugs. The police questioned Kelli, James, Vicky, and half the other riders whose horses were stabled nearby.

Kyle, it appeared, was the link. Clive had transitioned through Kyle's stable briefly but gone on to work for British rider Cole Kendrick before any of this happened. A major betting syndicate had weighed into eventing, a traditionally untapped market for gambling. To bet against Coalbridge in a big event was a gamble - unless he was taken out of the picture.

It was all hard to take in.

The men were charged with animal cruelty and fraud charges. Kyle had been lucky, insofar as his gunshot wound was pretty much a clean slice through. He would likely also face a lesser fraud charge by association.

With one of the Burghley stables a crime scene, the event was postponed for the first time since the coronavirus pandemic.

And it wasn't even lunchtime yet.

The sun rose slowly, painting the English countryside in glitter.

Kelli Holmes stood at her hotel window in her Winnie the Pooh dressing gown, a cup of mocha coffee in hand. Her wet blond hair was stuffed on her head. Her heart felt like it had finally returned to its rightful place.

Yesterday was the kind of day she wasn't sure she'd lived through until she saw her stressed face in the mirror. Until she saw the police tape in an old, familiar barn. Until she heard Jadin on the phone, asking her repeatedly if she was all right until she lost patience. And he snapped back, what he was supposed to do, when the woman he loved was in harm's way and he could do nothing?

Kyle was recovering after minor surgery. From what they'd discovered from the police, Kyle had gambling debts and had tried to find his way out in an ill-advised and ultimately dangerous fashion. Kelli had seen his change of heart at the crux, when the reality was closing in - but too late to take back a betrayal.

Coalbridge was recovering. The drugs could have done irreparable damage if not killed him, but the vet's counteraction had come just in time. His nervous system would take some time to recover, and they wouldn't know until down the track if he would ever compete to the top level again. But he would live a normal life.

Burghley would go ahead, a week later than planned with ramped-up security. But they were fairly sure it was all over.

Kelli took a deep breath of her coffee. It had taken a few hours for her hands to stop shaking. James had refused to let her - or Vicky, who had been the one to call the police, it transpired - out of his sight until he was convinced they were okay.

But she was okay. It was okay. Kyle's betrayal cut deep - but she didn't believe anyone was beyond second chances. She'd told James about Kyle's last-ditch effort to stop the attack. James was furious, and that did little to appease him.

Someone knocked on the door. 'It's open,' she called.

'Morning,' James stuck his head in the door. 'Are you okay?'

'Yeah, come in. Coffee?'

'Sure.' She saw him try to hide a smile at her Winnie-the-Pooh attire. She poured him a cup and handed it over. 'How are you?'

James sipped the drink and then let his head fall back against the wall. 'I feel like I've felt every emotion in the last 24 hours and 'drained' is the only one left.'

'I know the feeling.' Kelli sipped her drink.

He looked up at her. Beneath the fury was hurt. 'How could he, Kelli? I thought he was my friend.'

'I know.' She stared into the drink as if it had answers. 'I think he just got so entangled that he couldn't see a way out. Desperate times and desperate measures.'

'And that justifies betrayal?'

'Of course not. I'm just theorising.' She put down her mug and leaned against the open window. The first touches of warmth were just rising in the air. 'We know Kyle. We've known him, what, eight or nine years? What he did - it wasn't Kyle. It was desperation.' She raised a hand to stop his counterattack. 'I know, none of that excuses what he did.'

James put his head in his hands. 'Has anyone told you that you make terrible coffee?'

The tension and the strain manifested as giggles. When they got themselves under control, she asked, 'Do you want to hear some good news? At least, I think it's good news.'

'Heck yes.'

'Jadin told me he loved me last night.'

James grinned. 'And what did you say back?'

'I, um, said I loved him too.'

Amy held Chester at the edge of the ring, at attention. His mane was braided, and he was brushed to a sheen. Here it was, then: their first four-star.

She got the signal to enter and pushed Chester into a trot. He felt good this morning, as if he knew what a special occasion this was.

He was playing to the judges as they made their way through the steps. The flying change was one of his best. When they finished, he even bobbed his head to the judge.

'Good boy, Chester, good boy!' She praised him effusively as they made their way out of the ring. It was one of their best dressage tests since arriving in England. Dismounting, she saw the score - also their best since arriving in England.

'You look happy.' Her fiance appeared at her shoulder and took the reins.

She smiled. Fiance. She was still getting used to the word, and the fact that it made her happy was such a good thing. 'He did so well!' She rubbed Chester's grey neck under the pretty mane.

'So did you.' Damien patted her on the helmet.

'Thank you.' She smiled up at him and took back the reins. 'I'll just cool him down and take out his braids. He hates them.'

She walked Chester out and around the ring. She was floating. Life had been kind to her in the motherland. It had been such a major, scary decision - but it had flowed together.

She remembered something her high school teacher had told her. 'Happy people do beyond their best. Do something that makes you happy.'

She smiled. Her ring was in the car for safekeeping, but there was no doubt that she was happy with Damien, and it was flowing over to her eventing.

She talked to Chester as she pulled out his braids, rewarding him with another chunk of carrot. It was early days, but four-star level already agreed with him.

The next day, though - cross-country day - was wet. And muddy. Chester was not a fan. He was moody when she got him out to warm up. The news filtering back from the course was that jump 11, a big steeplechase-like hedge, landing on a slope, was the dangerous one catching the riders out. The reigning Olympic champion, Cole Kendrick, had taken a fall there on his new young horse, and several others had had refusals.

'Okay, Ches. Time to put on your big-boy pants and deal with it,' Amy murmured to her testy mount, in a soothing tone. They lined up by the starting box, waiting for the staggered interval clock to tick to three minutes. Thank goodness she'd remembered her goggles. At the hooter, she pushed him into a gallop.

The first 10 fences would be stock-standard on a dry track, but nothing was easy in the wet. Chester cleared the first two uprights easily enough, but the rain was driving and he was unhappy. She'd normally hold him to a canter on the first half of a course but thought better of it. The more freedom he had the better he'd run - and the main goal was getting to the finish without a refusal.

Six, seven, eight. The water jump at nine, Chester tried to veer sideways out of the pond, but she tightened her grip and squeezed her shins. He threw up his head, but he kept going. He may be stubborn and hate rain, but he had a big heart. Number 10 passed by almost without notice as Amy prepared for number 11. She pulled his pace right back until he was nearly trotting to the brush. He popped over and landed well, keeping well in control as he negotiated the slope. She let out a breath. The worst was over, but that meant nothing on a day like this.

Chester was running well and she decided she was less concerned with the time than with finishing. She slowed him at the big jumps and let him judge for himself at the small ones. The rain eased as they cleared the final hurdle and she gave him his head for the finish line, mud flying. A clear round, with only a couple of time penalties. She thumped Chester's neck.

'Attaboy, Chester. Good boy.' She slowed him to a trot to cool down.

'Good going!' one of the other riders called.

'Thanks,' Amy called back. She was so proud of her boy. Time penalties were the least of her worries. First four-star cross-country, and in the rain to boot. She wasn't sure, but she thought Chester was running in the top ten.

She took her time cooling him down and then gave him a lukewarm bath, again punctuated by lots of treats. By the time she left him for the night, Chester was warm and happy, tucking into his silage and hay. She kissed him on the nose and told him what a good boy he was.

'I'm thinking I have a rival for my affections,' Damien said seriously as he walked her to the car.

Amy stared at him. 'What are you talking about?'

'Whoa, easy. I meant that handsome grey gent eating hay back there.'

She grinned. 'Oh. Sorry. I'm still a little high-strung from today.' She put her arm through his. 'I'm just so proud of my little Kiwi horse that could.'

'As you should be.'

She smiled her thanks when Damien opened the car door for her and took her ring out of its hiding place. She slid it on, then sighed. They were going out for dinner tonight because Damien was reporting for duty in the morning.

'Requests?' he said as he slid behind the wheel.

She smiled a tired smile at him. 'Anywhere that serves food. I'm starving.'

'Coming right up, m'lady.'

She stifled another sigh. Though they'd tossed ideas around for their big day, they hadn't settled on a date. She knew the remainder of this duty tour would be a good six weeks.

Although they were yet to be intimate, and she wanted it that way, it had been nice having Damien around. The first couple of weeks, she was sure Jude had driven him crazy, but once he was more mobile, he became like another flatmate.

Just one that she'd get a kiss from when she came home, one who would hold her hand when they watched a movie, one that would do little things to make her smile.

'You're quiet for someone who's running second in their first four-star.' Damien sent her a smile.

She roused herself. 'Sorry.' She put her hand on top of his on the gearstick. 'I'm just thinking of what it will be like when you leave tomorrow. No more kisses when I come home, no more--'

'I'm sure Jude would if you asked her nicely,' Damien deadpanned.

She couldn't resist a giggle at that. 'Funny.'

He turned serious as he parked the car and took her hand. 'So let's set a date. Right now.'

'Why, because I'm hungry and I'll agree to anything to get to the food quicker?'

'Partly.' He grinned at her. 'But mostly because I don't want to leave without knowing when I get to make my fiancee my wife.'

Wife. The word gave her butterflies.

'Let's do it now,' he said suddenly.

'What?'

'Let's find a JP and get married right now. Then, when I finish my deployment, we'll go back to Enzed and have a party.'

'You're not serious.'

'Actually, I am.'

Amy shook her head. 'As much as I'd quite like to spontaneously marry you, I want it to be special. I want to wear a white dress. I want to look pretty. I don't want to have helmet hair and smell like horse and grass.'

'You always look pretty,' Damien said, predictably.

'Thank you. But no. I want to wake up in bed like some kind of Disney princess and think, I'm getting married today. I want the anticipation. The whole experience.' She leaned across the console to kiss him. 'After all, I'm only getting married once.' She reached for the door handle. 'Now, feed me.'

Amy tried to eat healthily when she was competing, but some days called for extra fries, and this was one of them. Damien raised one eyebrow as she helped herself to some of his fries on top of her own but wisely said nothing.

'Don't judge me. I'm carb-loading for tomorrow.'

'I didn't say a word. Want some T-sauce with that?'

She swallowed her mouthful before poking out her tongue at him.

They were just leaving when Amy's phone rang. She took it and gasped when the caller identified himself.

They didn't stay out late. Amy needed her sleep at the best of times, but the added stress of competing could wipe her out.

Show-jumping morning dawned fine. The ring would be damp underfoot, but not sodden. That was a bonus.

Chester was being obedient, which has a good sign. Generally, she had to hold him pretty tightly in showjumping because he liked to just run. Over the warm-ups, he was clean as a whistle. 'This could be our day, Chessy,' she murmured to the horse as they walked around the ring, watching the previous combination. The last obstacles were a triple -- jump-stride-jump-stride-jump. Few had jumped a clear round.

She got the signal from the starter and nudged Chester forward. Snuffling away he cantered towards the first jump.

It was only in the top echelons that the showjumping ran in reverse order of standing so that the leaders would jump last, adding to the drama. In four-star, there was not always the luxury of knowing that you won or lost as soon as you cleared or knocked a fence. Amy knew she had one fence in hand over the third and fourth placers, but she would not know until they had all completed their round whether she stayed ahead or fell behind.

One, two, three, four and five Chester popped over without a hitch. He was starting to pull against the tight rein, but Amy held him firm. The water double in the middle she heard a rear hoof clack against a pole, but no clang of a falling rail.

On the long approach to the troublesome triple, Amy pulled him right back and knew immediately she'd pulled back too hard. Chester's head went up and his stride wobbled just a little, but enough that he took off on a funny gait. His lead foot hit the pole hard and down it came - and a bad first jump in a triple usually meant there was no time to recover.

He got one stride in before jump two. Less of the hoof hit that, but the pole still came down. Jump three Chester pulled up his legs and just cleared it.

'Good boy, Ches.' She rose out of the saddle and patted his neck as they cantered out of the arena. Dropping two fences was disappointing, but they'd only made one real mistake. It dropped them to fourth.

She vaulted out of the saddle and rubbed her horse's neck. For their first four-star, she was proud of what they'd done.

'Well done, you two.' Damien patted the horse and hugged her. 'You'll be late!' Amy checked her watch. 'Have you seen what time it is? I thought you'd have gone.'

'Not without doing this.' Already in uniform, Damien cupped her head and kissed her. 'I'll see you soon. I love you.'

'I love you too.' She brushed a piece of fluff off his shoulder board and watched him walk away, smiling to herself at the double-takes he got. He was a good-looking man, and it was amplified by the uniform.

'All right then, work husband. Let's get you cooled down.' She patted Chester and led him back to the barn.

'Excuse me, Miss Williams?'

Amy turned. 'Yes?'

'You don't know me, but my name is Steve Merkell. I'm the chef d'equipe of the New Zealand eventing team -'

Amy's hand flew to her mouth.

'And we've been following you, you and your horse. We wondered how you would feel about coming to meet some of the riders in the development squad and considering the programme?'

Did he really need to phrase that as a question? Amy would have hugged him if she wasn't still holding Chester.

'You see, with recent developments, we need to look at expanding our rider base.'

'Of course I will!' All of her Christmases had come in a few days

Chapter Seventeen

A week was a long time in politics, but an even longer time in three-day eventing.

Kelli had tried to check on Kyle Rogers a couple of times, but he wasn't taking her calls. He had been released from the hospital and bailed by the criminal court, but suspended by the FEI pending an investigation. He'd also gone to ground, avoiding the media and all his teammates. She had decided she'd call into his farm on the drive down from Burghley.

The delayed event had gone off without a security hitch. Kaleido had run best of the Kiwis, finishing fourth, just ahead of James and Lacklustre, proving himself a rising star, in sixth. Coalbridge had been quite sick for a couple of days but then started turning the corner. Last night, James had even been able to ride him gently for half an hour. There was no guarantee, but the prognosis of him eventually competing again was looking better.

But that had done little to appease James' fury. For anyone to poison a horse was bad enough, but for it to come from someone James considered a friend was unforgivable in his book.

James had been in a bitter mood for days, ever since that fairly friendly conversation the morning after it all went down. All through Burghley, he'd been surly with the press, standoffish with officials and just barely polite with people he knew. Kelli had tried talking to him once but quickly gave up. He'd have to work this through in his own time.

On another front, she'd spent a lot of time on the phone with Jadin. Since he'd blurted out that he loved her the night of the arrests, they'd got closer, but only via phone calls. Kelli was somewhat surprised to discover, in response to his statement, that she loved him too - and differently from how she'd always loved him, as a dear friend.

Her mind cast back to her former boyfriend, Troy. He was a good man, and they'd gone steady for a couple of years, but when he proposed, she should've said no. She loved him, in a way - but not as a wife should, and she gave the ring back. She was too ambitious, and he wanted a traditional marriage with wifey staying home and minding the kids. Kelli was just not a housewife kind of girl.

But with Jadin, she'd be happier doing that, she felt. Oh, she'd never be barefoot and pregnant, but the idea of being a homemaker, at least when she wasn't riding, was no longer so appalling.

She checked the latch on her horse truck one more time and got behind the wheel. Her assistant, Henrique, had flown home immediately for a family matter, and she'd assured him she'd be fine making the three-hour drive on her own.

Ninety minutes in, she pulled the rig off the main road and down a rural side street. About a kilometre off the M6 was Kyle's farm where he ran beef cows as well as his eventing horses. She turned the rig into the winding driveway, parked and checked on the horses.

There was no answer to her knock at the door.

Kelli turned and surveyed the area. All was quiet. She could see the herd of beefies over in the corner field, and then her eyes latched onto something moving. The ATV. He was feeding the cows.

Kelli wandered over to the shed where the farm equipment was stored and sat on the fence. Eventually, he'd have to come back.

It wasn't that much of a wait, and he saw her from about 100 metres away, but he must have thought better than turning tail. He pulled the ATV into the shed in front of her.

'You're still alive, then,' Kelli deduced when the engine turned off.

'I have nothing to say to you.' He walked deeper into the shed, returned with a petrol can, and refuelled the quad bike.

'Well, I have something to say to you.' Kelli slid off the fence and walked up to him. 'How are you?'

'Fine.' He righted the petrol can and screwed the fuel tank cap back on.

'How is the court case?'

'Fine.'

'Have you heard from the FEI?'

'No.' He put back the petrol can and busied himself in the back of the shed. 'As you can see, I'm pretty busy.'

'For goodness' sake, Kyle, talk to me! You can't hide forever. You did a bad thing, but I happen to believe in second chances. You'd be surprised how many others do, too.'

Kyle put down what he was holding heavily and turned to face her. Anger and resentment radiated from every word. 'There is nothing to talk about. My deal to pay off my debts went sour, so I'll have to sell the farm. I'll have to sell my horses. I'll be lucky to even be able to keep Cetchco. I know, it's all my fault. I've screwed my life and lost all my friends and my livelihood. So forgive me if I don't want to engage in small talk.'

Kelli leaned against the barns. 'You haven't lost all your friends. I'm your friend. Bring Cetchco and come and stay in my sleepout.'

She thought she saw a glimpse of hope, even gratitude, in his eyes, but it was quickly gone and he shrugged indifferently. 'I don't need your pity.'

Kelli sighed. 'Okay, fine. Have it your way. But if you need anything, if you want a place to stay, call me. Text me. I'll be here.' She got in her truck without looking back, put it in gear and drove away.

The next day, she arrived at the hospital with a spring in her step. She was here to see Jadin - and to pick him up and take him to James' house.

He was still unsteady but there was feeling and movement in his legs again. He had wanted to go home, but his friends and doctors had ganged up on him and told him he needed some support at least for the first couple of weeks.

'Hey, stranger.' She smiled when she saw Jadin. He had lost a lot of weight at the start, but the extra physio and working out had put some bulk back on. He had a certain spark about him that had been missing for a long time after the accident.

'Hey, yourself.'

Kelli reached to hug him, feeling a little quiver as she did so. How, exactly, was she supposed to act? 'How are you feeling?'

'Great. I get to go home.' He grinned at her as she pulled away, but his face then became more serious. 'How are you?'

She smiled. 'I'm getting there. Shall we blow this joint?'

'Best idea I've heard all day.'

She took his suitcase and one of the nurses pushed the wheelchair. Kelli had to smile at the expression on Jadin's face. Six months after going into hospital fighting for his life, he was coming out almost under his own steam.

Her heart fluttered watching him get out of the wheelchair, thank the nurse, and get into her SUV on his own. She shut the boot and slid behind the wheel.

'So how's James?' Jadin asked as they pulled out.

She checked both ways twice before answering. 'I haven't talked to him in a few days. He took the whole thing hard.' She eased the vehicle out onto the main road, not looking at Jadin.

'I still can't believe it,' he said. 'I know we were never super close to Kyle, but to turn on your team?' He shook his head. 'I've got no time for people like that.'

Kelli bit her lip. 'Not even to forgive someone who used to be your friend?'

Jadin looked at her sharply. 'What do you mean?'

Kelli was not entirely sure how this would be taken. 'I went to see Kyle the other day. I don't want him to feel abandoned. I know he's done an awful thing, but I think we should all get second chances.'

There was a long silence. Kelli glanced at Jadin out of the corner of her eye. His jaw was set.

'I know how loyal you are to Jimmy. I am too. But that doesn't mean I can't show a little kindness.'

Jadin cleared his throat. 'I'm not sure I can agree with that.'

'Agree with what? I just don't think anyone deserves to be forever cast out because they made a bad mistake. And left without a friend in the world.'

Jadin shrugged. 'There are consequences to betraying people.'

'We've all made mistakes, Jadin.'

'That's not a mistake. That's an ongoing deliberate act to hurt someone. You can't just pretend it never happened.'

'You don't have to. But I'm worried about him, Jade. I'm not going to abandon him.'

She'd tried a couple more times to call Kyle and got no response. She was worried about how desperate he might get. She couldn't imagine how it must feel to be drowning in debt and alienated from all your friends.

'Well, I can't deal with him right now,' Jadin said.

She nodded. 'Just don't expect me to stay away out of loyalty.'

She parked in front of James' lovely Manorbrook homestead. Jadin surveyed the landscape. 'That's a sight for sore eyes.'

Kelli came around and handed him his crutches. Before he got settled there was someone he had to see.

Delaware tossed his head and whinnied when he caught sight of his owner. Kelli couldn't be sure but she thought she saw tears in Jadin's eyes. 'Hey, old man.' He rubbed the gelding's forehead under his mane.

She gave them a moment, popping down the aisle to check on Coalie. The big black was back to doing light work, but James was being very careful and taking it slow. He pricked his ears when he saw Kelli, his dark eyes asking for a treat. She obliged him with a piece of carrot.

'He looks so good,' Jadin said when Kelli reapproached the pair.

Kelli smiled and rubbed Delaware's ears, getting a whuffle in return. 'You big sweetie. James has been keeping him up to scratch for you.'

'I can see that.' He gave the grey one last pat, and Kelli saw the spark of determination in his eyes that had been missing since the accident. Despite the doctor's advice against riding again on his fragile spine, he wanted it again, she could tell.

She took his arm. 'Come on, let's get you set up. James is even ordering Hawaiian pizza.'

'A concession indeed.'

There was no more time for private discussions that night. They knew they loved each other, but that was as far as they were taking it for now. They'd agreed to take it slow and get used to them as a couple instead of just good friends.

Kelli drove home with a smile on her face. She dialled Kyle again as soon as she parked at home. To her, a friendship, a true friendship, was for better or worse. But again, it just went to voicemail.

She went down to the stables to check they were all bedded in for the night. After locking up, she wandered down to the paddock where Maximus was enjoying his retirement. He hadn't had a seizure in some time, but every time she started to think about competing him again, common sense won out. If he had another episode while on a cross-country course, it could kill both of them. Not to mention it just wouldn't be fair to put that strain on him.

He came trotting over when he saw her, keen for a treat and some affection. Kelli adjusted his blanket and then sat down on the big stone in the corner of his paddock to chat to him. He was a very good listener.

She told him about Jadin and about Kyle. Max listened, and nudged her shoulder with his nose, asking for more snacks. She fed him more carrots and asked him what else she could do to help Kyle. He whuffled helpfully.

'Good night, old boy.' She checked he had enough water and trotted back up to the house.

She lit the fireplace, tossed a TV dinner in the oven, and sat down to watch the news. There was a knock at the door.

She pulled herself up and opened it.

'Hi,' Kyle said quietly.

Kelli was sure she'd done a double-take, but just stepped forward and hugged him. 'Hi, yourself,' she said and invited him in.

Epilogue - six months later

Never in all his years had Kyle Rogers imagined himself attending a restorative justice conference - on the offender's side of the fence, no less.

He fiddled with his fingers; checked his cuffs were buttoned; checked the time. Again.

The door opened, and in walked the current champion of the eventing circuit, wearing a dress shirt and jeans and his New Zealand Olympic cap. James Blackman's jaw was set as he took a seat across the table.

Kyle didn't hear the opening line from the support staffer. He blinked and turned to the woman. 'I'm sorry?'

The woman smiled pleasantly. 'I asked if you'd like to start?'

No, he wouldn't, really, but what choice did he have?

He cleared his throat. 'There's nothing I can say except I'm sorry. So very, deeply sorry. I made bad choices which led to more bad choices to get myself out of the mess. I was so far in debt I had no way out, so I took a route I never should have taken. It was inexcusable. I'm sorry.'

James didn't look like he'd respond. Kyle idly wondered if he'd jump the table and punch his lights out instead. Finally, his steely eyes on Kyle, James spoke. 'I thought, even with the disagreements that had happened, that you were my friend.'

Kyle simply nodded.

'We had worked together, competed together. Looked out for each other. When everyone warned me it was an inside job, I could not fathom it because I was sure none of my friends would betray me.'

The support lady weighed in again, asking Kyle if he wanted to respond, but James held up a hand. 'I'm not finished.

'It took me weeks to even fully comprehend that not only was it a fellow horseman that had betrayed me, but someone that I trusted.'

He stood and came around the table, ignoring the staffer telling him to sit back down, and Kyle tried not to flinch. 'Stand up,' James said.

Kyle slowly rose to his feet. And of all the things that could have happened next, never in a million years did he expect James to reach out and hug him.

'I forgive you,' James said before letting him go. 'It's taken me a while, but I do. And I hope you get the help you need.'

Kyle sat back down, stunned. 'I...thank you,' he stammered.

'Coalie is doing fine,' James said conversationally as if the past six months and most of the past five minutes hadn't happened. 'I ran him at Adelaide last week and he was third. It seems like he won't have any major lasting effects.'

Kyle was not going to cry. 'That's great,' he managed.

'Jadin's back riding dressage and hoping to compete again after Christmas.'

Kyle nodded. 'I heard.'

James cocked his head to one side. 'And you?'

'I, um.' Kyle shook his head. 'I got community work in criminal court, but my FEI hearing is next week. My lawyer thinks it'll be a ban for at least two years, maybe more.'

James nodded. 'And what will you do?'

'My eventing days are probably over. I think I'll focus on farming, and maybe do a bit of breeding on the side.'

James nodded and rose. He held out his hand. 'Good luck.'

Kyle stood and took it. 'Good luck to you, too. And, Jimmy…'
He cleared his throat. 'Thank you.'
James smiled sadly. 'A mutual friend of ours keeps reminding
me about second chances. I've finally agreed we all deserve
one.' He opened the door. 'I mean it, Kyle. Good luck.'
Kyle nodded back, and slowly, gratefully, sat back down in his
chair.

The End.

Acknowledgements

Special thanks to my amazing beta readers, Delwyn, Sarah and Kym.

To my friends and family who have supported me, and been excited for me, and promised to buy my book - you know who you are. Thank you.

About the author

Christina Persico wrote her first book, a stapled, felt-tip pen creation, as a child and has loved the written word ever since. She was born in New Zealand and trained as a journalist, working for the country's largest news website for four years before joining a community newspaper. She lives in Auckland, with her black rescue cat, Nala.

Find out more about Christina on her social media channels: Facebook.com/christinapersicowriter and @cpersicoauthor on Twitter. You can email her at christinapersicowriter@gmail.com.

www.ingramcontent.com/pod-product-compliance
Lightning Source LLC
Chambersburg PA
CBHW022034240626
47154CB00007B/2403